Into the Po...
—101 Tales from Records of the
Taiping Era

Compiled by Li Fang and others of the Song
Dynasty
Translated by Zhang Guangqian

FOREIGN LANGUAGES PRESS   BEIJING

First edition   1998

ISBN 7-119-02011-0
© Foreign Languages Press, Beijing, China, 1998

Published by Foreign Languages Press
24 Baiwanzhuang Road, Beijing 100037, China

Distributed by China International Book Trading
Corporation
35 Chegongzhuang Xilu, Beijing 100044, China
P.O. Box 399, Beijing, China

Printed in the People's Republic of China

Foreword

Records of the Taiping Era is a nearly complete collection of all the written stories up to the beginning of the Song Dynasty (960-1279). It was named after the period's title "Taiping," which means "peaceful." It was compiled at the decree of the second emperor of the Song Dynasty and was completed in the third year of the Taiping Xingguo period (978).

It consists of nearly 7,000 stories in 500 volumes from more than 300 source books. The word "story (*xiao shuo*)" was used in a very broad sense to include accounts of geographical wonders, unusual natural phenomena, local customs, exceptional skills, anecdotes and quotations, and other categories that would not come under the modern heading of short stories. The principal focus of this present selection is on the more mature fiction of the Tang Dynasty (618-907).

The Tang Dynasty was one of the most prolific dynasties in China's long history. It was founded after almost two centuries of wars known as the Northern and Southern Dynasties, and a very brief interval of the Sui Dynasty (581-618). The Tang's borders extended beyond the Great Wall in the north down to what is now Vietnam in the south, and from the Pacific Ocean in the east to the present Xinjiang Uygur Autonomous Region in the west.

The history of the Tang Dynasty can be divided roughly into three stages. The early stage (618-741) is characterized by political stability and economic prosperity, which reached its height in Kaiyuan reign of Emperor Xuanzong.

More than 40 years of peace during the reign of Emperor Xuanzong turned him into a pleasure-seeker. Corruption crept in while regional powers gathered force. From Tianbao reign to the end of Yuanhe reign (742-820), the country was torn by the struggle between the central government and separatist warlords, culminating in the eight years of the An Lushan-Shi Siming Rebellion from 755 to 763, and sporadic but incessant local wars in its wake until Emperor Xianzong suppressed the major separatist force in the Huai River region.

Emperor Xianzong, however, was murdered by eunuchs in 820. This marked the beginning of the last stages of the dynasty when the eunuchs emerged as a powerful political force. Being closest to and most trusted by the throne, they not only held sway over the monarch and the fate of the crown prince, but usurped a great share of political power from the cabinet. Cabinet members aligned themselves either with or against the eunuchs, and prime ministers went in and out of office as though riding a merry-go-round. On the other hand, the country had never fully recovered from the disasters of the civil wars ongoing since the An Lushan-Shi Siming Rebellion. The national economy plummeted. Before the rebellion, salt was sold at one coin a liter, but after the rebellion, it rose to 11 coins a liter, and went up to 37 coins in Zhenyuan reign. Nationwide peasant uprising began as Emperor Yizong ascended the throne in 859. A peasant army led by Huang Chao even drove the emperor away from the capital and occupied it for three years. Though the Huang Chao Uprising was finally crushed in 883, the dynasty was too exhausted to regain its former glory. In 907, the Tang Dynasty fell and the country was once again plunged into the chaos of war and quick successions of one short-lived dynasty after another until the Song Dynasty reunified the land in 960.

Generally speaking, the rulers of the Tang Dynasty were relatively liberal and open-minded, especially in the early period. Cross-border commerce and travel flourished, and many new things were introduced into the country. The dynasty lived peacefully with the various ethnic groups within its borders and beyond.

Religious tolerance is obvious in these stories, though royal preferences did exist since the House of Li regarded themselves as descendants of Li Er (Lao Zi), the founder of Taoism. This preference is plainly reflected in the amazing number of stories related to Taoism and Taoist priests, which far exceeds those concerning Buddhism and Buddhist monks. But royal endorsement and religious contention did not take the extreme forms of one trying to eliminate all others. In "The Two Friends," for example, the monk visits the sacred mountain of Taoism as well as that of Buddhism. Unlike the previous and later dynasties, Taoist priests, Buddhist monks, and Confucian scholars could live harmoniously with each other.

In consequence of this political environment, literature in the Tang Dynasty boomed not only in poetry but in prose as well. Writing stories was no longer disdained by Confucian scholars as an inferior art. It even became a fashion for them to send their stories, in addition to their poems, to influential nobles as a way to win favor and recommendation. Stories finally became a conscious effort of literary creation.

The Tang Dynasty short stories developed from three chief sources, the historical records, myths and legends, and oral storytelling.

In China, keeping written official records of history is a practice perhaps as old as the written language itself. Since 841 B.C., a systematic imperial record has been compiled. There are two major styles of composition for these records. One is the listing of events chronologically, as in *The Spring and Autumn Annals*; the other is representing history as revolving around historical figures. The most famous representative is *Records of the Historian* by Sima Qian, which consists of five parts: The basic annals, tables, treatises, hereditary houses, and biographies, with emphasis on the last. As a matter of fact, these records are not bunches of cut-and-dried facts, but are good narrative prose. In ancient times, history books and literary works were not separated as they may be now.

What is written down in the historical records is considered to be the authentic facts, yet there are other "facts" too eccentric to be preserved in the official history. Confucius claimed that he would talk about neither prodigies nor spirits. And these off-the-official-record events, mostly passed down as myths and legends, developed into a literary genre of their own, known as "records of the strange," in the Wei Kingdom (220-265) and Jin Dynasty (265-420), and continued through the Northern and Southern Dynasties (420-589) up to the Tang Dynasty. Though they were all indiscriminately called "stories" by the ancients, the majority of them are still one step away from fiction, for the mysteries were treated as facts. Rather than make an artist's attempt at creative writing, the writers were "recording" events that might have interested him and might likewise be interesting to others.

Storytelling is an age-old popular entertainment. Because of its vocal and vulgar nature, very little has been handed down to reveal its earliest form. However, in the Tang Dynasty there bloomed a literary genre called *Bian Wen*. This written literature was discovered at the turn of the century in the Dunhuang caves. It is in a verse-prose form originally employed by Buddhist monks for liturgical purposes. Buddhism came to China in the late Han Dynasty (206 B.C.-220), and flourished in the Northern and Southern Dynasties. In order to popularize this alien religion, the monks had to make the abstruse doctrines easier to understand. Thus a kind of storytelling about the life and teachings of the Buddha, blended with singing and humming through the verses, became popular, somewhat like the liturgical plays in the churches of medieval Europe. And also like the fate of the liturgical plays when they spread out of the temples into the streets, the topics of *Bian Wen* were no longer confined to religious stories but expanded to include stories of lay heroes and ordinary people.

Traces of records keeping are still obvious in these stories.

A great number of them start by telling the reader unequivo-
cally the year and the place of the events and the family origin
of the protagonist. Some authors even go out of their way to
attach a postscript to the story in order to provide the reader
with the source of his information, as in "Ms. Wei's Dragon
Ride." This is not an artistic trick to make fiction sound like
fact. On the contrary, it is a sincere effort to prove that what
is related is not fictitious. This translation omits these post-
scripts.

Other traces of historical records remain. For instance,
most of the titles of the stories include the name of the main
character. Since a transliteration of those names into English
will be meaningless to readers unfamiliar with Chinese history, this translation has retitled most of the selected stories. A
few such as "Zhao Tai," "Mr. Li," and "Hermit Zhang" are left
unchanged.

The Tang Dynasty carried on the tradition of writing
about the strange and mysterious. But we can feel a subtle
change in its intent. The accounts are no longer attempting
an objective and impartial record of events. Now, the deities
and spirits are personified and put into a more or less realistic
setting that reflects human society. The authors now employ
these personified figures to tell a story and to pass on their
opinion about the world, and herein lies the fundamental
distinction between fiction and the historical records.

Pioneered by *Bian Wen*, poems seem to have embedded
themselves into these stories. They became a comfortable and
familiar vehicle for the writers to vent their feelings and
describe the scenes. This verse-in-prose style was further
developed in the later dynasties to become a conspicuous
ingredient in Chinese novels. Some of the poems, however,
are deleted from the translation because their rich idiomatic
references would require an annoying number of footnotes.

Stories composed up to the Tang Dynasty are usually very
short, often less than 200 Chinese words. Stories over 1,000

words are considered long, and stories of the length of "The Southern Bough," that is, over 4,000 words, are scarce. Succinctness is characteristic of classical Chinese writing. Western readers may feel the want of descriptive touches and transitional elements, which here must be filled in by one's imagination.

Much thought has been given to the arrangement of the stories. Though it would be best to arrange the stories according to the time they were written so the reader can gain a comprehensive view of the line of development, it is difficult, if not impossible, to do so because many source books have long since passed into oblivion, and even those still extant often lack both their publication dates and sufficient information about the author, if he is known at all, for us to pinpoint the dates. Furthermore, the dates of publication may not indicate when the story was written, as many of the source books are anthologies of still earlier works.

Neither would a listing in sequence of their original order in *Records of the Taiping Era* be desirable. The compilers of that great anthology arranged the stories into 92 categories, but Western readers may find its method of categorization rather unfamiliar. The translator has therefore reclassified the selected stories into the two major categories of "Gods and Spirits" and "Man and Life," that is, the romantic and the realistic. Of course, judged from a different point of view, one story could be assigned to either category. For instance, "The Lily" could be grouped with either "spirits" or "love," and in *Records of the Taiping Era* it is placed under "plants."

The present arrangement is not strictly chronological, but is an attempt to reflect the general trend and provide a binding thread between the stories. The reader can start with any story and does not need to worry about missing anything. Footnotes and explanatory parentheses in the text are kept to a minimum. Necessary background information, the dates of the emperors, and geographical names are all collected into appendices at the end of the book.

The selections begin with "Gods and Spirits," because that is more or less the tradition leading up to the Tang Dynasty; and the more realistic type of stories about people and their lives are a unique contribution by the Tang Dynasty. Love stories are a typical development from the middle period of the dynasty, sometimes known as *chuanqi* stories. The longer pieces in this category are placed under "miscellaneous biographies" in *Records of the Taiping Era*. As they are often published as separate editions under their own titles, and may already exist in more than one English version, they are excluded from this present selection.

From the numerous accounts of natural phenomena and technical wonders in this extensive anthology, a few have been chosen for the richness of their storytelling. This book covers 42 of the original categories with stories from 45 source books.

From these ancient Chinese writers to Sigmund Freud, dreams have fascinated people for thousands of years. The book ends with the world of dreams not because it is a late literary development, but because it may open up a treasure house of imagination for readers all over the world.

The translator

CONTENTS

GODS AND SPIRITS   1
Immortals and Magic
Old Zhang   3
The *Kylin* Rider   10
A Well Digger's Adventure   14
The Mountain God's Daughter-in-Law   18
The Ocher River God   21
Xue Zhao   26
A Hired Hand's Adventure   29
A Boat Ride on the Map   32
Priest Andao and His Two Disciples   35
The Priest Who Plugs His Ears   37
A Sigh for Millions   38
Hermit Zhang   47
One Who Paints Without Brush and Colors   50
The Old Man at the Inn   52
A Ride in a Goose Cage   54
A Dandy's Pleasure Trip   57
The Proprietress at the Wooden Bridge   60
The Carpenter and His Wooden Cranes   63
Ghosts and Spirits
A New Ghost   65
A Daredevil   67
The Traveler in Liyang County   70
Zhao Tai   73
The Courier in a Yellow Jacket   78
Mr. Tan's Bedmate   84
The Pink Sleeve   86
A Chance Meeting in Limbo   89
Mr. Li   91
Gentleman A   95

The Shattered Specter 98
General Liu 99
The Lily 101
The Girl in the Well 103
The Old Midget 107
The Fox Vampire 110
Who Is the Fox? 112
The Official's Wife 114
The Tribal Chief of Juyan 116
The Kingdom of Golden Elephant 119
A Mural in the Temple of Chrysanthemum 124

Animals

A Parrot Fights a Mountain Fire 127
The Turtle and the Mulberry Tree 128
The Long-beard Kingdom 129
The Mother Bear 132
The Hunter and the White Elephant 133
The White Ape 136
Mount Raven 142
MAN AND LIFE 145

People

The Wrestler 147
The Stutterer 149
The Princess' Stolen Treasures 151
The Rope Acrobat 154
The Corpse on the Coffin 156
Prince Ning 158
The Blacksmith's Money 160
Li Jing the Demigod 162
A Powerful Sneeze 167
The Scarred Monk 168
The Man with a Dark Countenance 172
Mr. Xiao 175
Ms. Wei's Dragon Ride 177
The Golden Berry 180

Stories from the Kingdom of Silla   181
The Pearl   185
The Blood-Stained Coat   188
The Two Friends   192
The Lis' Youngest Daughter   195
Red Strand   198
The Assassin   205
The Dark Slave   207
The Magic Bottle   211
Humor and Satire
Two Humorous Stories   213
  A) The Woman's First Mirror
  B) The Bitten Nose
The Muddlehead   214
A Potential Rapist?   215
An Old Man in the Han Dynasty   216
The Fox Tail   217
The Lucky Stones   218
The Lunar Goddess   220
The Meditator   224
The Erudite Gentlemen in the Capital   225
The Tiger at the Yangtze Gorges   227
The Disciplinarian   230
The Two Brothers   231
Love
Love-Knot Inn   234
The Blushing Cheeks   239
Re-matching the Broken Mirror   241
The Departed Soul   244
Mr. Shentu's Wife   247
The Conch Girl   251
Zhang's Daughter   255
The Maiden on the Painted Screen   257
Charcoal Valley   259
Knowledge and Skills

Sea Giants   261
The Snake on the Shoulder-pole   263
Appended: A Granny in Qiongdu County   264
The Tumor   266
The Polyps   268
The Monk in Jiang Prefecture   270
The Ingenious Carpenter   271
An Ancient Tomb   272
Water Painting   274
The World of Dreams
Into the Porcelain Pillow   275
The Southern Bough   280
A Kingdom in the Ear   293
Appendix I The Dynasties and Period Titles   298
Appendix II Glossary of Place Names   299
Appendix III Background Information   305
Appendix IV Source Titles in Chinese   310

GODS AND SPIRITS

Old Zhang

Old Zhang was a gardener in Liuhe County, Yangzhou Prefecture. Among his neighbors was a Mr. Wei, a retired official from the prefectural government, who settled there in Tianjian reign of the Liang Dynasty. Wei's eldest daughter was coming of age, so one day he called in a matchmaker, an old lady, to find him a good son-in-law.

The news excited Old Zhang. He waited at Wei's gate for the matchmaker to come out and ushered her into his house as soon as she emerged. A table was laid out with wine and food. In the heat of the meal he said, "I heard Mr. Wei's daughter is looking for a husband. Is that true?"

"Yes."

"Though I might look a bit too old, my garden provides enough to feed and clothe a family. Would you kindly make a proposal for me? I'll give you a hefty commission if you can have me engaged."

The matchmaker threw down her chopsticks and left the room with a stream of angry words. Yet, in a few days, he invited her to dinner again.

"Why can't you measure yourself properly?" said the frustrated woman. "What makes you imagine a girl from the high class would marry a gardener? To be sure, the Weis are not rich, but they won't have a problem finding a match among the gentry. You're far from her match. Do you think, simply because I've had a cup of wine at your table, I would bring shame upon myself by suggesting this crazy thing to Mr. Wei?"

"Just put in a word for me, please. If it's turned down, that's fate. I won't blame you."

Pestered by his entreaties, the matchmaker went over to

3

talk to Wei.

"How can you insult me so!" Wei exploded. "I am not so poor as to marry my daughter to a gardener! Go and ask around if any Wei has sunk so low. Who is he that he dares make such a proposal? A rustic laborer like him is beneath my reproach, but you, experienced and respected, how can you lose your sense of value?"

"I do know it was not proper for me to suggest this, but I was obliged and had to pass on his word."

"Tell him then," Wei accented his words, "if he can give me a bride-price of 500,000 strings of cash before the sun goes down, I will give him my daughter."

The matchmaker went out to tell Old Zhang.

"Fine," was all Zhang said, and in good time he had a cartload of coins sent to the Weis.

The Weis were dumbfounded. "How can a gardener have so much money, and in ready cash?" exclaimed Mr. Wei. "I was just kidding him. I never thought he could have that much. Now the money is here and the sun is still high, what shall we do?"

He had someone seek out his daughter's opinion. "That must be fate," she said calmly. So the marriage was agreed upon.

Old Zhang didn't give up gardening and selling vegetables after the marriage. He went on collecting manure and hoeing the field as he used to do, and his wife did all the daily cooking and washing without a word of complaint. The Weis and their relatives were ashamed of them, but the couple didn't give that a thought.

Several years thus passed, during which Mr. Wei was often censured by his more respectable clansmen. "We know you're not well off," some would say, "but isn't there any poor gentlemen in your neighborhood good enough for your daughter? Why on earth did you marry her to an old gardener? If you don't think much of your daughter, why don't you send her out of sight?"

So one day Wei invited Old Zhang and his wife over to dinner. With many cups of wine down, he had his misgivings confirmed.

"I thought you might miss your daughter," Zhang stood up and replied. "That's why we didn't move away right after our marriage. Now that you are bored by our company, we'll leave tomorrow morning. There is no trouble in moving, for I have a farm at the foot of the Wangwu Mountains."

Early next morning, he and his wife came over again to say good-bye. "In case you want to see us in the future," said Zhang, "you can send Elder Brother to look for us on the southern slopes." He placed a straw hat on his wife's head and helped her onto a donkey. He himself followed with a stick.

Thus they went away out of reach.

Before many years had passed, however, Mr. Wei began to miss his daughter, painting in his mind's eye doleful pictures of her haggard and shabby looks. He doubted if he could even recognize her now, so he asked his eldest son Yifang to go and see.

On the southern slopes of the Wangwu Mountains, Yifang came upon a dark slave tilling the land with an ox and plow. "Is there an Old Zhang who has a farm around here?" he asked.

The dark man dropped his whip and bowed, "Big Master, what took you so long to come? The manor house isn't far off. Would you please follow me?"

They walked east over a ridge and down across a creek. As more ridges and creeks took their turns, the view grew increasingly exotic. Descending one slope, Yifang saw on the northern side of the stream a complex of elegant brick houses adorned with red woodwork amidst what must be an enormous garden of flowers. Cranes and peacocks flew among the trees; sweet music floated in the air. "That's the Zhang's," the slave pointed. Yifang could hardly believe his eyes and ears.

An attendant in a purple gown met him at the gate and led him into the reception hall. He had never before laid eyes on such a lavishly decorated room. The hall and the entire valley seemed filled with an unnamable fragrance.

Suddenly, tinkling jewels and bracelets were heard approaching. Two waiting maids entered to announce the master of the house was coming. Next, a score of maids, all beautiful beyond description, filed into the hall in pairs as if leading a royal procession. Then a tall and handsome man stepped into the room, clad head to foot in fine silk and satin. Yifang bowed. At a closer look he found that this man with soft fair skin was none other than Old Zhang.

"A man labors in the world as if tramping over scorching fire," Zhang said, "and before he can cool down he is engulfed anew in the flames of worry and care, giving him not a moment of peace. I wonder how Elder Brother manages in that transient world. Your sister is refreshing herself. She'll attend you in a moment." They then sat and chatted.

Shortly, a maid came in to announce, "Her Ladyship is ready," and she led Yifang into an inner court.

The beams of the living chambers were of precious eaglewood, the doors were inlaid with polished sea-turtle shell, the window frames were carved out of jade, the screens were stringed pearls, and the doorsteps were of a glazy green, of what material he could not tell. His sister met him at the door, wearing layers of rich garments beyond compare. She made the routine greetings and asked after her parents with a note of indifference in her voice. A dinner was then spread out. The food tasted marvelous, though Yifang did not know what he was eating. After dinner, he was put up in a guest room.

Next morning, Old Zhang came to keep him company. Their conversation was interrupted by a maid who whispered into Zhang's ear. "We have a guest. How can we spend the night there?" he chuckled and turned to Yifang. "My sister wishes to make an excursion to Penglai, the mountain of the

6

gods. Your sister is going too. However, we'll be back before it is dark. Meanwhile, you can enjoy yourself here." He bowed and retired into the inner court.

Presently, a rosy cloud lifted from the courtyard and music sprang up. Yifang saw Old Zhang and his sister each riding a phoenix and a score of others followed on white cranes. Higher and higher they rose and gradually faded into the eastern sky, leaving only a trailing sound of music.

Yifang stayed behind and was meticulously attended to by the maids. As dusk descended, instruments were heard again and there they were, landing in the courtyard. Old Zhang and his wife greeted him, "It must be quite boring to stay alone, and yet ordinary folks won't be lucky enough to visit this fairy land. You have it in your fate to be here once, but it's not for you to stay long. You may go home tomorrow."

Next day, his sister came out to see him off, asking him to take her best wishes to their parents. "We are too far from your world to write," Old Zhang said as he handed Yifang 500 ounces of gold and a worn straw hat. "If Elder Brother should need money, you can take this hat to Old Wang and he'll give you 10 million. He owns a drug store in the northern quarter of Yangzhou City." In that way they parted. The dark slave led him to where they had first met and bowed his retreat.

Yifang carried the gold home and the whole family was more than surprised. They questioned him over and over. Some guessed that Old Zhang was a celestial being, others believed that he was a kind of sorcerer. No one of them could convince the others.

After five or six years, however, the gold was exhausted. They started to think about the money at Old Wang's, but most feared it was merely a hoax. "It's incredible anyone could claim such a huge amount for a hat without a note signed in black and white," some reasoned. Then things went worse for the family. "It'll do you no harm to try, even if you can't get a penny," they argued this time. Under their pressure, Yifang set out for Yangzhou.

He asked his way to the northern quarter of the city. In the pharmacy an elderly man was arranging herbs. "May I have the honor of knowing your family name?" Yifang asked as he entered the store.

"Wang," the old man replied.

"Old Zhang said I can get 10 million from you for this hat."

"The money is ready, but is the hat really Old Zhang's?"

"Why don't you see for yourself? You must be able to tell."

Before Old Wang could anwser, a girl emerged from behind a gray cloth curtain. "Once when Old Zhang passed by," she put in, "he asked me to mend the crown of his hat for him. It just happened that I'd run out of black thread, and had to sew it up with some red thread instead. I can certainly tell if it is the thread and my needlework." So she checked the hat and assured Old Wang that it was Old Zhang's.

So Yifang went home with the money and with a firm belief that Old Zhang was nothing less than a celestial being.

Again, the Weis grew anxious to see their daughter and Yifang was sent to the Wangwu Mountains. The hills and streams turned out to be more than a mere dozen, and there were no longer any roads. He asked many woodcutters, but no one seemed to have heard of Old Zhang and his manor. He turned home utterly disappointed. The family concluded that the celestial world was inaccessible to man, and their daughter was lost to them forever. Neither could they find Old Wang and his store again.

Years later, Yifang happened to be wandering through the streets of the northern quarter of Yangzhou when he was accosted by Old Zhang's dark slave.

"How's Elder Brother doing?" the dark man asked. "Though Her Ladyship cannot go home, she knows every family event, big or small, as if she were there herself." He took out 200 ounces of gold from his bag. "Her Ladyship asked me to give this to you. My master is chatting over a cup of wine with Old Wang in this pub. Please take a seat here and allow me to go in and tell him of your presence."

Yifang sat under the wine banner and waited till the sun dropped behind the roofs, but he didn't see Old Zhang come out. He entered the pub. It was packed, but neither Old Zhang nor Old Wang was there, nor the dark slave. He tested the gold and found it was real. He hurried home exhilarated. That sustained the family a number of years, and that was the last they heard from Old Zhang and his wife.

The *Kylin** Rider

There was once a servant of Zhang Maoshi, a native of Nanyang Prefecture, who lived at the foot of Mount Hua.

The servant was hired from the south market of the East Capital Luoyang during Zhang's visit there in the first year of Dazhong reign of the Tang Dynasty. This man, whose name was Wang Xiong, was in his forties, and he agreed to work for a mere five hundred coins a month. He was an earnest and diligent man. Furthermore, he seemed to take delight in working and never waited to be told what to do. Zhang liked him so much that he offered to double his pay, but that was declined. This made the Zhangs hold him in even higher regard.

At the end of the fifth year, however, after settling accounts, Wang told his master that he would like to quit. He had lived quite well-off in the mountains, he explained, but in the face of an impending twist of fate, he had to apply himself to hard manual labor in order to avert it. In this way he was unlike those deprived laborers who worked for pay. Now that misfortune had been warded off, it was time for him to go home. Mystified by the story, Zhang didn't venture to stop him.

At sunset that very day, Wang came in to make his farewells. "Sir," he said, "I'm very grateful to you for all the favors you've done me. In return, I would like to invite you to my place. It isn't far off, and does have a few scenes worth seeing. Would you like to come with me?"

---

* *Kylin*: a fabled and auspicious animal said to look somewhat like a deer with a scale-covered body.

"I'm much honored," replied Zhang, "but I don't want my family to know of it. Can we slip away without their noticing?"

"That's very easy," said Wang. He lopped off a bamboo stem several feet long and drew a few magic figures on it. Handing it over to Zhang, he said, "Take this with you into your bedroom and pretend a stomach ache. Send away the servants by asking them to fetch medicine. When they are all gone, hide this bamboo stick beneath the quilt and then come out to join me." Zhang carried out the plan perfectly. Satisfied, Wang said, "You're really the one who is worthy of a visit to my place."

They went south for less than a mile when they saw a groom holding the reins of a gray *kylin* and two orange-striped tigers by the roadside. The sight of them made Zhang wince, but Wang told him not to panic and just go forward. Wang himself mounted the *kylin* and bade Zhang and the groom ride the tigers.

"No fear," Wang encouraged. "I'll be at your side. The tiger is the most beautiful animal on earth. Just try it."

Zhang mounted and found the ride was smooth and steady. They scaled cliffs and canyons at will, as if traveling over level ground. By midnight they had covered more than a hundred miles. As they descended one peak, the scenery became phenomenal. The wind-fashioned pine trees, the rocks sculptured by nature, and the mansions and palaces all were fabulous.

In front of a gate a steward bowed and said, "Welcome back, Master." Hundreds of officers and officials in purple robes were kneeling by the driveway. Inside the gate were scores of maids playing an assortment of musical instruments. Their beauty and their clothing were unknown to man. After a banquet in the main hall, the host retired into a private room to change clothes, leaving Zhang at his seat to observe the place. The window lattice and door frame were elegantly carved and painted, the floor and steps richly carpeted, the

11

songs and dances heavenly. Hearing that music, one simply forgets all human worries and care. Soon Wang reappeared. He looked an entirely different man. In fact, he looked in every way as one imagines a celestial being.

"This is a celestial abode," informed the host, "and inaccessible to worldly beings, but you have it in your fate to be a guest here once. That's why I chose to spend five years at your place, to elude adversity. Immortals and mortals go separate ways, and earthly and heavenly things do not mix. So, you should go home and cultivate your moral characters. After three to five adversities, we'll be able to meet again. I am concluding my worldly affairs and will soon ascend to heaven. I've brought you into this Cave of the Haves just to give you a glimpse of heavenly pleasures. In a while I must send you back to the mortal seas. Listen: Though celestial pleasures are difficult to obtain, worldly sufferings on the other hand can be made easier to bear. It is as if we carry earth to build a mountain. Every handful contributes to its height. If you stop adding earth, it will cease to grow; if you dig under it, it will collapse. For the climber, isn't it far more difficult to ascend than to descend? From now on, cultivate your morals. After six or seven adversities, your soul will be purified. By then, when you look back, you'll see your earthly discards piled mountain high, and you'll discover that the four seas are mostly composed of tears from your worldly parents, wife and children. Never stop cultivating yourself and a lifetime is but a fraction of eternity. The more firmly you persist, the farther away you'll be from your mortal flesh, and the closer you'll be to success. Usually, when I meet someone with an aspiring heart and clean spirit who can be awakened, I encourage him and also provide him with 1,000 ounces of gold for his family's livelihood."

He helped Zhang onto the *kylin*, and with the groom leading the reins he accompanied Zhang home on foot.

Zhang's family was crying around his bed when they

arrived. Zhang dropped the gold into the well and Wang retrieved the bamboo stick and asked Zhang to slip back beneath the sheets.

"Tomorrow morning, I'm going to visit the Penglai Isle. You will be able to see rosy clouds on the Lotus Peak. That's my carriage," Wang whispered into Zhang's ear as he bowed his retreat.

Zhang suddenly let out a moan. His family was surprised and asked him how he felt.

"At first I felt a pain in my stomach," he invented, "and all of a sudden I sensed someone summoning me, and then lost consciousness. I really wonder how long it has been."

"It's seven days already," they replied. "We hurried to fetch medicine only to return and find you had passed out. But as your body remained warm, we didn't place you in a coffin."

The next morning, Zhang watched and indeed saw a patch of rosy cloud on the Lotus Peak. He resigned from office and went roaming among the sacred mountains. Later he returned home, dredged up the gold from the well and gave it to his family. He left again for the mountains, and never returned.

Translator's note:

To be an immortal is a Taoist dream. Some try to obtain that goal by experimenting with different longevity elixers, some insist on various kinds of self-realization. Immortality, according to one school, can be subdivided into three levels depending on one's "merits." Those who attain immortality after death are of the lowest level; those who roam the deep mountains are of the second level; and those who are able to lift themselves up into the air and ascend to heaven are the highest. Wang Xiong, the immortal being in this story, is probably at a transition point from the second to the highest level.

13

A Well Digger's Adventure

In the first year of Shenlong reign of the Tang Dynasty, a rich country gentleman in Zhushan County, named Yinke, hired workers to dig a water well behind the village. Two years had passed and the shaft had been already sunk to the depth of 1,000 feet, but, strange to say, no water was found. Yinke was resolved and wouldn't give up.

One month into the third year of digging, the digger at the bottom suddenly heard the muffled noises of roosters crowing and dogs barking coming through the ground. A few more feet down, a tunnel appeared in the side of the shaft and the digger ventured in. He fumbled ahead for dozens of steps. Then the darkness seemed to be dispelled by some natural light and he continued to descend.

The tunnel opened onto a high mountain peak. There he stood facing another world. Mountain ranges of glazy rocks unfurled before his eyes and in each valley there were palaces of gold and silver. There were gigantic trees too, whose trunks had joints like those of the bamboo, yet whose leaves were no smaller than those of a palm tree. Colorful birds, cranes perhaps, swooped amidst tree tops. Multicolored butterflies of the size of fans were dancing up and down among purple flowers larger than cushions. Among the rocks were twin springs. One in which the water was limpid and clear, the other milky white. He came down to the palaces, hoping to see someone who could satiate his curiosity. Above the gate arch hung a board inscribed in silver with the characters "Celestial Osmanthus Palace."

Out from the janitor's room hurried two men about five-feet tall, their faces bean-curd soft, their lips naturally red, their hair silkily black and their clothes light and filmy like smoke. On their heads they wore a coronet of gold, but they walked bare-footed. They asked the digger who he was and how he managed to come to this place. The digger did not have time to finish explaining when a throng gathered at the gate demanding to know why there was such a smell of filthy mortal. Blamed for not reporting sooner, the janitors meekly replied that a worker from the outside world, who had trespassed by accident, was just asking his way.

Presently, a messenger in red arrived with a decree, ordering the janitors to send the intruder away with due courtesy. The digger bowed his thanks.

"Since you are already here, why don't you ask for permission to have a look around before you leave?" one janitor suggested.

"I was afraid of being ill-mannered. If sightseeing is possible, do you mind putting in a good word for me?"

The janitor then threw in a jade slat, which returned as quickly as a boomerang. With the slat in hand, he led the worker first to the clear spring to wash himself and his clothes, and next to the milky spring to rinse his mouth. It tasted like cow's milk, sweet and natural. The worker drank several mouthfuls. It seemed to quench his hunger and at the same time brought on a slight feeling of tipsiness.

The janitor guided him from palace to palace without entering any. In about half a day, they reached a walled city on the outskirts of the mountains. Even the walls were made of bricks of gold and silver. Three huge characters in jade were inscribed above the town gate: "Stairway to Heaven."

"What place is this?" asked the digger.

"This city is where the newly converted immortals reside. They must live here 700,000 days preparing themselves morally before they can rise to the heavens and have a place in one of the various paradises. And only after that can they be appointed to heavenly positions with responsibility, and then they'll be able to travel freely through space."

"Since yours is a heavenly paradise, how come it is *below* my world?"

"My country is in fact the upper sphere of the underworld, just as there is a heavenly paradise above your world exactly like mine. ... Now, it's time for you to return."

They traced their way up the mountains. At the milky spring the janitor stopped to give the worker a chance to take a few more drinks. Reaching the peak, however, the digger could not find the tunnel through which he had come.

"Though it might have seemed only a moment to you here," said the janitor, "decades have crept by in your world. It's unlikely that you'll find the old tunnel. Let me find the key to the Heavenly Gate for you."

The digger thanked him for his trouble.

In no time, the janitor returned with a gold seal in one hand and a jade slat in the other. He led the worker up another peak to an imposing gate tower. The guards bowed most respectfully at the sight of the seal. The janitor pronounced a command from the jade slat. Instantly, the gate flung open, and as soon as the digger stepped across the threshold wind and clouds swept him off his feet so fast that all scenes were blurred and only a trailing string of words from the janitor's lips were caught: "Bon voyage. Remember me to ..."

Before long, the clouds dispersed and he found himself in a cave on top of Mount Lone Star, 10 miles to the north of Fangzhou Prefecture. Asking about Yinke, he learned that he was now in the seventh year of Zhenyuan reign and Yinke's great-grandson had come into inheritance of the farm. Nobody remembered that anyone had ever tried to sink a well behind the village.

He found his way to a huge pit where the well had once been—it must have caved in long ago. He looked for his own kinsfolk but they seemed to have passed into oblivion.

16

The mortal world no longer appealed to him. Food became distasteful. He wandered about for some time. Years later, rumor had it that he was seen in the Cockscomb Mountains, and that was the last anyone ever heard of him.

Translator's note:
This story is singular in that it goes against the common belief that gods live above in heaven. If they live beneath us, aren't we gods in their eyes?

Before science proved beyond doubt that the world is a globe with life spread all over its surface, people were always curious to know what was on the other side of the earth. The author was not far off in presuming that there was a world similar to our own down there, if only we dug deep enough.

The Mountain God's
Daughter-in-Law

In the early days of Kaiyuan reign, a discharged officer of the royal guards was returning to his hometown in the east from Chang'an, the West Capital.

Approaching the temple to the god of Mount Hua, he was accosted by a shabbily dressed lady's maid, who said that her mistress would like to meet him. He was then led to a young woman of about 17, pale and haggard. "I'm not any ordinary human being," she introduced herself, "but the bride of the third son of the mountain god. My husband is a real tyrant. You see, my parents live thousands of miles away at the North Sea, and for three years I haven't heard a word from them, so that my husband thinks he can mistreat and snub me as he pleases. As I learned you're going to the east coast, I hope you can do me a favor by bringing my parents this letter. My father will certainly reward your pains."

Filled with sympathy, he agreed to help, and asked exactly how and where he should deliver it.

"Knock on the second tree on the shore," she replied, "and someone will answer it."

The man kept his word and finally reached the North Sea. He knocked on the tree and a red door suddenly appeared in the trunk. A voice greeted him from within, and he handed in the letter. Presently, the doorman opened the gate and announced that the king extended his welcome.

A hundred steps or so brought him to another gate. Entering, he saw amidst thousands of serving maids a man over 10 feet tall, clad in a scarlet robe. He must be the king, he guessed, as he was offered a seat.

"I haven't had a word from my daughter in the past three years," the king said as he broke the seal and read. "How dare he!" he burst out in a terrible rage and shouted for his lieutenants, who appeared almost instantly. They were also 10 feet tall, with frightening looks and disproportionally large heads and giant noses. The king ordered them to deploy an army of 50,000 strong and attack Mount Hua on the 15th of the month. When they left the hall, he turned round and told the servants to bring the letter bearer two bolts of silk. "Please accept this token of my gratitude," he said.

Two bolts of silk were not much of a reward for all his troubles, he thought unhappily. Anyway, he thanked the king and stood up to leave. "Don't give away these two bolts unless you're offered 20 million coins," the king said in farewell.

Curious to see what would happen, he returned to Mount Hua. Toward dusk on the 15th he noticed dark clouds piling up over the eastern horizon and quickly spreading west. Soon thunder was heard rumbling in the distance. At the same time a howling gale rose over the mountain, pulling out trees by their roots and blustering east as if to repel the onrushing clouds. By now the mountain was overcast. Fire poured down from heaven; the earth quivered with the booms; even the slopes seemed to glow in the darkness. This lasted throughout the night.

At dawn, the mountain was scorched and charred. That was sufficient proof to make him continue his trip to the capital to sell the silk.

People thought him crazy when he asked for 20 million coins, but despite their ridicule he wouldn't sell it for a coin less. Not many days passed when there came a nobleman on a white horse, who accepted the price straightaway. He already had that sum in cash deposited in the market vault, he said. When asked why he was buying such expensive silk, the nobleman answered that the god of the Weihe River was going to marry his daughter, and this silk would be the best

19

gift, for silk from the North Sea is the world's finest. He added that he was just thinking of dispatching a dealer there to buy it when he learned that someone was peddling it right here in the market, and this saved him a lot of trouble.

With the money, the ex-officer went into trading. Months later, after selling out his wares, he decided to go home.

Passing by Mount Hua, he came across the same maid he had met before. She told him that her mistress was coming to express her gratitude in person. Then he saw a cow-drawn buggy descending the slopes, attended by a dozen maids. The buggy pulled up and out stepped a young lady. He could hardly recognize her, for this time her clothes were rich and elegant, and her eyes were bright and smiling. She made a deep curtsey and said, "Thank you, sir, for taking the trouble to bring my letter to my parents. Since that punishment, my husband has been quite sweet to me. I owe you a lot, and it'd be a shame if I couldn't do more for you. Listen now. Because you were the messenger, my husband has shifted his anger onto you. At this moment he is waiting for you at the Tongguan Pass with 500 soldiers. If you continue eastward you'll no doubt fall into his hands. Better return to the capital and stay there for the time being. His Majesty will soon pay a visit to the East Capital. Then you may find a place on the drum cart and go through Tongguan without harm. Nether spirits are afraid of drums." Having said that, she disappeared.

Scared, he immediately turned back to Chang'an. In a couple of months the emperor did set out on a royal visit to the East Capital. The man bribed the drummer and slipped through the Tongguan Pass in the emperor's train.

Translator's note:
In the Tang Dynasty stories we find that the gods are not always depicted as decent beings above worldly vices. In fact, they may look more like wicked lords familiar to human society. They bully the weak, they gamble (as in "The Courier in a Yellow Jacket"), and they have all the weaknesses of human beings (see for instance "The Ocher River God").

The Ocher River God

In the early years of Zhenyuan reign, among the administrative staff of Tang'an County in Shu, there was a Mr. Yuan. His tenure of office had just expired, giving him leisure to go sightseeing.

One day, he had just put up at an inn in Bachuan County when a man in white paid him a call. When they were both seated, the man plunged into an introduction. "My name is Gao. I live in Xinming County nearby. I served in the army for many years, but now I'm retired and I'm on a random tour." After chitchatting a while, Yuan was surprised to find that the man was extraordinarily intelligent. "I'm something of a fortune-teller," continued the man, "and I can tell your history quite accurately." Yuan asked him to make a try. To his utter amazement, the man recounted every detail of his life, event after event as if reading from a book.

That night when all was quiet the man confided to Yuan, "I'm not a human being. There's something I'd like to talk about with you. Shall I go ahead?"

Jumping to his feet in terror, Yuan babbled, "Not a human? Then you have to be a ghost! Have you come to lay a curse on me?"

"No, I'm not a ghost, neither am I here to fetch your soul. I came simply because I'd like to solicit your help. I'm the god of the Ocher River and my shrine is south of the county seat of Xinming. During last year's long rainy season my temple house leaked and crumbled and no one cared to repair it, leaving me to the mercy of the elements, buffalo boys and wood cutters. The villagers looked upon me as if I were a mere pile of dirt! Now that I've told you who I am, if you promise to help, I'll continue; if not, I'll leave you alone. I'll bear no grudge against you whatever."

"Since this is the god's wish," replied Yuan, "I don't see why I shouldn't pledge my help."

"Then listen carefully. Next year, you're to be appointed magistrate of Xinming County. I'll be much obliged if you can rebuild my temple and see to the seasonal sacrifices. You won't let me down, will you?" Having received Yuan's assurance he went on, "Upon your arrival at the county you ought to pay me a visit. However, we gods and you humans shouldn't be seen mixing company. I don't want to be debased by your servants. So you must leave them outside and enter the temple all by yourself. I look forward to another talk with you then."

"Your wish shall be honored," Yuan promised.

At the end of the year, as the river god had prophesied, Yuan was appointed magistrate of Xinming County. As soon as he assumed office he made an inquiry and learned that there indeed was a temple to the god of the Ocher River a couple of miles south of the county seat. Before a fortnight had passed he arranged for a trip to the temple. He dismounted a hundred yards in front of the temple and told his attendants to wait. Into the temple he went alone. The roofs had caved in; the walls were defaced; wild grass had sprung up unchecked. While he was looking around, a man in white walked out from behind the temple. It was none other than Mr. Gao, smiling radiantly. Yuan bowed.

"You're really as good as your word, and I'm most honored by this visit," said Gao as he led Yuan up the steps. On the verandah Yuan saw an old monk in shackles, watched over by a pack of guards. "Who is this monk?" he asked.

"He's Monk Daocheng from a temple to the east of the county, a sinner. I've had him here for almost a year, giving him a good whipping everyday at sunrise and sunset. He is to be released in a fortnight."

"Well, since he is not dead yet, how can you hold his soul

in chains?"

"When a living person's soul is apprehended, he is always found ill, and he has no way of knowing it is my doing. Since you've promised to rebuild my temple," the river god reminded him, "you'd better make haste."

"I will keep my word."

He returned to his office to calculate the labor and building materials needed for the project. It turned out to be far beyond his means. According to what the river god said, he thought that Monk Daocheng must be lying seriously ill in his temple, but that he would recover pretty soon. What if I should make up a story and talk him into undertaking the reconstruction project? He wouldn't even suspect me. Having thus made up his mind, he got on his horse and rode out of the east county-gate. Upon inquiry, he learned that there indeed was a monk called Daocheng, who had been lying ill for nearly a year.

"I'm dying," the monk told him. "Twice a day my whole body aches terribly."

"You do seem to be in bad shape with little chance of surviving," said Yuan. "Nevertheless, I may be able to rid you of your disease if you promise money and building materials to reconstruct the temple to the Ocher River god."

"If only I can recover," exclaimed the monk, "what money or materials I won't spend!"

"I'm good at communing with ghosts," Yuan lied. "The other day I happened to pay a visit to the Ocher River Temple where I saw your soul shackled to the wall. I summoned the river god and demanded an explanation. He said that it was because you had sinned in your previous life. Out of pity for your suffering, I told the god that since it's improper to hold a living person's soul in custody, an immediate release would be wise. I also said that you would rebuild his temple, a claim which I thought you would honor. The god seemed pleased and he agreed to forgive you and your crime in a fortnight.

23

That's why I told you that you could expect a speedy recovery. Just now you pledged money and materials for the reconstruction. If you should go back on your word when you've recovered, let me warn you, you'll be courting disaster."

"It's extremely kind of you to have told me all that," said the monk perfunctorily.

To be sure, the monk recovered in less than a fortnight. He called together his disciples and said, "It has been 50 years since I abandoned my home to devote myself to Buddhism. As you all know, I was struck down by an illness. The other day, the magistrate told me it was caused by the god of the Ocher River, and I should repair his temple after I have recovered. A temple is built for gods to give their blessings to man and to answer people's prayers. Now that it has inflicted such adversity on me, it should be demolished!" Having said that, he led his disciples to the temple with spades and picks. They pulled down the statues and halls. Nothing was left standing.

The next day the monk went to see Yuan.

"Glad to see you've recovered, Master," Yuan greeted him joyously, "so I was not cheating."

"Right you are. You saved my life. I'm much indebted to you."

"So it's high time you repair the temple, otherwise misfortune may befall you again."

"We worship the gods because they can extend our happiness and avert bad fortune. In a drought we can ask them for rain; when suffering a deluge, we plead for sunny days. That's why in ruling his land His Majesty decrees a temple in every locality, big or small. All is for the happiness of his subjects. How can we put up with such gods as this one of the Ocher River, who makes people ill rather than happy! I've razed his temple to the ground."

Yuan was dumbfounded and humbled. His fear then increased with each passing day, while the monk seemed to become ever more robust.

One day, more than a month after the monk's visit, a subordinate of Yuan's was charged with an offense and brought before him. Unfortunately, the man died under interrogation. The enraged family of the dead man lodged a complaint against him at the prefectural government, and in consequence he was exiled to Duanxi, a remote county on the southern frontiers. Passing through the Yangtze Gorges, he saw in the distance a man in white standing by the roadside. A closer look affirmed that it was none other than the god of the Ocher River.

"I asked you to repair my temple," said the river god reproachfully. "Why on earth did you make that monk demolish my statue and house? It's all your fault that I've become a homeless vagabond! How gratifying it is to see you also banished to the barren areas!"

"It was the monk who tore down your temple," muttered Yuan sheepishly. "Why blame me for that?"

"At present, Monk Daocheng is swelling with good fortune so that I can't affect him. But as you're at the ebb of fate, I certainly can take my revenge." So speaking, he disappeared.

Yuan was greatly annoyed by this encounter. A few days later he succumbed to an illness and died.

Translator's note:

In this story we see an inversion of the norm—a god is overpowered by a human being, and a monk at that. The monk takes such a pragmatic attitude toward the god and temple that his approach borders on atheism.

Xue Zhao

Xue Zhao and Cui Yu studied together at Mount Lu. There had been four of them, but two had quit halfway. Cui exercised great diligence in the Confucian classics and successfully passed the imperial examination. Only Xue devoted himself entirely to the study of Taoism. We have no idea who his teacher was, but after many years he seemed to have attained the Way.

At the foot of the mountain there lived a man who had been paralyzed for years. Medicine failed to show any effect, and he was reduced to a living corpse, waiting for the final hour to come.

One day Xue came along the road and happened to take a rest in the tree shade by the sick man's gate. When he learned about the case he asked for permission to see the paralytic. "It's nothing serious," he said to the patient. "I can cure you." He took out a pill, which was smaller than a grain of rice, and handed it to the man's family. "Let him take half of this pill with water tomorrow morning, and his condition will improve. If he is not fully recovered in three days, give him the other half." The sick man's family was incredulous. They had engaged doctors by the dozens and wasted tens of thousands on medicine, and still the patient was no better than a bundle of bones puffing its last. How can half a pill work? Anyway, they gave him half of the pill the next morning. By noon, the sick man could sit up and start to eat, and then, leaning on a stick he was able to walk! Thus in three days' time he seemed to have recovered. The other half of the pill restored a glitter to his eyes, his hair turned jet black and his skin jade smooth as if he were again in his twenties.

Xue returned in a month and said to the man, "You're just the right person to study Taoism. My pill has not only driven away your disease but has purged your body." He then taught the man the fundamentals of Taoism. As it happened, the man later became a hermit at Mount Lu.

Cui, on the other hand, having succeeded in the imperial examination, was appointed lieutenant of a suburban county of the East Capital. On his way to take office he came across Xue at the Sanxiang post house. They talked about the old days. Cui, full of pride at his success in official circles, could not help but show pity on his old friend's unkempt and time-worn looks. They chatted till the sun declined in the west. "It's a long time since we met last," Xue said. "Why don't we go over to my humble cottage and have a good night's chat? It's not far away." Cui agreed and followed, leaving his horse and attendants at the post house.

First they went along a narrow footpath through barren fields. After half a mile or so they came upon rare trees and flowers. Finally there appeared an imposing gate tower and high walls. The buildings were august and magnificent like a king's palace. Cui hesitated while Xue went straight in. Scores of attendants came to wait on him and accompanied him to his seat in the main hall. He invited Cui in and offered a seat beside him. "You've got a good position in official circles," he remarked, "so this is not a place for you to remain. But for this one night it won't harm your career." He gave orders for a banquet and music and everything was ready in minutes. Together they went into another hall where an elaborate feast was spread out. Besides the two of them, there were no other guests. Around them were over 40 girl musicians playing soft tunes on their various instruments while another 10 served wine and food. Sitting nearest to Cui was a girl playing the harp. He judged her the best looking of the whole band. He also noticed that there were two lines of verse inscribed on

27

her harp, which read:

Afar I know you by the boat you ride;
Atop the clouds I watch trees greet the tide.

After the feast, Xue asked if there was any girl he liked in particular. Cui mentioned the harp player. "You'll have her all right," Xue laughed, "but not tonight."

The day was dawning and it was time to move on. Xue offered 500 ounces of gold as a farewell present. So reluctant were they to part that they walked hand in hand till they hit the main road.

Hardly had a month slipped by since Cui assumed office when he was engaged to a local beauty, whose surname was Liu. He always felt that he had met her somewhere before, but simply couldn't recall the occasion. One day, his wife took out her harp to play him a tune, and on her harp he saw the two lines of the poem that he clearly remembered. "Have you played at a party recently?" he asked.

"On a certain day some time ago," his wife recalled, "I was in bed with a fever. I dreamed of a herald coming after me. Taoist Master Xue to the west of town is entertaining an important guest tonight, he announced. All virgins within 100 miles with some musical talent must go to serve the occasion. He had already collected more than 40 girls, so I followed. We served a night at the banquet in honor of a Mr. Cui. When I woke up, the fever was gone. That Master Xue must be an immortal, and that Mr. Cui, as I think of it now, looks like you!"

The complementary parts of their stories surprised them greatly. Only then did Cui realize that Xue Zhao had attained immortality.

A Hired Hand's Adventure

Early in Zhenyuan reign of the Tang Dynasty there lived in Guangling County a man called Feng Jun who, made his living as a hired hand. He was sturdily built and reliable, so it was not difficult for him to find work.

One day, an elderly Taoist priest who had purchased a heavy sack of ores in the market was offering an attractive sum of 1,000 copper coins to anyone who would help him carry the sack to Liuhe County, some 40 miles to the west. Feng volunteered. He then rushed home to tell his wife that he would be out of town for a few days.

"Now come with me," said the priest when they were ready. "Instead of taking the more direct land route, I'd rather follow the water course up the river. If we happen upon an upstream boat, you can rest your muscles. I won't take a coin out of your pay."

They found a boat all right, but once out on the open waters the wind dropped.

"How can we go against the stream without a good tail wind?" remarked the priest. "Let me invoke some magic power."

Feng and the boatman were ordered to lie face down in the cabin while the priest remained on deck, managing the sails and rudder. The two in the cabin could only hear the sound of whistling winds over the waves. The boat seemed to be lifted out of its element and flying. They shut their eyes tight, transfixed with fear.

After a while the priest called them out of the cabin. They were on a serene lake, facing row upon row of sun-kissed mountains. It took the boatman quite a while to realize that

29

they were in Meteor Bay at the foot of Mount Lu.

The priest jumped ashore and took out his pouch to pay, but the boatman was too awed by his magic power to accept the fare.

"Take it," said the priest. "I took liberties with your boat because I knew you live in Xunyang and wish to get home as early as you can. You've done your job, and here's your pay." The boatman accepted with a most grateful bow.

The priest then told Feng to shoulder the sack. They threaded their way through a beach of boulders until they came upon an enormous table rock at the very foot of the mountain. The priest picked up a stone and knocked on the flat rock in a sort of code. The rock split open and out stepped a neophyte. "Welcome back, Master," he beamed.

The priest then led Feng into a cave. At first, the way was difficult, a treacherous and long descent. Then it leveled off and the tunnel became wider. Further on, it grew brighter. There was a spacious hall in which scores of Taoist priests were rollicking about, some playing chess. When they saw the elderly priest they all asked why he was so late. They told Feng to put down the sack and ordered him out immediately. The elderly priest intervened, saying that having traveled all day Feng must be hungry, and now that it was almost dinner time, better let him eat something before he set off again. So Feng was given a bowl of sesame rice and a bowl of soup. Thick and sweet, the milky soup was like nothing he ever had before.

"Thanks for carrying that heavy sack for me. Here's the 1,000 coins I promised you," said the elderly priest as he accompanied Feng to the cave mouth. "Tuck this pouch in your belt. Remember, don't look at the contents until you get home. It will bring you good fortune." Then he asked Feng about his family. Feng replied that he had a wife and four children.

The priest also poured out 100-odd tiny pills from his

medicine gourd and handed them to Feng. "One pill," he said, "will sustain you a hundred days without the need to eat any food."

"So far from home now, how shall I go back?" Feng muttered to himself as they emerged from the cave.

"Don't worry. I'll take care of that, too," said the priest, leading him to the rocky beach where he looked around and picked out a boulder shaped like a crouching tiger. "Climb onto it," he commanded, and wrapping a piece of cloth around the tiger's head, he placed the ends in Feng's hands as if they were reins. "Don't open your eyes until your feet step on firm ground," he warned. So saying, he whipped the rock with his horse-tail whisk and Feng felt the rock taking off into the air.

His feet touched ground again. He opened his eyes to see that he was at the gate of Guangling County, where people were just starting to light candles.

His family was amazed to see him back so soon. He untied the pouch and poured out the coins—they were all gold. He no longer needed to work as a hired hand and could have his own land to farm!

His overnight riches, however, aroused the suspicion of his neighbors. So when a case of robbing was reported, they believed that Feng was involved and dragged him to the magistrate.

It happened that the magistrate himself was an alchemy and magic enthusiast. He was only too pleased to hear Feng's story and requested to see the pills. But strange to say, once the pills were placed in his hand, they slipped through his fingers and vanished. Feng then referred to the tiger-shaped boulder which was still standing outside the county-gate. The magistrate was convinced by this and acquitted him.

Encouraged by Feng's evidence, the magistrate became even more devoted to alchemy, but he never managed to produce a magic pill. Feng and his descendants enjoyed long and comfortable lives.

A Boat Ride on the Map
(abridged*)

Chen Jiqing, a native of southeast China, had tarried in the capital for 10 years. He remained for the imperial examination, and he felt ashamed to go home, for he had sworn that he would not return until he accomplished something of consequence. He managed a living by writing letters for the illiterate and copying lawsuit documents. Occasionally, he would go to the Black Dragon Temple to visit the abbot.

On one such visit it happened that the abbot was out. He decided to wait in the inner room. As he lifted the door curtain, he found an old man already waiting by the fireplace who introduced himself as a hermit in the Southern Mountains and invited him to take a seat by the fire. It was a long wait. The hermit turned to him and asked, "The afternoon is waning. Aren't you hungry?"

"Oh, indeed," replied Chen, "but the abbot is not back yet."

The hermit removed a small pouch from under his arm and took out a piece of dried herb about an inch square. He stewed it in a cup of water and handed it over to Chen. "This might cure your hunger," he said. As Chen sipped it down, he felt a sense of release. Cold and hunger were entirely swept away.

On the eastern wall of the room was a map of the country. To kill time, Chen traced the map with his fingertip to locate his hometown. "If one could actually sail down along these rivers," he sighed, "starting right here from the Weihe River,

---

* Five poems have been deleted from the text.

32

into the Yellow River, passing through the East Capital, then down the Huaihe River into the Yangtze River, and all the way home by boat, it would be the accomplishment of a lifetime."

"Your wish is not that difficult to attain," smiled the hermit. He asked a neophyte to bring him a bamboo leaf from the courtyard and folded it into the shape of a boat. He placed the boat on the map where the Weihe River lay and said, "Sir, now concentrate your mind and keep your eyes fixed on this boat, and you'll be able to fulfill your life-long wish. But, remember one thing: Don't stay too long at home."

After staring at the boat for a while he felt that waves were rising on the Weihe River and the leaf-boat had expanded. A sail was hoisted and he felt himself stepping aboard. The boat set sail, floating down the Weihe River to the Yellow River. Everything happened exactly as he had traced it over the map. On his way he stopped over at scenic spots and historical sites, and paid visits to famous temples, leaving a poem here and there on the walls.

He reached home in about 10 days and his wife and brothers welcomed him at the gate. In his excitement he penned a poem on the white walls of his study lamenting the swift passage of time and his uneventful life. That evening he said to his wife, "The date set for the imperial examination is drawing near. I can't stay. I must return tonight."

When it was completely dark, he boarded his leaf-boat and disappeared up the stream. His wife and brothers wailed at the riverside, thinking that his ephemeral appearance was but an apparition of his ghost.

The leaf retraced its route upstream back to the Weihe River. Once off the boat, he chartered a coach and rode up to the Black Dragon Temple. There he saw the hermit sitting by the fireplace with a shaggy cape tightly wrapped round his shoulders.

"I'm back from my visit home," he exclaimed gratefully,

33

"but wasn't all that a mere dream?"

"You'll be able to tell for yourself in 60 days," replied the hermit with a smile on his lips.

The day was getting late, yet there was still no sign of the abbot's return. The hermit had left, and Chen went back to his rented room in town.

Two months after that incident, his wife suddenly arrived from southeast China. She was surprised to find him alive, for she had thought him dead and had come with sufficient money to take his remains home. She explained that she came because he showed up unexpectedly at home one day and vanished the same night leaving a doleful verse on the wall of his study. Only then did he believe that what he experienced was not a dream.

Next spring, as he was once again disappointed in the imperial examination, he decided that it was really time to go home. On the temple walls he located his poems in his own handwriting. The ink still looked fresh.

He made a name for himself the following year. Thereafter, he abstained from food and social life, and disappeared into the Southern Mountains.

Priest Andao and His Two Disciples

In the Tang Dynasty, a Taoist, Mao Andao, lived in Mount Lu. He was not only versed in the art of drawing magic figures and employing ghosts, but was also a master of transformation. Among his hundreds of disciples there were two whom he had taught the magic arts of invisibility and visual penetration. These two, however, soon thought of quitting, excusing themselves on the grounds that their aged parents at home needed to be taken care of.

The priest permitted them to go, but warned, "I've taught you the art of invisibility to facilitate your learning Taoism. It's not a trick for you to go around and show off, or for any other indecent purposes. Should you go against my teaching, I can revoke your power the moment you attempt it." The two nodded and left.

Run Prefecture was then governed by the Duke of Jin who held adverse opinions about Taoism and its practitioners. After leaving the mountains, however, the two went straight to the Duke's official residence to solicit favors, thinking that if the Duke should show any displeasure, they could slink away with the help of invisibility.

The Duke did receive them, but did not treat them as important guests. Feeling slighted, the two behaved audaciously. They even swaggered up to the Duke's seat. The Duke was infuriated. He ordered the guards to have them tied up. It was then that the two resorted to their art of invisibility but, as the priest had warned, their art wouldn't work. So they were seized and detained for execution.

"We wouldn't have dared to behave like that if we hadn't been taught by our master. It's his fault," the two contended.

The Duke had long wished to have the whole Taoist school rooted out, so he said, "Probably you can save your neck, if you just tell me the name and whereabouts of your master."

The two were about to speak when the guards announced that a priest was at the gate. Overjoyed by this opportunity to have them all here and exterminated once and for all, the Duke immediately asked the priest to come in.

The priest entered with an air of nobility. His beautiful flowing long beard and thick eyebrows gave him a venerable look. For a moment the Duke forgot he was receiving a hated priest. He rose from his seat to extend his welcome and offered the priest a chair beside him.

"I heard," the priest said, "my two disciples acted foolishly in front of Your Excellency and now their lives hang upon your mercy. But before Your Excellency carries out the execution, may I first talk to them and make them realize they were wrong?"

Escorted by a troop of guards, the two in heavy pillories and shackles were led to the hall steps with naked swords pressed against their necks. They kowtowed and pleaded for life.

"May I have some water?" the priest asked the Duke's attendants. He was refused, for fear that water might be a medium of escape.

The priest didn't seem annoyed. He picked up the inkslab from the table, took a sip and sprayed the ink over the two, who turned on the spot into a couple of black mice, scurrying hither and thither in the courtyard. Before anyone realized what was happening, the priest himself changed into an eagle. Clenching one mouse in each claw, he soared up into the sky.

The stunned Duke shook his head and sighed.

The Priest Who Plugs His Ears

Outside the south gate of Lizhou City was a thriving market. One day, amidst the throng of peddlers a shabby Taoist priest was hawking gourd seeds. He claimed that in a year or two his gourds could be put to great use. Besides, all one needed to do was put the seed in the ground without going to the usual trouble of constructing a trellis. Each seed, he emphasized, would sprout and bear only one, but giant, gourd. He also drew on the ground the size of his promised gourd, which was incredibly big. Nevertheless, despite his persistent efforts no one bought even a single seed. "Don't be taken in by that crazy priest," was the crowd's comment.

Then the priest covered both ears with his hands and scurried through the market, shouting that the din of wind and torrents was deafening. He was trailed by a swarm of laughing kids, who thought him good fun.

One autumn night the following year, the Jialing River flooded. Water rampaged as far as the eye could see and hundreds of families were either drowned or washed adrift. In the distance, they beheld the priest sitting in a scooped-out gourd, his hands over his ears, crying that the noise was too much to bear.

Nobody knew where he sailed to.

A Sigh for Millions

Du Zichun, a man who lived around the time between the Northern Zhou and Sui dynasties, was a loafer in his youth with no sense of responsibility and no thought of a career. He squandered away his days and his inheritance in wine and idleness, and his relatives were soon tired of his incessant pleas for assistance.

Winter set in. With rags on his back and an empty stomach, he wandered aimlessly through the streets of the capital, Chang'an; his famished looks had long been a familiar sight from the east end to the west gate of the city. From dawn to dusk on that particular day, he had not had a single bite, and could not think of anyone to turn to. He stared into the blankness of the firmament and let out a deep, long sigh. Just then an old man approached, leaning on a stick. "Sir," he asked, "what makes you sigh so mournfully?" As Du poured out his grievance, his disgruntlement at the coldness of his relatives was unconcealed.

"How much do you think is needed to make a good living?" inquired the old man.

"I can live on 30,000 or 50,000."

"That probably won't be enough. Why not ask for more?"

"A hundred thousand, then."

"Raise it."

"A million?"

"Raise it."

"Three million?" uttered Du in breathtaking disbelief.

"Well, that might do," said the old man calmly as he pulled out a string of 1,000 coins from his sleeve. "Take this. You'll need it tonight. At noon tomorrow, I'll be waiting for

you at the Persian Mansion in the west end. But don't be late."

Du went as he was bidden. The old man handed him the three million and left without even disclosing his name.

Money rekindled his old habit of lavishness, and he imagined he would never again have to live a vagrant's life. He was seen riding fine steeds through the streets, wearing expensive furs, drinking in taverns, and wallowing in music and songs in brothels. His enterprising ambition was flung to the winds. In a year or two the money had slipped through his fingers. His grand carriage and costly clothes were replaced by cheaper brands. Next, he gave up horses for donkeys. Then, he trudged on foot instead of riding. Before he realized it, he had exhausted his means. What could he do but have the heaviest sigh? At that moment the old man reappeared. Clasping his hands, the old man exclaimed, "Sir, you are a real marvel. How can you be so poor so soon? I'll give you another chance. How much do you think you'll need this time?"

As shame clutched his throat, he kept his head bowed no matter how earnestly the old man entreated him. "Come tomorrow at noon," said the old man soothingly, "to our last meeting place."

Overcoming his embarrassment, Du kept the appointment and this time received 10 million. He had made up his mind to turn over a new leaf and invest wisely so as to outshine the wealthiest men in history. But as soon as the money was deposited in his hands, his determination wavered. He sank back into his old spendthrift self. In another year or two he was worse off than before.

Once again, he came upon the old man in the street. Covering his burning cheeks with his sleeve, he turned round and took to his heels. The old man gripped him by the hem of his gown and said, "You're really a bad manager of your life." Placing 30 million in his hand, he warned, "If you can't do better this time, you are incurable."

He had been down and out, and none of his affluent relatives or friends gave him a coin, while this old man helped him not once but thrice. How could he repay his beneficence? He said to the old man thoughtfully, "With this money, I'll be able to embark on any project a man could wish to undertake. The old and homeless could be fed and clothed, and the Sage's teachings can be carried out. I'm deeply indebted to you, and I'll be at your service when these things are accomplished."

"That's just what I have in mind," replied the old man. "When you have completed your plan, come to see me under the two entwined juniper trees by the Temple of Lao Zi on the full moon night of the seventh month next year."

Du calculated that the area south of the Huaihe River was the most distressed. He therefore invested his money in Yangzhou, where he bought 100 hectares of rich farmland, constructed mansions in the city proper, and built hostels at the main country-road intersections. He offered the old and homeless free board and lodging, provided for the weddings of his nieces and nephews, and for the funerals of his poorer relatives. He rewarded those who had been kind to him and revenged himself on those who had maltreated him. When all was done, he went to his appointment with the old man.

The old man was practicing whistle calls in the shade of the entwined juniper trees. He led Du on a climb up the Cloud Terrace Peak of Mount Hua. About a dozen miles into the mountain, Du saw a courtyard of unusual solemnity and serenity set off by a backdrop of rosy clouds. Snow-white red crowned cranes soared above. In the main hall there was an alchemist's furnace about nine feet tall. Purple tongues of fire licked out from the stove-door, tinting the window panes with their flickering hue. Nine maidens stood around the furnace while a black dragon and a white tiger crouched in front and behind. The sun was then setting behind the peaks. The old man had changed into full Taoist attire complete with yellow hat and cape. He gave Du three white pills and a goblet of wine to wash them down. Then, pulling out a tiger skin and laying it by the west wall of the room, he asked Du to sit on it and face east.

"Don't utter a sound," he cautioned, "no matter what you might see, be it a god, a demon, a carnivore, or infernal tortures of yourself or those dearest to you. All those are nothing but illusions. Don't budge, don't say anything. As long as you keep composed, you won't be hurt. Remember what I said." So saying, he left the hall. As Du looked out into the yard he saw nothing but a gigantic vat filled to the brim with water.

The priest was hardly gone when tens of thousands of flags and armored cavalrymen came pouring over the hills and valleys toward Du. Their war-cries reverberated among the peaks. At the head of a large group of sword-brandishing, arrow-ready soldiers, a man about 10 feet tall clad, along with his horse, in shining gold armor rode straight up to him. "Who are you that dare block my way?" he blustered. His soldiers wielded their swords and pressed for an answer. Du made no reply. The horde was so enraged that they vied with one another in an attempt to chop him to pieces or to shoot him to death. The noise was deafening. Du, however, kept his mouth shut. At last, the general left in a fury.

In a moment pouncing tigers, venomous dragons, lions, vipers and scorpions by the thousands came snarling forward to bite and kill. They bore down on him and some even leaped over his head, but he kept perfectly calm and collected. After a while, they had spent themselves and vanished as fast as they had come.

Presently, the sky grew ominously dark and rain came pelting down in buckets. Fireballs bounced left and right; thunderbolts dashed before and behind. He was almost dazzled by the glaring lights. The booming torrents sweeping down the hillsides joined the thunder above as if the mountains had cracked and crumbled. The water in the yard rose 10 feet high and the waves began to lap at his seat. Yet, he did not move a muscle.

Then the general in gold returned with a group of eerie ox-head devils. They placed a big cauldron filled with boiling oil in front of him. With their iron forks pointed at his heart they surrounded him and yelled, "Tell us your name and we'll let you off, otherwise, we'll throw you into this cauldron!" Du gave no response. Then the devils brought forth his wife, and threw her down on the ground before the stairs. "Tell us your name," they bellowed, "if you want us to spare her." Du made no answer. They started to whip her. Blood oozed out at once from her fair skin. They made gashes in her soft body and jabbed her with arrows; they dipped her in the cauldron and scorched her on the fire by turns. It was beyond endurance.

"I might be stupid and ugly," pleaded his wife hoarsely, "and an unworthy wife, but at least I have been attending to you for more than a decade. Now you see me suffering so at the hands of these most respected devils. Can't you put in a word to save my life? I am not asking you to prostrate yourself at their feet. A man must have feelings. Why grudge me even a word?" Her tears rained down her cheeks as she begged and scolded in the yard. But Du seemed unaffected.

"If you think I have no other ways to torture her," croaked the general, "you are mistaken!" He called for a file and pestle and mortar and started to file his wife from her feet up. She shrieked at the top of her voice, but Du simply ignored it. "That knave's black art is accomplished," groaned the general in disappointment. "We must not allow him to continue his life in this world." He ordered that Du be put to death.

After his execution, his soul was brought before the King of Hell. "Is this the evil soul from the Cloud Terrace Peak? Throw him into jail!" the King commanded. What followed was a succession of tortures: He was tied to a red hot copper stake, lashed by iron whips, pestled in a mortar, ground in a mill, baked in a pit of fire, submerged in a cauldron of boiling oil, pulled over a mountain of knives and driven through a forest of swords. However, as he kept the priest's word in mind, it seemed that the miseries were somewhat bearable —he didn't even let out a moan. Finally, the devils reported that they had exhausted their implements of punishment. The King decreed, "Since this soul is of a purely negative nature, it shouldn't be reincarnated as a male, but as a female.* Let it be born into the family of Wang Quan, deputy magistrate of Shanfu County."

Du was born a weak baby. Acupuncture treatment and bitter herbs were her daily fare. She had fallen off the bed, stumbled onto a frying pan, but no matter how great the pains, she never uttered a sound. In this way she gradually grew up as a girl of exceptional beauty. Mouth she had, but it never issued a sound. Her family thought she was mute. And she was never able to retort to the gibes and insults from flirts and rascals.

Also living in that county was the learned young scholar Lu Gui. He had caught wind of her beauty and was enamored. A matchmaker was dispatched, but the marriage proposal was at first declined by her parents on grounds of her muteness. "What is important for a wife," remarked Lu, "is her virtuousness. There is no need for her to talk. Moreover, talkative wives usually turn gossipy." So the marriage was agreed upon. Lu personally went to her door to bring her home in a grand wedding ceremony. Their love grew with their years of marriage, and a son was duly born—a very bright child.

One day when the boy was a full year old, Lu held the child up to her hoping to wheedle out an utterance of affection. Yet she remained silent and wordless. Whatever he

---

* According to the dualistic outlook of Taoism, the world is made up of the complementary forces of yin and yang. Yang represents the sun, the positive, the male, etc., while yin represents the moon, the negative, the female ....

tried, he just couldn't get a response. Finally he cried out in exasperation, "History tells of a Mr. Jia whose wife refused to smile because he looked ugly. But when she saw how he excelled in archery, she gave him a big smile. I am not nearly so ugly as that Mr. Jia. Besides, my learning is not something that Jia could have dreamed of and yet you refuse to speak to me! If a man is so despised by his wife, why should he raise her child?" So saying, he grabbed the child by the legs and dashed the boy's head against a rock. The head exploded at the collision, and blood splashed several feet. Her motherly love made Du forget his obligation and he let out an "Ouch!" Even before that "Ouch" had died down, she found herself sitting on the tiger skin in the room. The priest was standing beside him. It was almost daybreak.

Purple tongues shot out from the furnace and leaped onto the roof. A fire broke out on all sides and the house went up in flames. "You meager wretch. You have let me down!" moaned the priest. He grabbed Du up by the hair and dropped him in the water vat. Before long the fire burnt itself out. The priest approached him and said, "Sonny, you have almost overcome all the weaknesses of a human being, those of joy, anger, sorrow, fear, hate and desire, all except one, and that is love. If you had kept your mouth shut a moment longer, my magic pills would have been made and you and I would have become celestial beings by now. Oh, heavens! How difficult it is to find a qualified person! Though the tempering of magic pills can be started anew, you have to return to the realm you've come from. There is no help about that." So saying, he waved his hand toward the trail leading down the peak. Du insisted on having a final look, and was allowed to ascend the foundation of the ruined house. Where the furnace once stood, only an iron rod was left erect. It was several feet long and as thick as one's arm. The priest had taken off his gown and was scraping the charred pole with a knife.

At home, Du was haunted by shame as he could not

forgive himself for his breach of faith. To redeem himself, he resolved to try again. Cherishing that determination, he once again ascended the Cloud Terrace Peak, but there was no trace of human activity there. He returned home with bitter regret.

Translator's note:

Alchemy was very popular among Taoist priests in the Tang Dynasty. As sulfur, realgar, and niter were the most widely used components, and temperature control during calcination was still at a rudimentary stage, fires were not uncommon. Incidents of houses burning down and serious physical injuries are recorded in the books on alchemy of the time. The latter part of the story could be a reflection on the difficulties of controlling furnace temperature and the consequent frustration on the part of the priests.

Hermit Zhang

During one of his many hunting trips in the mountains of Heng Prefecture, the Prince of Cao, who had been banished from Court, flushed out a dozen deer and had them surrounded. However the herd simply disappeared from what he thought was a sure catch.

As there lived in the mountains Hermit Zhang, a highly reputed master of magic arts, the prince summoned him to explain this uncanny event.

"The deer are concealed by someone who is versed in the Taoist arts," said the hermit.

He asked for a bowl of water, chanted an incantation and danced with his sword. In a while, to the surprise of everyone present, there appeared in the bowl a Taoist priest about an inch tall trudging in the water with a stick in one hand and a bag over one shoulder. The hermit took out a sewing needle and pricked the priest in the left foot. The priest limped on in the bowl.

"Now you can overtake him," said the hermit. "He is only a few miles away to the north."

The prince's men galloped off in that direction. In less than three miles they caught up with a limping priest who looked exactly like the miniature figure they had just seen in the bowl. They summoned him in the name of the prince and the priest smilingly obliged.

"No harsh words, please," the hermit advised the prince. "It may be better if you treat him respectfully."

"Does Your Honor know where the deer are?" the prince asked when the priest was brought before him.

"I do," replied the priest. "I've had them concealed, be-

47

cause I hate to see them die for no good reason. Yet, in spite of my personal feelings, I didn't dare release them into the forest without Your Highness' consent. They are now on the other side of the mountain."

The prince dispatched a couple of guards to check this out, and they reported that the deer were all lying quietly on the slope.

"What happened to your foot?" the prince teased.

"I've been walking a couple of miles and it suddenly started to hurt."

The prince beckoned the hermit to come forth and found that the two were in fact acquaintances. The priest turned out to be the abbot of the Chain-Peaks Temple in neighboring Chen Prefecture. The pain in his foot was gone, and the prince saw him off with due courtesy.

Not long after that event, a traveler passing through Chen Prefecture dropped in at the Chain-Peaks Temple for the night. His horse, which he left tied to a post by the gate, made a mess with its excrement. When he was censured by the abbot in the morning, he flared up and spewed out a mouthful of profanity before he departed.

Several days later the traveler chanced upon Hermit Zhang. "An imminent threat overhangs your life," the hermit observed. "You must have offended someone." The man then related his squabble with the abbot.

"That priest is no ordinary priest," remarked the hermit. "He can bring misfortune to you. If you don't hurry back and make a timely apology, I'm afraid you won't be able to avert it. Your adversity comes from the thunder. If you take my advice, wherever you put up tonight, find a length of cypress tree as tall as yourself, lay it in your bed and cover it with your clothes and quilt, while you yourself take shelter in another room. Hack out seven date-wood spikes, stick them in the ground in the pattern of the Big Dipper, and squat under the second star. Only this may save your life."

The stunned traveler immediately reversed his course. By nightfall he arrived at a mountain inn in Chen Prefecture with a cypress log and date-tree timber, which he arranged as the hermit had told him.

At midnight a storm broke out. The house trembled with the rumble of thunder and lightning flashed into the room. The man held his breath, his muscles scared stiff. Several more bolts struck in succession, as if searching for a target. Then the lightning gave up.

Day broke before the man ventured to look about—the log was smashed to splinters. Appalled, he rushed all the way to the temple to beg forgiveness. After his repeated pleadings, the priest finally spoke, "Never slight anyone, much less insult someone without cause. What if he is a man with the heart of a scorpion? Now you are pardoned. Better move on."

The man bowed his way out. He then looked up the hermit and loaded him down with gifts.

One Who Paints Without Brush and Colors

At the end of Zhenyuan reign, a General Ran was garrisoned at Kai Prefecture. His hospitality and generosity had won him many friends among the literati.

Among his entourage were two scholars of the Confucian school, a Mr. Guo and a Mr. Liu. The two had always been jealous of each other.

One day, the group gathered at the general's sitting room to view a new painting entitled *Seven Saints Amidst the Bamboo Grove*. Liu turned to the host and commented, "Though this painting is scrupulously done in the details, it has no life. I may be able to show you a hand of art today. What do you say if I polish up this painting without resorting to brush and colors?"

"I never knew you are an artist," remarked the general somewhat surprised. "But how can you paint without applying the colors?"

"I know better than that. I will go into the painting in person to do the job,"

Guo clapped his hands in a fit of laughter, "Do you take us for poor little kids who will be swindled by your nonsense?"

Liu proposed a bet, which Guo gladly accepted and laid down a wager of 5,000, with the general as a witness.

Before the crowd realized what was happening, Liu leaped up into the painting on the wall, and disappeared. The stunned crowd fumbled all over the surface but could not locate where Liu was hiding.

Presently, Liu's voice came out from the painting. "Mr.

Guo, now do you believe me?" it said.

After about the time it took for a meal, Liu jumped out from the painting. He pointed to the prominent figure of Ruan Ji in the painting and said, "That's as much as I can manage."

Upon closer inspection the group noticed that Ruan's figure was indeed different from the others in that he was more lifelike—his lips pursed as if giving a high-pitched whistle. Even the painter himself agreed that it was far superior to what he had originally done.

The general and Guo made a deep bow to Liu. A few days later, Liu was gone without leaving a word of farewell. The general believed that he had attained immortality.

The Old Man at the Inn

This is a story recounted by Wei Xinggui of the Tang Dynasty about his own youthful experience.

At sunset one day as he was traveling west of the capital, he dropped in at a roadside inn for a meal and was ready to set off again.

"Don't travel at night. Bandits roam this area," warned an old man making a bucket in the hallway.

"Don't you worry. I'm expert with the bow and arrow," replied Wei as he stepped out into the thickening twilight.

It was completely dark before he had covered many miles. Suddenly, he sensed there was someone following him in the tall grasses along the road. He shouted at the figure but got no response. He raised his bow and shot in quick succession, believing that he must have hit his target. The figure, however, kept following him. In no time he was out of arrows and out of his wits. He began to run for dear life.

Soon a strong wind rose up and thunder was heard approaching. He jumped off his horse and pressed his back against a big tree. Lightning flashed like lashes across the sky, chasing one another to the top of the very tree under which he was hiding. He felt things falling all about him. An intent look told him that they were wood chips, and before long, the chips had piled up to his knees. Unnerved, he threw down his bow and bowed and bowed to heaven begging for mercy. Gradually, the clouds seemed to be lifting, the thunder trailed off and the wind died down. He raised his eyes and examined the tree, which by then was bare of all its branches. His horse was nowhere in sight so he had to walk back to the inn. The old man was just beginning to hoop his bucket.

Believing that the old man was behind all this, Wei thanked him for sparing his life.

"Never be self-deceived by your archery," the old man smiled. "Swordsmanship is also very important."

He led Wei into the backyard and showed him his horse. "Here's your nag. Hope you aren't offended. I was just testing your art," the old man said as he picked up a stave. Wei saw his arrows sticking in it.

The old man refused to accept Wei as an apprentice. However, from what he revealed about his art, Wei learned a thing or two.

A Ride in a Goose Cage

In the Eastern Jin Dynasty Xu Yan, a native of Yangxian County, once traveled through the Suian Mountains, carrying on his back a pair of geese in a cage. He came upon a student-scholar about 18 years old lying by the roadside and complaining of sore feet. He didn't take the young man seriously when he asked for a lift in his goose cage. But while he was musing over this whimsical notion, the youth had slipped through the bars into the cage and sat side by side with the geese. Strange to say, the geese showed no alarm and the cage did not in any way expand, neither did the scholar seem to contract. As he picked up his load to continue his trip, he was surprised to find that it was not any heavier.

Having traveled thus for some distance, he stopped for a rest under a shady tree. The scholar stepped out from the cage and said, "How about me offering you a quick snack?" "That'll be fine," Xu replied. Then from his mouth, the young man produced a round, bronze food-container, from which he extracted delicious dishes of the rarest sea and land produce, and laid them out on the ground before Xu—all on shining bronze plates. It would have taken a very large table to hold them all. The smell of the food itself was appetizing enough to attract the gods. After drinking a few cups, the youth said, "I've a habit of bringing a mistress along. You won't mind if I call her forth?" "Do as you please," said Xu.

Finding no objection from Xu, the scholar disgorged from his mouth a girl of the budding age of 16, her clothes bright with color, her features of celestial beauty. She sat down and dined with them.

Soon the scholar seemed to be overcome with wine and dozed

off. The girl turned to Xu and said, "Though I'm his mistress, I've got a lover of my own choice, and I always sneak him along. Now that he is asleep, I shall invite my man. Hope you won't mention this to the scholar." "Do as you please," was Xu's reply. Thereupon the girl extracted from her mouth a young man about 24 years old with a handsome and intelligent look, who cordially exchanged compliments with Xu. Just then, the scholar stirred as if he were about to wake up. The girl immediately took out a brocade portable screen from her mouth and set it up. She then went behind it to sleep with the scholar.

The handsome man turned to Xu and whispered, "A lovely girl, isn't she? Yet, a man, you see, sometimes may have more than one mistress. I keep another woman. This seems a good opportunity for a fast date. Please don't give away my little secret." "As you please," Xu said dutifully. The man opened his mouth and brought out a woman in her early twenties. They sat and dined, hugging and kissing all the time. A good while passed when a rustling was heard behind the screen. "They're waking up," the man said. He grabbed up the woman and stuffed her back into his mouth.

In a moment, the girl reappeared from behind the screen. "The scholar is going to wake up," she said to Xu as she swallowed her man and sat down opposite Xu. The scholar then emerged and said apologetically to Xu, "Sorry for napping so long and leaving you unattended. You must have been bored. Now it's getting late, I must say good-bye to you." He threw the girl and all the bronzeware back into his mouth, except for one king-size plate about two feet across which he handed to Xu and said, "I've nothing else to show my gratitude. Please accept this plate as a souvenir."

Xu became an archivist during Taiyuan reign of the Eastern Jin Dynasty. He showed the plate to a palace officer who figured out from the plate's epigraph that it was produced more than three centuries before in the third year of Yongping reign of the Han Dynasty.

A Dandy's Pleasure Trip

During the early years of Zhenyuan reign of the Tang Dynasty, the Shu Prefecture bred a handful of super-rich families. Matchmakers swamped their doors and any young woman with a pretty face would sooner or later be dragged to their dens. There were no means they would not resort to —fishing out beauties by portraits was not an unusual practice. Nevertheless, they often complained that they could not find even one good-looking girl.

Someone recommended Zhang He, a district constable with a reputation for chivalry, saying that he was a know-all, and there were no secrets in the boudoir that could escape his knowledge. A show of sincerity would probably enlist his assistance.

So one night a dandy from one of those rich families arrived at Zhang's place with presents of gold and silk. Zhang consented to help forthwith.

The next morning, he took the dandy out of the west gate of town to a deserted temple. Though the building was in disrepair, the main Buddha statue still stood intact and majestic. They climbed up the pedestal and Zhang reached out for the statue's nipple and pushed, revealing a hole the size of a plate. Holding the dandy by the arm, he stepped in. Everything happened in a flash and they were walking through a tunnel. All of a sudden, high walls and broad gates like those of a major town loomed up in front. Zhang knocked several times. A handsome lad appeared and bowed respectfully to Zhang, saying that his master had been expecting him. Presently, the host streamed out with a train of attendants. He wore a purple robe with a shell-studded belt around his waist and seemed very submissive to Zhang.

Pointing to the dandy, Zhang said, "This is my young gentleman friend. Treat him well. I'm not staying, for I've got urgent matters to attend to." With that, he disappeared. The dandy was bursting with questions but he dared not ask.

The host led him into the hall. Decorated with jade beads and pearls, silk and satin, the room was luxurious. The table was laid with delicacies from the high mountains and deep seas. The host called in singing girls and told them to pour wine for the guest. What hair! Softly curled like ripples over a lucid lake. How they walked! Lightly as if on cottony clouds. Fairies could not match them. The lithe movements of their bodies when they danced, the silvery voices when they chirped, oh, the elaborate way they entertained was like nothing he knew. What's that vessel they served wine in? A gold bowl set in a constellation of pearls, wide mouthed and deep-bellied to hold several liters? Never seen that before. His host laughed and told him that this wasn't the biggest cup they used. A bigger size had been intended. It was all very puzzling.

The strokes of midnight rang out. The host suddenly left his seat and excused himself. "Please don't let my absence interrupt your enjoyment. I've got to leave you a while." He bowed himself out of the room. The splendor of his mounted honor guard exceeded that of a general as the procession marched out with torches lit.

The dandy took the opportunity to relieve himself in a corner of the yard. One of the older singers came up to him. "Alas!" she sighed. "How did you, a gentleman, fall into this place? We poor beings are entrapped by his magic and have no hope of escape. But if you want to go home, do as I tell you." She handed him seven feet of white silk. "Take this. When he comes back, greet him politely. While he returns your bow, he'll almost certainly do that, loop this length of silk around his neck and throttle him."

At daybreak, the host returned. The dandy did as he had

58

been told, and the host dropped to the ground, begging for his life. "The old hag has betrayed me and ruined my designs. This place is no longer fit to live in." So saying, he rode off.

The singer and the dandy took possession of the place and lived together there for about two years when he suddenly became homesick. The singer showed no objection to his leaving. When the grand farewell banquet was over, she picked up a spade and dug a hole in the east wall, like the earlier one in the statue's breast. She pushed him through, and he found himself lying at the foot of the capital's east city wall. He had to beg his way back to Shu Prefecture.

As he had been missing for a number of years, his family thought him dead. He had to refer to the particulars of his earlier life to convince them that he was not a ghost.

The Proprietress at Wooden Bridge

To the west of Bianzhou City there was a tiny village called Wooden Bridge. There, a widow in her thirties, popularly addressed as Third Sister, had opened up a small inn with several rooms. No one knew where she came from. She had no children, nor did she seem to have any relatives or kinsfolk. Yet she was quite wealthy, and could afford to raise a herd of donkeys. Whenever a beast of burden failed a traveler, be he on private or public business, she would happily offer him a replacement at a bargain price. Thus she gained a high reputation for virtue and a steady stream of clients from far and near.

During Yuanhe reign, a man named Zhao Jihe from Xu Prefecture happened to put up at the inn on his way to the East Capital. By the time he arrived there were already half a dozen guests there who had occupied the best beds. So he was left with the bed at the far end of the room against the partition board separating the guests' room from the proprietress' room.

The proprietress provided them with a rich dinner, and later joined them in their revelry late into the night. Though he habitually abstained from wine, he did not withdraw from the party but chatted and joked with the others. At midnight, drunk and tired, the travelers took to their beds. The proprietress also retired to her room, locked her door, and blew out the candle. The other guests snored, but Zhao was not able to fall asleep. As he tossed and turned in bed he heard slight noises like rat movements coming through the partition. Putting his eye to a chink, he saw the proprietress retrieve a lit candle from beneath an overturned pot and trim its wick. Then, from a bedside trunk she took out a plow, a wooden bull, and a carved wood figure,

60

each no more than half a foot tall and placed them before the fireplace. Next, she took a sip of water and sprayed them. Directly, the little wood figure jumped to his feet, grabbed the plow, and started to drive the bull to till the patch of ground before her bed. After a few turns of the plow, she reached for a bag of buckwheat seeds in the trunk and handed it to the little man to sow. In a blink of the eye, wheat grew, flowered and ripened. The little man was ordered to reap and thresh, bringing in a harvest of about one peck. Subsequently, she installed a tiny mill and had the wheat ground into flour. With that done, she placed all the diminutive objects back into the trunk and started to bake pancakes.

Cock crow was soon heard in the distance, and the travelers got up to continue their journey. She lighted the lamps and placed the oven-fresh pancakes on the dining table for their breakfast. Zhao had second thoughts and made an immediate departure. However, he did not go far, but hid right outside to see what might happen next.

He saw the travelers sitting around the table eating the pancakes. But before they had finished, they collapsed to the ground, and brayed! In a moment, they all turned into donkeys. The proprietress then drove them behind the house and took possession of their wares. Secretly admiring her magic art, he did not inform against her.

A month later, he returned from the capital. Approaching Wooden Bridge, he stopped to prepare some buckwheat pancakes of the same size and shape as he had observed last time. Thereupon, he took up lodgings at the inn. Third Sister was as hospitable and courteous as she had always been. That night, as he was the only guest staying at the inn, she seemed even more attentive to his needs. At bedtime, she asked him whether he wanted anything else. He said that he would like to have a simple breakfast before he left early next morning.

"No problem about that," she replied. "Have a good sleep."

When he peeped through the chink after midnight, he was satisfied to see that she was going over her old tricks again.

At daybreak she appeared with a plate of pancakes. When she retreated into the kitchen he quickly replaced one of her cakes with one of his own. He called out to her that he happened to have some pancakes with him, and would rather eat his own so that she could save hers for other guests. While he was eating, she re-entered with tea.

"Please have a taste of my cake," he said politely, and offered her the one he had replaced. No sooner had she swallowed a bite than she dropped on all fours and brayed. She was quite a strong donkey, he mused. He jumped on the donkey and rode off, of course not forgetting to collect the wooden figure, the bull and plow. But he was not able to make them work, for he had not acquired the magic.

He traveled around the country on his donkey, often covering scores of miles a day without ever having the slightest trouble with the animal.

Four years later, as he crossed the Tongguan Pass and was nearing the temple of Mount Hua, an old man turned up by the roadside, laughing and clapping his hands. "Third Sister from Wooden Bridge, how come you have fallen into this shape?" Catching hold of the donkey, he turned to Zhao, "She does deserve a punishment, but your treatment of her has been harsh enough. Show some mercy now and let her go." He spread the donkey's mouth wide open by pulling at its lips, and the proprietress leaped out from the skin. She looked not a bit different from her old self. She made a deep bow to the old man and went away. Nobody has ever seen her since.

Translator's note:
Stories about "black" inns where travelers are murdered for their money are not scarce in ancient Chinese literature. In this one, touches of fantasy distinguish it from those of darker horrors.

The Carpenter and His Wooden Cranes

In the Tang Dynasty, a carpenter named Bing Hua lived in Xiangyang Prefecture. One fine spring day he took a leisurely stroll out of town, got drunk somehow, and fell asleep on the bank of the Hanshui River.

"Get on your feet, young man!" The stern command of a venerable elder startled him out of his soddenness. "You look talented. Don't squander your life in drinking or gambling. Here is an ax for you. As long as you use it, it'll bring magic to your work. But remember, never get tangled up with women." The carpenter bowed in acceptance.

With this ax, his skill became astonishing. He could make objects that would move by themselves and even fly, not to speak of building houses and towers that came from his hand without the least seeming efforts.

On a trip to Anlu County, a local squire of the Wang family, who had heard of his ingenuity, invited him to stay at his place and build a single-pillar pavilion by his garden pond. On the day of completion, the whole family turned out to watch. Among the gathering was Wang's widowed daughter. Such was her beauty that the carpenter felt a strong urge to possess her.

That night he climbed over the wall and slipped into the widow's chamber. "If you make a fuss, I'll kill you!" he threatened, and the terrified woman succumbed. Every night he would come after it was dark and sneak away before dawn.

It didn't take long for Wang to learn about these goings on. He decided to dismiss him by offering him an extra bonus.

63

Bing took the hint and said, "I'm very much indebted to you for having put me up so long. Now you're giving me such a fat bonus, I feel all the more obliged to do something for you in return. Let me show you my prized skill. Give me some wood, and I'll make you something really wonderful."

"What is it? I won't accept something I've no use for."

"I'll make you a pair of wooden cranes that can fly! In case you need to travel and are time-pressed, just ride it. It'll carry you to wherever you wish in a wink."

Wang had long been fascinated by such legendary things, so he readily agreed.

Bing hewed and chiseled with the ax, and a pair of wooden cranes soon took shape. They looked exactly like real ones except for the eyes, which were left uncarved.

"Why's that?" Wang asked.

"Because you need to fast and pray first, or they won't take to the air."

That night, while Wang was reciting his prayers in seclusion, Bing grabbed his daughter and flew back to Xiangyang on the cranes.

Wang found his daughter missing the next morning. There was no trace of her in town. He made a secret trip to Xiangyang and reported the incident to the prefect, who ordered a search throughout the town, and Bing was caught.

The angry prefect had the carpenter beaten to death, but he could by no means make the cranes fly.

A New Ghost

A new ghost, weary and bony, ran into an old friend in the nether world. His friend had died 20 years ago but now looked quite plump and healthy.

"How are you?" inquired his former friend.

"I'm starving," replied the newcomer, "and it's getting beyond endurance. You must know your ways around here. Hope you can give me some tips."

"That's no problem," said his friend. "All you need to do is to play some tricks on the living beings. When they are put in fear, they'll offer you food."

The new ghost thanked his friend and went to the first house at the east end of a village where he saw a stone mill in the western wing. He bent his back to it and pushed like a live human being. The father, who happened to be a devout believer in Buddhism, said to his children, "Buddha must be taking pity on our impoverished conditions, and has sent a ghost to help push the millstone." So they brought him cartloads of wheat to grind.

When dusk fell, the ghost had already done a dozen bushels. Exhausted, he shambled back to the nether world, sought out his friend, and blamed him for lying.

"Try again," his friend encouraged, "and this time you'll get your reward."

This time the new ghost started from the west end of the village. By the gate of the house was a mortar and pestle. He took up the pestle and pounded right away, as a good laborer would have done.

"I heard," said the master of the house, who turned out to be a Taoist disciple, "yesterday a ghost helped the family at the east end. Today it must be our lucky turn. Give him plenty of rice to hull." His housemaid was told to provide the ghost with baskets and sieves.

Night set in and no food was offered. The ghost, more tired and hungry than ever, dragged himself back to vent his rage on his friend.

"Don't forget we are related by family ties!" he shouted in his old friend's face. "How dare you treat me worse than a total stranger! Because of you, I've been working two whole days without getting a single bite."

"Don't blame me, but blame your own foolishness," soothed his friend. "Those two families you chose are strong believers in either Buddhism or Taoism. They won't be easily affected. Tomorrow, go and find an ordinary family. I guarantee you won't be disappointed."

The new ghost went again and picked a house with bamboo poles at the gate. He entered to see a group of girls eating by the window. In the courtyard there was a white dog, which he grabbed and made it paddle its legs in the air. The family was astounded, saying that they had never seen, or even heard of, a dog behaving like that. They sought an oracle, which read: "A stray ghost is demanding food. He can be appeased by sacrificing the dog and offering it with food, wine and fruit in the yard." The family took the advice and the new ghost got his first treat.

Thanks to his friend's teaching, one more ghost haunts the world.

Translator's note:

Ghosts are invisible and their existence is unsubstantiated. Nonetheless, they strike horror into many hearts. Or should we say rather, it is our fear that created them?

A Daredevil

In Nanyang Prefecture, there lived a man named Song Dingbo. Once in his youth, while traveling in the depth of night, he ran into a ghost.

"I'm a ghost," acknowledged the ghost when greeted, "and who are you?"

"A fellow ghost," Song hoaxed.

"Where to?"

"To the market."

"Me, too."

So they shared each other's company.

"Walking like this is too slow," grumbled the ghost after a mile or two. "Why don't we take turns carrying each other?"

"Great idea!" Song responded.

The ghost led off by carrying Song on its back and scurried ahead. "You seem too heavy to be a ghost," it complained after a couple of miles.

"I'm a new ghost," remarked Song, "and you know new ghosts are heavy." When it came to his turn, he found that the ghost was virtually weightless.

They thus changed places every few miles.

"Excuse me," said Song, "I'm new in this world. Do you mind telling me what we ghosts dread most?"

"The most dreadful thing is being spat on by a living person," answered the ghost frankly.

Across their way lay a river. The ghost walked right in and waded through without making the slightest sound, while Song made loud splashes.

"Why are you making so much noise?" asked the ghost somewhat annoyed.

67

"Sorry, pal. Haven't learned the ways in water yet," he replied.

It was Song's turn to carry when they drew near the market. He clutched the ghost tightly by the legs. Alarmed, it cried out hoarsely, begging to be let down. Ignoring its pleas, he marched straight into the market place. As he settled the ghost on the ground, it turned into a goat. For fear that it might escape by transforming again, he spat on it several times. He then sold the goat for 1,500 copper coins.

So goes a popular rhyme of the day:

> Song spat and caught a ghost,
> Half'n' thousand for the goat.

The Traveler in Liyang County

In Kaiyuan reign, a poor scholar rambled to the north of the Yellow River in hope of securing a job, but nobody cared to hire him.

One day he arrived in Liyang County. Darkness was closing in and he seemed to be in the middle of nowhere. Suddenly, a magnificent house with a spacious yard appeared by the roadside. Thinking that this might be his only chance for a night under a roof, he went over and knocked at the gate.

It took quite a while before a servant came to answer the door. "It's getting late," explained the traveler. "I'm afraid I can't reach a post house or an inn before it's completely dark. May I spend the night in a wing room?"

"You'd better ask my master yourself," the servant replied and led him into the hall.

Presently, scuffing footsteps were heard. A well-dressed gentleman entered the hall. He was a handsome man, with leisurely and lordly manners. He greeted the traveler politely and told the servants to make tea.

"A long trip must be exhausting," said the gentleman. "I hope Your Excellency will find my humble residence comfortable enough."

This man sounds queer, thought the traveler. With necessity and curiosity, he decided to stay and see what might happen. The gentleman turned out to be quite eloquent, prattling about things that happened in the previous dynasties as if he had lived through them himself. When asked his name, he told the traveler that he was Xun Jihe, a native of Yingchuan. His father first came and settled here as an official, and the family stayed ever since.

A banquet was given in honor of the guest. The dishes were delicate, but rather tasteless.

The guest room was ready when dinner was finished. The host showed him to the room and appointed a maid to attend to his needs.

When he felt familiar enough with the maid, the traveler asked what official title her master presently held. "Chief of staff under Lord River," murmured the maid, "but don't mention this to anyone else."

By and by cries of pain and agony were heard outside. The traveler peeped through the window and saw his host sitting on a couch in the yard lit by candles and lamps. In front of the couch stood a naked man in a pool of blood, his hair was disheveled, and flocks of birds were pecking at his eyes at the bidding of the servants. The host seemed very angry. "See if you dare trespassing against me again!" the traveler heard him shout.

"Who's that man there?" the traveler asked.

"Why ask about things you need not know," replied the maid.

But upon insisting, he learned from the maid that the man was the magistrate of Liyang County, who loved hunting, and had several times invaded the host's ground while chasing wild animals. Now he was being punished for his offense.

Waking up in the morning, the traveler found that where he had spent the night was nothing more than a majestic tomb. He asked the first man he ran into and was informed that it was the tomb of a gentleman named Xun.

Arriving at the county seat, he was not much surprised to hear that the magistrate was declining audiences on account of an eye disease. The magistrate was overjoyed to hear that someone knew how to treat his disease. When summoned, the traveler recounted his weird experience.

"So it was," remarked the magistrate, and he gave the

traveler a generous reward.

Then, without the traveler's knowing, the magistrate issued orders to the local village head, demanding that thousands of bundles of firewood be placed around the tomb. He himself led the troops there to set fire and level the tomb. Soon enough, his eyes recovered.

Later, when the traveler once again passed by the site, he saw a ragged man crouching in the bushes, his hair scorched, his face severely burned. The man accosted him in a familiar way, but the traveler simply could not recall where he had met such a man.

"Don't you remember you once spent a night right here under my roof?"

"Heavens!" the traveler exclaimed in astonishment. "What has happened to you since?"

"Well, that was the magistrate's revenge. I know it was not your intention, just that my fortune was running low."

Feeling deep remorse, the traveler bought wine and food for a libation, and burned up some of his old clothes as an offering. The ghost accepted the gifts gratefully and disappeared.

Translator's note:

In the Tang Dynasty stories, ghosts are not always portrayed as dark, fearful figures, but rather as normal human beings. In this story, the magistrate seems more vicious than the ghost.

Zhao Tai

At midnight on the 13th day of the seventh lunar month in the fifth year of Taishi reign of the Jin Dynasty (265-420), Zhao Tai, a well-known scholar in Qinghe County, died of a sudden heart attack at the age of 35. But, strangest of all, his body remained warm and his limbs flexible.

Ten days after his death, his throat let out a loud gurgle, his eyes opened, and he asked for water. Then he was able to sit up.

He told his family that the moment he passed out he saw two men galloping toward him on two sorrels, followed by two footmen. "Catch him!" they shouted, and the footmen grabbed him under the arms and raced eastward. Whizzing through space for heaven knew how many miles, they reached a magnificent walled-city built with what looked like iron and tin. They entered through the west gate and came upon rows and rows of office buildings. He was led through two black gates into a courtyard amidst several dozen tiled houses. There were some 50 or 60 men and women standing in the yard and an officer in a dark robe was tagging them with numbers. He was assigned No. 30. Then they were ushered into a big hall where a lord sat facing west. Their names were checked against a list, and he was sent on through another black door in the south.

Under a massive roof, an official in scarlet was making a roll call. He asked each one what he or she did during their lifetime, whether they sinned or achieved merits. He warned that they had to tell the truth, for their words would be compared with their records. "There are observers constantly walking the land," he said, "and noting down every deed one performs, good or bad." "Of the six ways of reincarnation," he continued, "three are bad, and to kill is the most serious crime. On the other hand, if one devotes himself to Buddhism and sticks to the five don'ts and 10 do's, and is kind and charitable, he will be reborn in a happy land and be exempt from all sufferings."

The crowd's confessions varied from person to person. When it came to Zhao's turn, he said that his whole life was devoted to books, and that he had never sinned.

When the interrogation was over, Zhao was appointed supervisor of the water bureau, overseeing the reconstruction of river banks. Under his watch, 1,000-odd half-submerged sinners carried sand from the shallows up the bank night after day without a break. They wailed with unendurable pain and regretted that they did not do good in their lives to have sunk so low.

Later on, he was promoted to commissioner of the water bureau in charge of all prison camps. He was given a horse and told to inspect these camps. He saw sinners whose tongues were pierced by needles, blood trickling over their bodies, or a group of the naked, driven by officers holding heavy clubs, walking in pairs toward white-hot iron beds and glowing copper pillars. As they stretched out on the bed or hugged the pillar, their skin and flesh were scorched and seared, but the moment their charred bodies were peeled off, they healed themselves, only to go through the agony once again. And there were huge caldrons on whirling furnaces, heads and severed limbs bobbing up and down in the boiling oil. Three or four hundred men and women stood in lines waiting their fate, and *Yakshas* with long forks rhythmically flopped them in, one at a time, despite their howling and clinging to each other. And there was a giant tree with twigs of swords and leaves of knives. Arguing among themselves, the damned climbed up as if in competition, while their bodies were cut to bleeding pieces. He saw his parents and a brother whining among the crowd.

Then came two messengers with papers in their hands, which they delivered to the jailer and mentioned three names. They said that their families, having been converted to Buddhism, had offered joss sticks and banners* in the temple and had been chanting the Buddhist scriptures to mend the bad deeds those three had committed, so they should be transferred to the happy land. So saying, Zhao saw that the three men already had nice clothes on their backs, and out they went to a place called Hall of Revelation. He followed them through three red gates set in white walls and arrived at a radiant palace decorated with shining jewels. In the hall were two crouching lions bearing a marble couch, on which sat a golden man over 10 feet tall with a halo circling his head. Numerous monks stood around with bent heads. He saw the Lord of Hell saluting the golden man in a most respectful way. "Who is the one on the couch?" he asked an attendant.

"He is Buddha, who possesses the power to save all souls on or below the earth."

Just then Buddha opened his mouth to speak. "He has come to convert and save," he said, "and any soul detained in hell is allowed to attend his sermons. The sermons will last seven days, within which period all those converted will be delivered in time, depending on the extent of their previous merits and sins." Nineteen thousand turned out to listen, and even before Zhao left the compound he saw 10 men rise up into the heavens.

He moved on to another walled city called the City of Reincarnation. Those who refused to be converted but had gone through the infernal trials were held here before they were transmigrated. Entering from the north gate he saw

---

* The banner referred to here is a long rectangular strip of embroidered cloth hung vertically on a post. It is employed at religious rituals to recall the lost soul.

thousands of earthen huts encircling a tiled brick mansion about 50 yards wide. Over 500 officers were busy checking names and documents, and dispatching individuals on their respective ways. Those who killed would become mayflies that are born in the morning and meet their death at the end of the day; those who robbed would be reborn as pigs and lambs to repay with their own flesh; those who indulged in luxury would be hatched as wild geese or snakes; those who slandered or cursed would be turned into owls or crows whose voices only induce loathing from anyone who hears; and those who repudiated a debt would be beasts of burden. The mansion had a basement facing north and a door opening onto the south. Those summoned entered from the north, and by the time they exited in the south they were either beasts, birds or insects.

He traveled on. At another walled city he found people living in brick houses who seemed to be enjoying their time. He was told that they were the ones who did neither good nor bad things during their lifetime. After 1,000 years as contented ghosts, they could be reborn as humans.

There was still another walled city about 10,000 yards across, called Earth Center. Held here were 50,000 to 60,000 naked figures languishing in the pangs of eternal hunger. On seeing him, they kowtowed and shrieked for mercy.

Completing his tour, he reported back to the official in scarlet who asked him whether he found everything in order, and told him that his privilege as an administrator, instead of being one of those tortured, was simply because he never sinned.

"What is happiness?" Zhao asked.

"One's happiness lies in his devotion to Buddhism and abiding by its principles," the official replied.

"What if one has committed mountains of sins before he is converted? Can he still be pardoned?"

"No doubt about that," the official assured him. Then he

turned to a secretary and asked him to look up the cause of Zhao's death. After fumbling through the records which were kept in a cane trunk, the secretary reported that Zhao was in fact abducted by two villainous devils while were still had 30 years of life in store. Zhao was thereupon sent home.

After his recovery, Zhao and his family became pious adherents of Buddhism. He chanted the scriptures and held services to redeem his parents and brother.

Translator's note:

This story may remind one of the Inferno in Dante's Divine Comedy, but despite their similarity in the description of the horrors of afterlife punishments, this one is Buddhist. In Buddhist belief, a soul goes through infinite cycles of birth, misery, and death known as samsara, *and depending on how it behaves during a lifetime, its next existence is to be in one of the six "ways," or worlds, namely, inferno, animal, starvation, antigoasura, human or heaven.*

There are two stories of rather similar content under the same title "Zhao Tai" in Records of the Taiping Era. The present translation is based on the one from "You Min Lu" in volume 109 and supplemented for some details by the one from "Min Xiang Ji" in volume 377.

The Courier in a Yellow Jacket

The magistrate of Fuliang County, a Mr. Zhang, had amassed an amazing fortune in grain and gold during his term of office, and his property extended from the Yangtze valley to the Huai River.

At the end of his tenure he set out on a journey to the capital, and as always, he had an advance party prepare for his lodging and meals—his elaborate recipes demanded the rarest produce of land and sea.

His advance party, having reached the foot of Mount Hua one day, had a room cleaned and curtained. Wine cups were laid out and the chefs had a lamb roasting over a fire. A man appeared from nowhere and seated himself at the table. The servants tried to drive him away, but their scolding and cursing seemed to fall on deaf ears.

"He must be one of those royal falconers," the landlady whispered. "They run amuck around the capital. Nobody dares to argue with them."

The servants were going to seek the authority of Zhang when he arrived, and they clamored about the stranger in a yellow jacket.

"Don't annoy him," Zhang said, and turned to the stranger. "Where are you from?"

The man slurred out something while he kept motioning the servants to warm up the wine. When it was warm, Zhang himself poured it out into a big gold cup and handed it to the man. Though he made no explicit articulation of thanks, a glint of gratitude welled up in his eyes. He gulped down the wine and fixed his gaze on the roast lamb. Zhang cut off a leg and offered it to him, which he finished off with hunger still apparent on his face. Zhang took out more than a dozen meat-stuffed griddlecakes from a food hamper and placed them before the man, and he washed them down with jars of wine.

Seemingly satiated, he looked up at Zhang. "The last good meal I had was at East Camp 40 years ago."

Puzzled by that offbeat remark, Zhang insisted on striking up a closer acquaintance.

"I'm no human," said the intruder finally, "but a ghost courier carrying the death roll to Mount Hua."

"I don't understand," Zhang said with a start.

"When the God of Mount Tai* recalls a soul, he entrusts the death roll to couriers like myself, and we take it to the respective mountain gods governing the area."

"May I see what a death roll is like?"

"I don't think it matters if you have a peep." So he untied the leather bag he was carrying and retrieved a scroll. The title line read:

The God of Mount Tai to the God of Mount Hua:
Then came the name:

> Zhang, ... , ex-magistrate of Fuliang County,
> greedy with no shame, unrestrained in
> slaughtering and killing.

It was his name! Zhang implored the courier for help. "I know," he said, "the length of one's life is predestined. I'm not afraid of death, but, you see, I'm in the prime of life and was totally unprepared for the end. I haven't even made arrangements for my vast property. Is there any way death can be postponed? I have with me hundreds of thousands. You can have it all."

"I have no use for your millions, and I'm already indebted to you for this meal. A kindness must be returned in one way

---

* The God of Mount Tai, in Taoist belief, is supposed to be the Lord of Hell.

or another. Now, listen carefully. There is an immortal named Liu Gang living in exile from heaven on the Lotus Peak. Your Excellency may crawl your way up to his feet and beg him to write a petition for you and send it to heaven. That probably is the only way I know to save you. Also, I heard yesterday that the God of Mount Hua had lost 200,000 to the God of Mount Heng in gambling. He is very much pressed. So, if you go to his temple and offer to pay his debt, I'm sure he'll drop that Liu Gang a clear hint. Even if it doesn't work, at least it'll make your climb easier, for the hills are thorned and cliffed. Few can reach his abode."

Zhang rushed to the temple of the mountain god with sacrifices of cows and lambs, and promised millions in reward. Then he made for the peak and, luckily, found a hidden path. Miles of winding mountain trails led him to the summit. He discerned a thatched hut on the southeast slope where a Taoist priest was sitting by a low table.

"How did you, a soulless walking corpse, manage to intrude upon my peace?" was the priest's greeting.

"True as you have put it," Zhang said, "I'm no better than a drained-off water clock at the end of a day, or morning dew before a rising sun, but I hear Your Highness can reunite the soul with its shell and restore flesh and blood to a skeleton. Such benevolence emboldens me to think that you won't grudge writing a petition for my sake."

"You know why I was banished to this bleak place? Because I once penned such a petition for a cabinet bigwig of the Sui Dynasty. What do I owe you that you should think I would risk myself for your sake and live forever at this place?"

The more humbly he pleaded, the more furious the priest seemed to become.

Just then, a messenger appeared with a letter from the God of Mount Hua. The priest grinned as he read. "Once money is promised, one has to oblige," he commented to himself. Having sent the messenger back with an acknowledgment of receipt, he sighed, "I hope this time I won't be blamed by His Almighty again."

He opened a jade box and wrote something. Kneeling and offering joss sticks before the altar, he burned up the message. In the time it takes for a meal, a folded sheet drifted down from heaven bearing a seal. Offering another bunch of joss sticks, he knelt again and spread out the sheet to read:

"Zhang has betrayed the teachings of his ancestors, ignored all decencies of life, and usurped a respectable social position through ignominious means. This person is greedy and stingy, dishonest and faithless. To govern a hundred villages is already beyond his lot, not to mention the thousand cartloads of riches that should not belong to him.

"All the above has been proved beyond a shadow of a doubt, and his soul is to be fetched and punished. How can someone send in a petition to extend such a life!

"Nevertheless, it is a tenet of the Way to assist the needy and rescue the drowning, and it is also in the spirit of Taoism to withhold punishment and to forgive. Thus, by pardoning one, our creed shall radiate many. Let him renounce the evil and reclaim the virtues. Let his life be extended five years, but, he who spoke for such a person shall not be forgiven."

The verdict thus pronounced, the priest said to Zhang, "An ordinary human being should be able to live for 100 years, but all too often such emotions as joy, anger, and sorrow weaken the fountain of his heart; love, hate especially, and other desires chop away at the root of his life; vanity and scorn, in addition, constantly disturb his mind, exhausting its spirit and destroying its harmony; just as pure water from the source of a river is always corrupted by added tastes of sweetness, saltiness, bitterness and sourness. In that case, how can a life sustain its vitality? Now that you've gained new life, don't let us down." Zhang bowed a farewell. When he lifted his eyes, the priest was gone.

The way back seemed less difficult. Halfway, he encountered the ghost courier, who congratulated him.

"May I have your name so that I should know who to thank?" Zhang brought up the question once again.

"My family name was Zhong. I was a messenger for the Xuancheng County government, and fell dead during an errand at the foot of this mountain. Because of my former experience, I was employed after my death as a nether courier. I am worked as hard as I ever was."

"Is there any way I might have you relieved from your present toils?"

"All you need to do is pray for me to the God of Mount Hua, wishing me to be reassigned as a janitor. Then I would enjoy the privilege of sampling the offerings to god. Sorry that I must say good-bye to you now, for I'm already half a day behind schedule." So saying, he vanished in the mulberry woods south of the temple.

That night, Zhang made up his mind to return home the next morning. He calculated that it would cost him more than 20,000 if he were to keep his promise to the mountain god. "Twenty thousand would be enough to cover 10 days' traveling expenses," he confided to a servant. "Why should I give it to an earthen statue in a temple while I have the blessing from His Almighty?"

So east he went.

One night, he had just put up at a county guest house when the yellow jacket courier kicked open the door and strode in. "How dare you cheat god!" he shouted at Zhang, waving a scroll in one hand. "Now you're doomed. And because you failed to keep your word, you made me unable to repay your meal. That debt will forever be like a scorpion bite poisoning my heart!" He vanished without another word.

Instantly, Zhang fell ill. He grabbed a brushpen and tried to write a will, but he never finished it.

Translator's note:
This story provides us with a glimpse of the widespread corruption

in the Tang Dynasty. A county magistrate could collect a fortune during his term of office; the royal falconers, because of their special position, had the license to bully the common folk; humble as janitors are, they could abuse their power to embezzle the offerings to the gods; immortal beings succumb to backdoor tips; and even the gods themselves gamble heavily and rely on "black" money to pay off their debts.

Mr. Tan's Bedmate

Mr. Tan was already 40 years old, but was too poor to get married. His solitude goaded him into a more fervent study of the Confucian classics, and he often sat up late into the night.

During one of these nocturnal studies, a girl of about 16, with features more beautiful than tongue could describe, emerged and presented herself as his wife. "I'm no usual woman," she introduced herself, "so don't try to expose my body to light, not for three years' time. After that, I don't mind you looking at it."

In that way, Tan had a wife, and a son was duly born.

One night two years later he could no longer suppress his curiosity. He lit a candle and lifted a corner of his wife's quilt while she was fast asleep. Flesh had filled out on the upper part of her body, but below the waist, she was a skeleton.

His wife awoke startled, "You abused my trust! I've almost regained a human form. Why can't you just wait one more year! Why do you have to look at my body?"

Tan apologized humbly.

"Our marriage is finished now," she sobbed. "But, for the sake of my son, come with me. I'll give you something. I'm afraid you're too poor to feed both of you."

He followed her into a grand chamber, elegantly decorated and exotically furnished. She handed him a robe of stringed pearls. "I think this might sustain you two for quite a while." So saying, she tore off a strip from Tan's garment and waved him out.

He later sold the robe at the market and got 10 million coins from the House of Suiyang. When the robe was later presented to the prince, he recognized it as the funerary object of his diseased daughter. Tan was arrested and interrogated on a charge of grave-robbery. He recounted every detail of his story, but the prince brushed it aside as sheer nonsense and went in person to inspect his daughter's tomb. Though it appeared intact, the prince still ordered it to be opened up. The shred from Tan's torn garment was seen sticking out from beneath the coffin lid. Tan's son was summoned, and the boy's distinguishing features of his daughter finally convinced the prince.

Tan was released and given back the pearl-robe. The prince formally accepted him as his son-in-law and petitioned the throne to enter his grandson's name into the peerage.

The Pink Sleeve

The military commissioner of Jiannan Region after the An Lushan-Shi Siming Rebellion was a Mr. Zhang. With the advent of the *Ullambana* Festival on the full-moon of the seventh lunar month, he ordered that all temples in the city be decked out and throw their doors open to the public during the festival season.

The whole town, old and young, men and women, turned out for the occasion, all except the wife of a Mr. Li, a county official under Zhang's jurisdiction. As Li's wife was reputed to be the most beautiful woman in the region, Zhang had long coveted a look. He was pretty sure that she didn't come out because he had his subordinates' households watched, and any of their movements would be immediately reported to him.

Her seclusion fascinated him. He approached her neighbors through middlemen and the reports they brought back confirmed the gossip that her beauty required her prudence. Yet, he was determined to bait her out.

He gathered the best carpenters from all over the region to the Kaiyuan Temple and told them to pool their minds and make a whole band of wooden musicians which, operated by an internal mechanism, could play the various stringed and wind instruments. Upon its completion, he had it proclaimed in the streets that the band would be put on public display for three days, and three days only. After that, it would be sent to the capital as a tribute to the emperor.

For two days the streets leading to the temple were jammed with people from as far as a hundred miles coming on foot, on horseback, in sedan chairs and in carriages. But Li's wife did not show up.

In the twilight of the third day when the last crowds were dispersing, Li's wife finally emerged from the gate of her house in a sedan chair, accompanied by a serving maid. Zhang was immediately notified. He took off his official robe and hurried to the temple in disguise, where he hid himself in the cavity of a hollow Buddha statue and peered out.

Li's wife soon arrived. Having first sent in the maid to make sure that the hall was vacant, she got off the sedan and walked in. How could she be anyone but the goddess of beauty herself!

Once home, he secretly summoned the nuns and women soothsayers who had any contact with Li's wife and bade them convince her of his admiration. However, all his advances were bashfully turned down.

It just happened then that Li was accused by his servant of taking bribes. Zhang had a confidant preside over the trial, who dutifully exiled Li to the remotest frontier with 60 strokes across his back, all in the name of law. Li died along the way.

Zhang showered Li's mother with gifts, and with her acquiescence he was able to gain Li's widow as a concubine. The widow, on the other hand, did not put up a fight, because, Li being unpolished and plain-looking, she had often rued her low marriage. Zhang kept her in his official mansion and petted her with jewelry and favors.

Their good days didn't last long, for Zhang soon fancied that he saw Li around. He hired sorcerers to drive away Li's spirit, but to no avail. In about a year, Li's widow died. A few years later, it was his turn to fall ill. In his sickness, Li's image flickered on ever more frequently and vividly. Then one day he saw Li's wife standing before his eyes, as beautiful as she had always been. He greeted her with a thrill of joy and surprise.

"I owe you a lot," she said, "and would like to do something for you in return. Li has brought his case before His Almighty, and the final verdict should come out before the end of the year. But don't worry. You have people up there defending you. If only you can make it into next year, you'll be all right. His spirit is already here waiting for an opportunity to fetch your soul, but as long as you stay within doors, you're safe, for he dares not enter an official mansion. Take care. Don't venture out." So saying, she disappeared. A venerable Taoist priest from Mount Hua, who had set up an altar in the courtyard at Zhang's request, had said the same thing. So, for several months, with the assistance of Li's wife and the priest, Zhang carefully refrained from crossing the threshold.

At dusk one day, Zhang saw a pink sleeve beckoning to him from the bamboo grove in the yard. Thinking that it must be Li's wife, he ran out from his room toward the grove, forgetting all the warnings and ignoring the desperate calls from his attendants for him to come back. Who he met behind the grove was none other than Li in woman's clothes. Li caught hold of him and gave him a good long beating, saying, "Only a pink sleeve can make you voluntarily come to your death."

Overpowered by a sense of drunken numbness, Zhang's attendants watched him* being dragged out of the gate. When they were able to move again, they discovered Zhang's body prostrate in the grove, his nose and ears bleeding, but not quite dead yet. By the time they carried him back into the room, he had drawn his last breath.

---

* This "him" refers to Zhang's soul, while his body lies in the bamboo grove. It is a Buddhist belief that the soul can be separated from the body. The former, though unsubstantial, can assume the shape of the latter. See "The Departed Soul."

A Chance Meeting in Limbo

During mid Jian'an reign of the Han Dynasty there was a man named Jia Ou in Nanyang Prefecture who died of an illness—a nether courier had come to bring him to Mount Tai, where all souls return. The nether judge fumbled through his records but could not match them with Jia's dates and address. Finally he turned to the courier and scolded him for fetching the wrong person—it must be a namesake from another prefecture, and the one he snatched should be immediately released.

As the day was already getting dark when he was escorted out of the town gate, Jia decided to spend the night under a big tree. Soon he saw a lone maiden hurrying along the path. "Who is it over there?" he called out as she approached. "Judging from your elegant appearance and fine clothes, you ought to belong to the high class. How come you're trudging on foot? May I have the honor of knowing your name?"

"I'm a native of Sanhe District. My father is the magistrate of Yiyang County and I was summoned here yesterday, but today they told me to go back. I know, a prudent young woman should shun the company of men to avoid rumors, but as I see you are a gentleman and it is getting late, I hope you won't mind my staying with you under this tree."

"I have a liking for you. Why don't we make love?"

"My aunts told me that the virtue of a maiden lies in her chastity, and her name cannot afford to be stained."

In spite of his coaxing and pleading, she did not give in. At daybreak, they went on their respective ways.

Jia had been dead for two days, and was laid out on the bier ready to be coffined. His family then discovered that color was returning to his face and, placing a hand over his heart, they felt his body warming. In a while, he came round.

Intending to check out whether his nether experience had been real, he made a trip to Yiyang County and requested an interview with the magistrate.

"Has Your Excellency's daughter just recovered from death?" he asked, substantiating his bluntness with a careful description of her looks and dress, and the conversation they had. The magistrate went in to question his daughter, and received a similar account. After the initial shock, the magistrate consented to their marriage.

Translator's note:
It's only human to err. Well, so do the supernatural beings.

Mr. Li

Mr. Li, a native of the region north of the Yellow River in Zhenyuan reign of the Tang Dynasty, was a tough man when he was young and loved a good fight. As decency rarely bothered him, he was often seen mixed up with the local rascals. He did not begin to read books until he was in his twenties, yet the poems he composed won praise from many. With that, he was able to obtain a job in the local government as a clerk, and gradually rose to a position as minor official in the government of Shen Prefecture. He was a capable official and quite discreet when it came to office policy. He also had a graceful deportment and a good sense of humor. As for games and drinking, he excelled most, and in this respect he was known to the prefect.

At that time, the governor of Chengde Region was a General Wang Wujun, an arrogant and impudent man who did not hesitate to bend the law to his own desires. The prefects under his jurisdiction were subjected to his constant tyranny which they could not but grin and bear. In addition, he often sent his son, Wang Shizhen, on inspection tours through the prefectures.

On one such inspection, Shizhen arrived in Shen Prefecture. Cowed by the father, the prefect took exceptional pains to please the son. A luxurious banquet was held in Shizhen's honor with fragrant wine and roasted calves. Musicians and singers were collected to entertain. Still, the prefect was afraid that someone might forget his manners when sodden with wine, and unwittingly offend the distinguished guest. He therefore kept the size of the company down to the minimum.

Shizhen was pleased with the banquet, thinking that it was

better than at other prefectures. Drinking late into the night, he turned to the prefect and said, "Thanks for this cordial reception. Let's thoroughly enjoy ourselves tonight, but I don't see much company here. Why didn't you summon more?"

"I beg Your Excellency's pardon. My poor jurisdiction doesn't have any celebrities to boast of. On the other hand, with regard to Your Excellency's high position, I didn't dare invite anyone of low status. Among my subordinates there is a Mr. Li. He is a good companion at the table. If you don't mind, I'll send for him."

"Do, please," Shizhen rasped.

Li bowed deep and respectfully as he entered the room, but the smile disappeared from Shizhen's face the moment he caught sight of him. Then Li was offered a seat, and he sat humbly at the table. Shizhen seemed even more displeased. Li held his hands stiffly and stared vacantly ahead, entirely different from the jolly man he used to be.

Not knowing what was wrong, the prefect was scared to death. He tried to catch Li's eye, but to his surprise he saw beads of sweat oozing out on his forehead, and his hands shook so that he could not even hold his cup. All those present were stunned. Then Shizhen burst out to his attendants to have Li tied up and thrown into prison. The attendants grabbed Li by the sleeves and whisked him out to jail. With Li out of the room, Shizhen regained his cheerfulness and started to drink again.

When the banquet finally came to an end at daybreak, the prefect was more worried than relieved. He secretly dispatched a confidant to the jail to question Li: "You behaved most respectfully, and you didn't even say a word, so you couldn't have offended that man in any way. Is there some reason I don't know?"

It was quite a while before Li could control his sobs and pull himself together to reply. "There is a Buddhist saying that retribution doesn't have to wait till one's next life. I believe it now. As you know, I was very poor when I was young and had no means to support myself. So I associated myself with bad company and we often stole and robbed in the villages. We sometimes would prowl a good stretch of highway on horseback with arrows and bow. One day, I saw a youth driving two beautiful mules. Each mule was carrying a bulky sack. As it was getting dark and it happened to be a craggy stretch of road, I thought he was easy prey. I dashed forth and shoved him down the cliff. Then I galloped away with the mules. When I opened the sacks in my tavern room, I found more than a hundred bolts of silk. I became well off. So I discarded my arrows and bow, and turned to the books. Thanks to that, I became a clerk and rose to this position today. It all happened 27 years ago, but yesterday, at my lord's banquet, as soon as I saw His Excellency Mr. Wang, I recognized the youth I killed. When I bowed to him, I actually bowed with my deepest regret. I know I can't escape this time. I'm waiting for the headsman with my neck stretched. I don't want to defend myself. Please bring my heartiest gratitude to the prefect for treating me well. My only wish is that he'll take care of my remains."

Meanwhile, Shizhen had awakened out of his hangover. The first thing he did was send his adjutants to the jail to fetch Li's head. After Li was beheaded his head was presented to Shizhen who examined it with a contented smile.

Then he was invited to another feast at the prefect's place. Seeing him intoxicated, the prefect sighed. He rose from his seat and ventured, "I should say I am an incompetent governor. It's only by your favor and leniency that I can continue to hold this position, for Your Excellency must have found many unsatisfactory things during your inspection. As Your Excellency sees, my prefecture is deprived and has little to offer. So yesterday when Your Excellency told me to summon more company, I thought of that Mr. Li. He used to be fun at the table and a good drinker as well. Who knew he would be so ignorant and without manners as to affront Your Excellency. It was really my fault for having him come. He deserved his death, as Your Excellency has punished him. Yet I wonder, excuse my ineptitude, in what name he was executed. I hope Your Excellency will enlighten me so that I might be wiser next time."

"As a matter of fact," Shizhen chuckled, "that Mr. Li did not do anything wrong. I don't know why, but as soon as I saw his mug, I felt a kind of revulsion and wanted to have him eliminated from earth. Now that he is dead, do not mention it again."

After the feast, the prefect probed and learned that Shizhen was 27 years old, that is, he was born into the Wang family in the very year Li killed the youth.

Amazed by the workings of providence, the prefect gave Li a proper burial.

Translator's note:

Stripped off its Buddhist principle of retribution, this story reveals the corruption and brutality of the Tang Dynasty officials. Human life was so cheap that they could kill a person for no reason at all.

Gentleman A

During the reign of the first emperor of the Eastern Jin Dynasty there was a Gentleman A of a noble clan who died of a sudden illness and was brought to the celestial court.* As the heavenly judge reviewed his case it was discovered that his life span was not yet completed; it was a mistake to have summoned him. The prosecutors were told to send him back, but he had hurt his feet on his way there; the pain was so sharp he was unable to stand on his feet, much less walk all the way home. The prosecutors were annoyed. "If he can't go home," they said to each other, "and should die here because of his foot trouble, we would be accused of a miscarriage of justice." So they turned to the judge for advice. After lengthy contemplation, the judge at last hit upon an idea and said, "We have just summoned a barbarian named Kang B. Right now he is waiting outside the western gate, and he is destined to die this very moment. He has a pair of good strong feet. Why not have them exchange theirs? Neither will suffer a loss by this."

The prosecutors retreated from the hall, very pleased with the idea. They told A to prepare himself for the swap, but the barbarian looked so ugly, his feet in particular, that A objected.

"If you don't," threatened the prosecutors, "you'll be confined here forever."

Seeing no alternative, he finally consented.

The prosecutors told the two of them to shut their eyes.

---

* It is rather unusual for a soul to go straight to heaven. It should be brought to Mount Tai first as in other stories of the time.

Straight away, their feet were switched. Without delay A was dispatched home where he came back to life. He told his family what had happened, and as they lifted his coverings they did discover a pair of barbarian feet, hairy and smelly.

As a gentleman, he had taken particular care of his hands and feet. Now that he had acquired such a pair of feet, he felt too ashamed even to glance at them. The fact that he regained his life could not console him for his loss of pride. He lived like the dead.

Someone who knew the barbarian told him that the man lived nearby Eggplant Bend and was not buried yet. So A went in person to have a look at the corpse. Indeed, it was his feet that were on the dead man's body. He cried over the pair of feet which had once been his, while people dressed and placed the corpse into the coffin.

The barbarian turned out to have a very filial son. On the first day of each new month, and on every festival, he would ride over to A's place, clasp his father's feet and wail for hours. Even if they met on the road, he would cling to A and make a show of tears. Therefore, A had to place a guard at his gate to fend off the young man.

All through the rest of his life, his abhorrence of his feet never abated, and on no account would he let his eyes wander in their direction. Even on the hottest days of high summer he would don layers of clothes so his feet would not be exposed to the light.

Translator's note:
   Unlike "A Chance Meeting in Limbo," this mistake by the supernatural beings does not effect a happy turn of fate. A person's family origin was considered a very important social factor during the Jin and the Northern and Southern Dynasties, and "high" blood was not supposed to mix with the "low."

The Shattered Specter

Yuan Jiqian, imperial carpenter of the Jin Dynasty, told of an event that occurred during his stay in the eastern provinces.

He and his family then lived in a rented house which they later learned was rumored to be haunted. The whole family lived under the shadow of fear and they kept themselves indoors as soon as night fell. Their nerves were on edge, even in their sleep.

One night, wild, hollow howls suddenly reverberated throughout the courtyard, as if a frenzied voice was locked in a barrel. The family shook with fear, thinking that it must be the monster people had talked about. Peering out from a window they saw a dark specter running wildly in the yard. By the dim light of an obscured moon it seemed to have the body of a dog, but with a disproportionately large, sagging head.

Yuan picked up a club and hit it hard on the head. With a loud crack and a sharp howl, their family dog bolted away.

So it was that during the day, the farmhands had been bringing in the year's harvest and had dined in the courtyard. A little food was left in a pot and their dog somehow pushed its head into it, but wasn't able to pull it out.

That night, the family had a hearty laugh and a sound sleep.

Translator's note:
Ghost stories arise from ignorance and fear. What if the man does not have the courage to give it a hit?

General Liu

There was a noble old house with spacious rooms, large windows and broad stone doorsteps in the East Capital, yet it had been unoccupied and locked up for many years because strange deaths would befall those who ventured to live in it.

In spite of friendly warnings that the house was haunted and not fit to live, Lu Qian, commissioner of the supervisory committee during Zhenyuan reign, was thinking of buying it. He claimed that he could get rid of the evil spirits, if there were any at all. So late one afternoon he moved in, bringing with him only one adjutant who was courageous and an accurate marksman. All the other servants were left outside.

The adjutant seated himself in the foyer facing the door and windows with a ready bow. The night advanced when suddenly a knock was heard on the door and he demanded who it was.

"General Liu sends a note of greeting to Commissioner Lu," a voice answered.

As Lu didn't pick up the conversation, the creature dropped a slip of paper in through the window. The characters were slender and faint, as if written by licking a dry brush. Lu asked the adjutant to read it:

"I have been living here for many many years. The rooms, the steps and the whole courtyard all belong to me. The deities patronizing the doors and rooms are all my subordinates. And now for no reason at all you are intruding upon my premises. How do you justify yourself? Suppose you have a house and I should force my presence onto you. Would you like that? You may not be afraid of me, but aren't you ashamed of your deeds? Better leave immediately or you'll bring disaster upon

99

yourself." As soon as it was read, the paper decomposed like ashes.

Presently a voice spoke out again, "General Liu would like to speak to Commissioner Lu in person." Then a monster many times the height of an ordinary man appeared in the courtyard, holding in one hand what looked like a long ladle. The adjutant drew his bow to its full and let fly an arrow. It must have hit the object, for the monster dropped it to the ground and backed away.

Before long it approached again, stooping over the house to peep into the window. It had a strange look. The adjutant shot again, this time hitting the creature in the torso. That seemed to have taken it by surprise and daunted it, for it retreated toward the east.

Soon after daybreak, Lu ordered his servants to look for traces, which led them to a vacant lot east of the house. There stood a hundred-foot-tall willow tree with an arrow sticking out of its trunk. So, that was the so-called General Liu. Lu had it chopped down into firewood and the house became habitable again.

The following year while the house was under renovation a dried bottle-gourd about 10 feet long with an arrow through its neck was found beneath the tiles among the rafters.

Translator's note:

In the old days, it was believed by the superstitious that everything, old things especially, including plants and even inanimate objects, may have a spirit, and those spirits may bewitch people. Here is a typical example in the ancient willow tree.

"Willow," pronounced [Liu], is a common family name in China.

The Lily

Far away from worldly hustle and bustle, up on Culai Mountain was a Buddhist temple named Guanghua. Once, a young man of the Confucian school took up residence there to concentrate on his books, brushing up for the imperial examination.

One cool summer day while he was perusing the murals on the temple walls he bumped into a beautiful girl in pure white about 16 years of age.

"Never seen you around here," he said admiringly. "Are you from afar?"

"No. I live just down the hill," she smiled back.

The answer amused him, for he knew there was no such girl living there, and yet that didn't set off an alarm in his mind. Her features were too appealing, and he felt the urge. What with teasing and what with seriousness, he led her to his room. Before long, they became glued to each other.

"I appreciate it very much that you didn't treat me like a low-bred country lass," she crooned. "I swear I'll be at your service for the rest of my life, but tonight I must leave. Next time I come, I'll be able to live with you forever."

Though he exhausted his gifts of scholarly eloquence to make her stay, it seemed she could not be swayed. He took off the white jade ring he was wearing and handed it to her. "Hope this ring will remind you to return soon," he said.

At the gate of the temple compound, she insisted that they part. "No further, dear. My parents may come at any moment to meet me."

He then ascended the gate tower and hid behind a pillar to see where she was heading. After having walked 100 steps or so she suddenly disappeared off the face of the earth. He made a mental mark of the place and traced her steps.

The temple lay on a stretch of flat incline. The young trees and tender grass could not hide anything. He paced the distance many times but could not make out how she could have vanished altogether.

Night was descending and he was about to give up when he noticed a remarkably beautiful white lily among the grass and he pulled the plant out. Unlike ordinary lilies, its roots were clustered into a ball. Back in his room he untwined the roots which disclosed in their grip the white jade ring he had just given the girl!

How surprised he was! And how he hated himself for destroying the flower! He then dropped into a trance and died in less than a fortnight.

The Girl in the Well

During Tianbao reign of the Tang Dynasty, there was an industrious young scholar named Chen Zhonggong from an affluent family in Nanjing. He had come to the East Capital to further his studies, and had rented a house in Qinghua District.

In front of the house was a deep well, notorious for having drowned many. That, however, did not bother him, for he did not have family and kids to worry about. Usually, he would shut himself in his room to study his books.

As days grew into months, he noticed that every morning a neighbor's teen-age maid would come to fetch water from the well. It was peculiar that she was apparently reluctant to leave even after her pails were filled, and one day she fell headlong into the well and was drowned. So deep was the water that her corpse was not dredged up until the next day.

This provoked his curiosity. So one day he strolled over to the well and peeped down. All of a sudden a girl appeared in the water. She was quite a beauty and dressed in the latest fashion. Her eyes were engaging, her lips full. A transient smile flashed across her face, which she coyly attempted to conceal with her flowing robe sleeve. It was soul-catching! And he felt himself pulled toward her. Now realizing why so many had so willingly plunged to their death, he pulled himself together and backed away.

It was a hot and dry summer. The drought was serious, yet the water level of this well remained as high as ever. Then one night it dried up without the slightest warning.

Early in the morning, he heard a knock on his door and

a voice announced itself as a Miss Jing Yuanying.* He opened the door and standing before his very eyes was the belle he had seen in the well, her clothes in style and her face powdered and rouged. Politely he offered her a seat, but didn't mince his words in accusing her of killing innocent people.

"That wasn't my doing," she replied. "This well has been occupied by a venomous dragon ever since it was dug in the Han Dynasty. To be exact, he is just one of the five bad dragons in town. Like the other four, he enjoys the patronage of a dragon adjutant to His Almighty. So every time he was asked to report to heaven he was able to excuse himself from going. That's how he managed to survive till now. He loves sucking human blood, and so far has killed 3,700 people altogether. In that way, he maintained a high water level. My poor self was dropped into this well in the early years of the dynasty, and had since been enslaved by him and employed as a decoy. You must understand, I was abused against my will. Yesterday, as it was time for the beginning of a new term of office, all dragons on earth were obliged to go up to heaven to pay homage to the new commissioner. He left at midnight and probably won't be back for a couple of days, since he'll be detained to account for the severe drought plaguing this region. Now that the well is dry, if you can have it dredged and have me released from this endless suffering, I promise you my service throughout your lifetime. All your wishes will be granted." Having said that, she disappeared.

Diggers were immediately called in. He had his most trusted servant go down with the men. "Bring up whatever you find unusual," he instructed.

The only thing unearthed was an antique bronze mirror seven inches across. Careful washing revealed an elaborate pattern on its back side. Around the rim were 28 ancient characters, each representing a constellation, encircling the

---

* The name in Chinese puns on homonyms which can be translated literally as Mirror (*jing*) Round (*yuan*) Image (*ying*).

sun and the moon in the center. The inner ring consisted of the four icons—a dragon, a tiger, a sparrow and a tortoise, symbolizing the four bearings of the earth. He gently placed the mirror in a case in a niche and offered his homage and incense, thinking that it must be somewhat related to the girl.

As night fell, a shadow slipped through the door and made straight to the niche and bowed. It was Jing. Turning to face him, she said, "Thanks for raising me out of the mud and mire. Honestly, I'm the seventh of a series of 12 mirrors cast by the famous artisan Shi Kuang more than 10 centuries ago. Each of us was cast on a certain date of each month. I was cast at high noon on the seventh day of the seventh lunar month. In mid Zhenguan reign, this house was occupied by a Court minister. Accidentally, his maid dropped me into the well. As the water was deep and the well was filled with noxious gas, all those sent down to retrieve me were suffocated. So there I remained until now. It must be a stroke of luck to have you take this house, and I owe my deliverance to your virtues and moral strength. As a piece of advice, you'd better move out of this house by tomorrow morning."

He argued that he had put down a hefty deposit and an unscheduled move would deprive him of the means to rent another house.

"Don't worry," she assured him. "I'll see to it. You just pack up and get ready." And she got ready to leave.

"Since you're a mirror, how did you come into a human form, and a pretty one at that?" he asked, in the hope of prolonging her company.

"I can change into any form I wish, but we're not going to discuss this now." So saying, she vanished from sight.

Early next morning the house agent made an unexpected call, followed by the landlord himself who apologized for the inconvenience of having to ask him to change residence at short notice. Porters were waiting outside and before noon he was comfortably resettled in another district in a house of exactly the same size and rent. The agent already had the new lease drawn up.

Three days later, the well at his former dwelling caved in, bringing down a wing of the house with it.

From then on he succeeded in every exam he took and rose to a high position. Anything he wished would be carried out with the same planned smoothness as his first change of residence.

The Old Midget

In Dali reign, Mr. Lü, a former official of Shangyu County, was staying in a rented house in the capital. He had been recalled to the Court for reassignment.

One evening he invited several friends over to his new residence. They had finished their dinner and were about to turn in when a very old woman, less than two feet tall, emerged from the foot of the northern wall. Her face was as pale as her spotless white dress. As she swaggered slowly forward, Lü and his friends could not help grinning at each other at this unusual sight. She approached Lü's couch and said, "Sir, since you're having a party, why didn't you send me an invitation? Am I to be so looked down upon?" At Lü's rebuke, she retreated till she was lost in the northern wall. All were amazed, and no one could tell who she was.

The next evening Lü was at home by himself when he once again caught sight of the old midget at the foot of the northern wall. She seemed rather indecisive, as if she were afraid of something. Lü reproached her as he did the previous night and she disappeared without further ado.

She must be some kind of goblin, Lü thought in the morning, and it was most likely that she would come again at night. If he could not get rid of her once and for all she would probably haunt him night after night. So he hid a sword under the mattress. As expected, she did walk out of the northern wall that night. When she came within reach he quickly pulled out his sword and made a swing at her. The old midget leaped onto his couch and smacked him on the chest. As she skipped and danced around him, another old dame sprang onto the couch and gave him one more stroke on the chest. He felt as if he were struck by frost. He wielded his sword frantically only to have more and more dames join in the dance. Their numbers increased with every futile stroke while their sizes shrank to an inch or less, each having exactly the same appearance. He could no longer tell which was the original one. Panic caught hold of him as he saw the little figures closing in on him. There was no escape! Just then, one of the miniatures spoke, "Behold sir, I'm going to merge back into one." Thus speaking, all the diminutive figures converged before his couch and massed into the old midget whom he had seen before.

"What kind of goblin are you?" he muttered in escalating fear. "How dare you harass a living person! Better leave me now, or I'll call in a sorcerer to subdue you with his magic arts. Then it'll be too late for you to regret."

"You're misplacing your confidence, sir," remarked the old dame with a sarcastic smile. "If such sorcerers as you believe do exist, I'd certainly like to meet them. I was just having a little fun with you, with no intention of doing harm. Don't be alarmed. I'll leave you right now." So saying, she retreated into the northern wall.

The next day Lü related his experience to others. A Mr. Tian, well known in the capital for his magic arts in expelling evil spirits, was delighted to hear of the story. "That's my business," he told Lü. "It's as easy as catching an ant. Tonight I'll go to your place and wait for her."

That night, Lü and Tian sat in the room waiting. Before long, the midget appeared and moved up to the couch they were sitting on.

"Evil spirits off!" commanded Tian.

The old dame simply ignored him. Pacing indifferently before the couch, she slowly said to Tian, "You are really disappointing!"

All of a sudden, she waved a hand. It snapped off and dropped to the ground, turning into a tiny old dame like herself. It hopped onto the couch, and before Tian had time to shut his shocked mouth, it jumped in and down his throat. "I'm finished!" cried Tian, gasping.

"I promised I wouldn't hurt you," reproached the old dame, "but you didn't believe me. Now that Tian is ill, can it be helped? However, you'll profit by this." So saying, she withdrew herself.

The next day Lü was advised to excavate the spot where the midget emerged so as to find and eradicate the source of evil. Lü appreciated that idea and directed his servants to dig and search. Ten feet down they discovered a big jar more than half filled with mercury. Only then did he realize that the old midget was a mercury spirit. Poor Tian died from that chill.

Translator's note:

It is a characteristic of mercury that it can be cut into smaller and smaller balls without losing its features, and can be rolled back into one again. It can also dissipate into tiny holes or cracks in the floor and remain unsoiled. It is interesting to note how the author carefully weaves these features into the old midget.

The Fox Vampire

In Changning County there was a Buddhist monk named Yan Tong who practiced *dhuta*, an ascetic way of living. One of the 12 requirements was spending nights in the open, especially in the wilderness or in a graveyard. Be it rain or snow, his exercise was never interrupted; be he among ghosts or demons, his mind never wavered.

One moonlit night he was reposing by a roadside heap of skeletons when he saw a fox vampire staggering along his way. It didn't notice him because Yan was in the shade of a tree. It picked up a skull from the heap, slipped it over its head, and gave it a violent shake. If the skull disintegrated, it would simply try another one. Having thus tested four or five, it chanced upon a durable one which it donned joyously. Then it plucked leaves and flowers to cover its body. At the touch of its vision they turned into flower-patterned clothes and in no time the fox turned into a young woman and walked off to the roadside swinging its hips. There it waited for late travelers.

Before long, the clattering of hoofs was heard coming along the road and the fox affected a noisy cry. The rider halted to make an inquiry.

"I'm a singer," replied the fox in a flood of tears. "My husband and I were summoned to perform in Court, but he was killed by a gang of bandits in the morning and all our possessions were seized. I'm alone and helpless. I'd like to return north, but I don't have the means. If you take me along, I pledge my word I'll be a good serving maid."

The rider happened to be a soldier stationed in the north. He dismounted and looked the woman up and down. It seemed that he was rather pleased with her features. They exchanged a few more words and he helped her up to sit behind him. Just as they were about to ride off, Yan jumped out from the shade and shouted, "Look out, man! This is a fox vampire. How can you be so trusting!" With one stroke of his walking stick he knocked off the skeleton skull, and the fox changed back into its original form and fled.

Translator's note:

Stories about fox vampires that can change into beautiful maidens to seduce men become increasingly popular and reached their acme in Pu Songling's Strange Tales from Make-Do Studio (c. 1679). Reading behind the lines, however, we may see a society where skeletons pile high and bandits thrive, in contrast to the music and songs in the palace.

Who Is the Fox?

Business once took a distant uncle of mine to Mianchi, and he seized the opportunity to visit an old friend, a Mr. Tian, who was living some 10 miles northwest of town. To get to the village one had to scale a steep and thickly wooded ridge. The oak forest, if one believes the local legend, was haunted by fox vampires. People were so scared that they would usually gather into groups to cross the woods.

Having a guest, Tian dispatched his old butler to town to shop for groceries and wine. The man left early in the morning, but did not return until late afternoon, limping badly.

"What happened to you?" his master asked in concern.

"I was not far into the woods," the butler mumbled in reply, "when a fox vampire tripped me. I fell and hurt my ankle."

"How do you know it was a fox vampire?" Tian asked incredulously.

"Once down the hill, I looked back and saw it had changed into a woman. She was chasing me! I ran, and she ran, too. She quickly caught up with me. I dropped to the ground and was hurt. I knew if I didn't strike back, I would be her prey. So I gathered myself up and fought. You guess what, she called me a fox, and begged for mercy. 'Have mercy, Lord Fox. Have mercy, Lord Fox.' she kept whining. How cunning she was! But little tricks like that can't fool me. I punched and punched till my hands were sore. And that's how I escaped death."

"If you had a brawl with someone in town, just say so. Don't throw the blame on a fox," coaxed his master.

"It was real strange," the butler rambled on. "No matter how hard I beat her, I couldn't make her show her true colors."

"I'm afraid you were mistaken, but for the present get back to your room and have a good rest."

The sun had sunk below the horizon. A haggard woman in torn clothes and with blackened eyes appeared at the gate, begging for a bowl of water.

"I was entering the forest," she explained to Tian, "when I saw an old man not far ahead. I thought he would make good company to cross the woods together. I didn't suspect anything when I approached him, but he turned out to be a fox vampire in man's form. See how I was beaten up. Thank heaven that he seemed to have some more urgent call, or I wouldn't be able to keep body and soul together. I live in the village to the north. Can I have some water? I'm dying of thirst."

Fearing that she might recognize the butler, Tian himself fetched her a ladle of water and hastily sent her on her way.

The Official's Wife

This happened in Kaiyuan reign of the Tang Dynasty. An official of the Ministry of Revenue had a beautiful wife, and he also had a fine steed. For no obvious reason at all his wife contracted an unusual disease and his horse suddenly started to eat twice as much as it used to, but was growing ever thinner.

The puzzled official went to see his next-door neighbor, a Persian who was reputed to be something of a sorcerer. When asked, the Persian chuckled, "Ten miles will exhaust a horse, won't it? Not to speak of racing a thousand miles a day. It couldn't but be reduced to bones."

The official protested that he seldom rode out and there was no other male in his house.

"Every time you were on the night shift," confided the Persian, "your wife would go out. Well, if you don't believe me, you may make an unexpected return next time you're supposed to be on duty, and see for yourself."

The official took this advice and returned one night, hiding out at a neighbor's. When night fell, his wife started to make up and ordered the maid to saddle the horse. Then she came out onto the steps and mounted. The maid straddled a broom and followed. They rode up into the night sky and disappeared from sight. The stunned official went to see the Persian early in the morning, announcing that he was now fully convinced and begged for further advice. He was told to make another secret return.

That night when his wife was out, the official slid home and hid himself behind the hall curtains. All of a sudden, his wife reentered and asked the maid why there was the smell of a living person in the house. The maid lit the broom and used it as a torch searching from room to room. In a pinch, the official slipped into the big vat in the hall and replaced the cover above his head. Presently, his wife jumped onto the horse and was ready to set off again. Since the broom had burned up, this time the maid had nothing to ride.

"Broom or no broom, it's all the same. Ride whatever is at hand!" his wife commanded.

In haste, the maid got onto the vat and followed. The official inside was numbed with fear.

Before long, they landed at an opening in a forest on a hill top. There, in front of a tent, a rich banquet was laid out. A group of seven or eight young men were sitting at a table, each holding a belle on his lap. The feast continued into the small hours of the night. Then his wife got up, mounted the horse, and ordered the maid to get onto the vat.

"There's a man in the vat!" the maid shrieked in surprise.

Sodden with wine, his wife told the maid to push the man down the hill. The maid, also drunk, dragged the official out of the vat and rode away. The official was too frightened to say a single word.

Day broke. All was quite and there was nothing but smoking ashes at the site to remind one of the midnight revels. The official had to find his way out the mountains. It was only when he finally reached a human habitation that he learned he was in Lang Prefecture, hundreds of miles from the capital. It took him months before he begged his way home. His wife asked in amazement where he had been for so long. He made up a pretext, and went straight to the Persian for help. The Persian told him that next time his wife was going, he should be able to catch the evil spirit possessing his wife and throw it into a fire.

That moment came. A voice was heard in the sky pleading for mercy. Then a gray crane fell out from the blue and dropped dead in the bonfire. His wife recovered immediately.

The Tribal Chief of Juyan

During the reign of Emperor Jingdi of the Northern Zhou Dynasty, Juyan, an important outpost in the Northwest Corridor, was controlled by a tyrannical tribal chief called Bodu Gudi who led a sumptuous and sensual life.

One day, dozens of strangers came to the gate of his grand mansion. Their leader sent in a card introducing himself as Phil More Chambers, Chief of Namesake Tribe. Bodu invited them in and asked why the tribe was called by such a funny name.

"That's because we share our first name," Chambers replied. "Since we come from different origins, we bear different family names, such as Horse, Deer, Bear, Riverdeer, Donkey, Tiger, Hide, and so on. Therefore it is unnecessary to give each a different first name. We're all called Phil,* except me the chief. I've got a middle name More."

"Your family names make it sound like a whole circus. Are you good at performing?"

"We can do plate-spinning, somersaults with bowls piled on the head, and all the usual tricks, but we like creative work and we fill our shows with quotes from the sages."

"I certainly would like to watch some tricks I've never seen before," said Bodu eagerly.

One of the Phils stepped forward and said, "We're hungry. Our bowels are tied in knots; the skin on our bellies can go around our waist three times. If my lord cannot let us have our fill, better not feed us at all."

Bodu was fascinated and he told the servants to bring in

---

* Phil puns on "fill."

116

more food.

Another Phil stood up and said, "We'll show you a trick called the Sequence of Size and the Order of Life." So saying, the taller ones swallowed the shorter ones, the stouter gorged down the thinner till only two of the group were left. Then the tall one said, "Now, the Order of Life." So he disgorged a shorter one, and the shorter one in turn spewed out an even shorter one until all of the group reappeared.

Shocked by its sinisterness, Bodu hurriedly sent them away with a handsome tip. But the next day they were at his gate again, and played the same old trick. So they did everyday for a fortnight. Bodu became very upset and could no longer afford to satiate their tremendous appetite.

They were offended. "If you take our great performance as nothing but magic," they bellowed, "we can prove it on your wife and children." They grabbed his sons and daughters, brothers and sisters, nephews and nieces, wife and concubines, and swallowed them all. Muffled cries and pleadings could be heard from their stomachs. Bodu was helpless. He descend the steps and bowed apologetically, begging for the lives of his family and relatives. The performers laughed, "No harm will be done to them. Don't be so alarmed." And they disgorged them intact.

Bodu was furious and murder sprang up in his mind. He had them shadowed to the ruins of an ancient building where they disappeared. He then ordered his men to dig up the site. Several feet beneath the rubble they came upon a big wooden crate in which were several thousand leather bags. Beside the crate was a store of wheat grain, which turned into dust at the slightest touch. A bundle of bamboo slips were also found in the crate, but the words on them had long since faded. He could only make out a few, one of which was the word "Ling." It suddenly dawned on him that the performers were but the apparition of the bag spirits. He was about to have them hauled out and burned when the bags cried out in the crate,

"We were not destined for longevity, and should have decayed long ago if it were not for the quicksilver General Li Ling* stored here with us. It's the quicksilver that preserved us. We are the general's grain bags. The storehouse collapsed and buried us here for centuries, so long that we have gained lives of our own. The god of Juyan Mountain has adopted us as his performers. With respect to the mountain god, please spare our lives. We will not bother Your Highness with our presence any longer."

But Bodu had his mind on the mercury. The bags were set to flames. Moans and wails filled the air and blood stained the ground. For months afterwards, every pivot and hinge in his house would let out a groan or shriek on each turning.

Before the end of the year, all the Bodus had succumbed to a fatal illness of some kind. Within a year, none survived to preserve the family line. The mercury also mysteriously disappeared.

---

* Li Ling (? - 74 B.C.), a renowned general in the war against the Mongolian nomads (Xiongnu). In 99 B.C. he led an expedition deep into enemy territory and was outnumbered and surrounded in the deserts beyond Juyan. He capitulated after putting up a last-ditch fight.

The Kingdom of Golden Elephant

Now getting older, Cen Shun, a learned man from Runan County, became deeply absorbed in war strategy. Too poor, however, to afford a house of his own, he moved to Shan Prefecture to live with his maternal relatives. They had an abandoned cottage on the hill behind the village in which he persuaded them to let him take up his quarters.

"I'm not afraid of ghosts, because one's fate is always predestined" was his answer to those who tried to dissuade him.

There he resided for a year, and had developed a habit of sitting alone by the window in his study. He would not let anyone, even his relatives, come to disturb him. For a few nights he had caught the faint sounds of drums and bugles. Though he could not figure out the source, he discovered that as soon as he walked out of his study into the yard, the sound stopped. He was very much excited, cherishing high hopes that it must be an auspicious omen to have a nether legion privately in his support. If a great fortune is in store for me, he prayed, let there be some sign.

A few days afterward, he dreamed of a man in armor approaching him, saying, "The King of Golden Elephant has dispatched me to bring Your Excellency the following message: As war is imminent, we have been making a lot of noise during the nights. We do appreciate your tolerance and the interest you show in our affairs, in that you have won our respect. You have good fortunes ahead. Watch out for it. Yet, for one with lofty ambitions, I wonder if you would stoop to assist a miniature kingdom like mine. In face of an immediate invasion, I beg you to take command. We'll follow your orders and I'll be your servant."

"I'm much honored," he replied courteously, "but His Lordship is a wise man himself. He knows best the guiding rules of truth. Please convey my deepest gratitude to him for deigning to seek opinions from such a humble man as myself. If in any way my martial knowledge may be of help to His Lordship, I won't hesitate to apply it." With this promise, the envoy retreated.

Suddenly, he woke up. So confused was he that he sat long in his bed trying to figure out the implications of the dream. Soon, drums and bugles were heard again. The noise grew deafening. He slid off his bed, straightened his robe, and bowed in prayers.

A wind picked up, flapping the curtains and bamboo drapes. In the lamplight suddenly appeared hundreds of heavily armored cavalrymen several inches tall dashing across the floor. In a short while, they arrayed themselves into battle formations. Amazed, he held his breath and watched. Soon, a messenger came up with a scroll in hand, saying that the king had a letter for him. He spread it open and read, "Our territory unfortunately borders upon aggressive neighbors. They have forced us to bear arms for decades on end. My generals have lost their youth and my soldiers their households. Though we are tired of wearing armor through the four seasons of the year, heaven has set us against unrelenting and ever recurring enemies. Your Excellency being learned and cultured, we have benefited from your timely and frequent advice. We hope your blessings will bring us good luck. Your Excellency is a man of great prospects in the living world. We wouldn't dare to have you involved if it weren't for the joint invasion by the Kingdom of Beyond-Horizon and the North-Mountain Bandits. The decisive battle is to take place at midnight tonight. The outcome is unpredictable. But if the worst should come, let me die."

He made an acknowledgment and brought out more

candles to light up the room. Then he sat down to wait.

Midnight arrived. Drums and bugles flared up. First, the rat hole at the foot of the eastern wall became the gate-tower of a fortified town. After three cheers, formidable troops poured out from the four gates. Innumerable banners and colors flashed around as troops maneuvered into position. Finally, two distinct battle formations were formed. By the eastern wall was the army of Beyond-Horizon, and by the western wall the army of Golden Elephant. A figure, who must be the chief-of-staff of Golden Elephant, said to the king:

"The divine horse flies oblique across columns three;

To the four borders the king moves horizontally.

The chariot dashes straight ahead with no return;

In good order the six pawns march forth one by one."

"Good," the king said. The drums boomed. Each side had a horse that moved obliquely over three feet. After another round of drums, a pawn from each side moved one foot across. Then with another round of drums, the chariots dashed forth. The booming of drums became more and more urgent. Every element in the forces was put into action. Arrows and projectiles flew across the field. Before long, the Beyond-Horizon troops took to their heels, leaving their wounded and dead behind. Their king fled south alone. Hundreds of the Beyond-Horizon army ran toward the southwest corner and surrendered themselves to save their skin. There had been a stone mortar for pounding herbs in the southwest corner of the room, in which the king of Golden Elephant had taken up positions. Now it was transformed into a castle. The Golden Elephant army was exhilarated. The enemy soldiers were rounded up. Broken chariots strewed the ground. As he bent low to observe, a mounted messenger from the king rode up to him and proclaimed, "Yin and yang have their ways. Those who master them will thrive. With the blessings of providence, we have smashed the enemies at one stroke. What does

Your Excellency think?"

"Bright as the shining sun," he replied, "His Lordship knows how to exploit time and space. I am most pleased to have been an observer to the show of his military wonder."

The military campaigns did not end in one day, and there were many victories and defeats.

The king had an unusual air of dignity and pride. He was taller and sturdier than the others. He invited Cen to feasts on rare and most delicious dishes and gave him innumerable gifts of gold and pearls. Cen had whatever he desired, and was quite content to be one of them.

Thus he lived, hardly setting foot outside his room, and renouncing the company of his relatives. Though they became very suspicious, they could in no way put their finger on what was happening. One thing they were certain about was that he grew pale and haggard as if his spirit had been fogged by the devil. They agreed that something must have gone wrong, but he always held his tongue whenever asked.

One day they got him drunk and he gave away his secret. His relatives came to his cottage with hidden spades and picks. When he happened to go to the outhouse, they barred the door and started to poke around and dig up the floor. Reaching down eight or nine feet, the ground caved into an ancient tomb. It was a brick-lined tomb. Among the numerous funerary objects were hundreds of suits of armor. In front of the suits, there stood a table on which a chessboard was laid out with the chess pieces in position—all gold. That was the wars, and it suddenly occurred to them that what the chief-of-staff had spoken was the guiding rules of elephant chess.* Then they burned down the grave and filled up the

---

* Elephant chess is a literal translation of the name for Chinese chess. It is related to "elephant" because the chess pieces were originally carved out of ivory. Today, the game consists of 16 pieces on each side, including a king, five pawns, and guards, elephants, horses, chariots, and cannons in pairs. In its earliest form, each side had only six pieces.

pit.

Cen was awakened by the discovery. He felt a tightness in his stomach as he thought of the delicious food he had enjoyed, and vomited violently. The treasure they retrieved from the tomb provided him with an easy life through his remaining years, and the cottage was no longer haunted.

All this happened in the first year of Baoying reign.

A Mural in the Temple of Chrysanthemum

When Emperor Xiaowen of the Northern Wei Dynasty ascended the throne, there lived in Wei City a Taoist priest named Yuan Zhao. It was said that he could subdue all kinds of demons and evil spirits with his "Magic Arts of the Nine Heavens."

A soldier of the garrison force stationed in Ye County near Wei City had a 14-year-old daughter who had been suffering from a strange disease for years. None of the scores of practitioners she went to could provide a cure for her illness, so her father brought her to the city to see the priest.

"Her malady," said the priest, "was not caused by such things as a fox vampire but by an evil painting. How do I know? I know all the tricks of the deities in heaven, the devils in the nether world, the elves in the forests and the nymphs in the waters. From what you described, it must be a painted figure among the train of the four guardian gods on a Buddhist temple mural. Am I right?"

"Indeed, sir," the father replied. "For some time I had been praying before the God of Orient painted on the east wall of the Temple of Chrysanthemum. I sometimes took my daughter with me. She seemed to be afraid of a particular figure in that picture—it filled her with nightmares. She would dream of a monster clutching her with sinister laughter. That's how she contracted this illness."

"So it is," the priest burst out laughing. Then, all of a sudden, he started to talk with someone in the sky. All those in the room could hear the other voice speaking in the air.

After a lengthy exchange of words the priest raised his voice and demanded sternly, "Why don't you just bring it here immediately!"

"The God of Orient," the invisible voice responded, "asks me to convey to Your Excellency that he will take it upon himself to discipline any culprit under his patronage without inquiring assistance from Your Excellency."

The priest flared up and shouted into the sky, "Please tell the God of Orient explicitly that this offender must be sent to me. I am going to punish him myself. Bring him here in chains at once!"

"Send two Long-fangs and eight Red-brows," he added. "There is no need to obtain permission from the God of Orient."

The sound of winds and rain soon approached from afar. "You miserable thing!" the priest ridiculed merrily. "You didn't even have a shape until you were painted. What face do you have to charm a living person?" Then he turned to the girl, "Now tell me if this is the thing that haunts you."

"Show yourselves!" he commanded.

Eight deities clad in red with even redder brows and eyes appeared in the courtyard, as well as two others in black and red with pairs of long fangs sticking almost three feet out of their lips. They pushed to the steps of the hall a tightly held creature with teeth protruding from a broad mouth under a giant nose, its eyes red, its hair disheveled, its hands like the claws of a bird, its feet hairy, and wearing something that seemed to have been made out of leopard skin.

"That's exactly what my daughter often sees," the father remarked.

The priest ordered the creature to step forth. "You were but formless," he said, "and it is the painting that gives you some definite shape. How is it you acquired such devilish ways?"

"This form is but the result of painting," the creature

retorted. "A painting is but the reflection of a verity. What the verity shows is a spirit. Therefore, it's nothing strange that a spirit should inhabit a painting. In that way I acquired feelings, and feelings of many kinds. I won't deny my guilt."

Enraged by its defiance, the priest had a houseboy fetch a jar of water to rinse it, yet it did not even change color. The infuriated priest then told the assistant to use boiling water and pour it over the creature. This time it dissolved, leaving on the ground something like an empty sack, which he ordered to be cast away in the wastelands. The girl recovered on the spot, and her father took her home happily.

Later, the man revisited the temple. Standing before the mural he was very much astonished to see that the place where the image had been looked as if it had been washed. Seeing his expression, the abbot sidled up to him and asked politely, "Is there anything unusual about this mural, sir, that makes you gaze at it with such startled looks?"

"My daughter was possessed by an evil spirit," the man replied as he pointed to the wet stains. "Mr. Yuan, the great master, said it was a painted deity in this temple."

"You must have unusual perceptions!" the monk exclaimed. "To tell you the truth, one day last month, without any warning, the sun was blocked out by menacing dark clouds and fierce winds. Thunder cracked right above the roofs for a fearfully long time. I heard wrestling sounds coming from this very hall. 'Mr. Yuan is more powerful than me. Better give up and go,' I heard a voice say. As soon as that was said the clouds dispersed and sunlight bathed the temple again. I inspected the halls afterwards, and saw that the figure painted here had been washed off. What you said explains it."

A Parrot Fights a Mountain Fire

There was once a parrot living on a mountain. He was well respected by his fellow birds and beasts. Though that seemed an ideal place to inhabit, the parrot thought he should not be stuck there all his life, so he flew away.

A few days later, a terrible fire broke out on the mountain. Seeing this from afar, the parrot dipped his wings in a water hole and flew over to drench the fire. God said, "Determined as you might be, what use will your efforts come to?"

"I know this is of little use," answered the parrot, "but as I once lived there as a member of a congenial brotherhood, I can't watch them suffer unmoved."

God was so impressed that He extinguished the fire.

Translator's note:
This story and "The Turtle and the Mulberry Tree," both written during Lin's Song Dynasty (420-479), might be the earliest of China's fables.

The Turtle and the Mulberry Tree

In the reign of Sun Quan, king of Wu in the Three Kingdoms Period, a man in Yongkang County caught a giant turtle in the mountains.

"It was the wrong time for me to take a stroll," sighed the turtle, "otherwise I wouldn't have been caught by you."

Surprised that a turtle could talk, the man decided to carry it out of the mountains and offer it to the king. At nightfall, he moored his boat to a big mulberry tree on the shore. Deep in the night, the mulberry called out to the turtle, "Had a long trip, Mr. Round Shell? How come you've fallen into such a disgraceful state?"

"Just a stroke of ill luck," replied the turtle, "and I think they want to make soup of me. But no one will be able to have me cooked, even if he should burn up all the firewood in the mountains."

"Look out for a Mr. Zhuge Ke, a learned counselor of the king. You may suffer at his hand. What if he should send for venerable people like myself?"

"Shut up!" snapped the turtle. "If you can't hold your tongue, your days are numbered." The tree fell silent.

The turtle was brought to the Court, and the king ordered his men to boil it. A hundred cartloads of firewood were burned, but the turtle remained unscathed and talkative. Mr. Zhuge Ke came forth and said, "Cook it with the wood of an old mulberry tree." The man then told of the conversation he overheard between the turtle and the tree. At the king's mandate, the tree was chopped down. Once its wood was fed into the fire, the turtle was cooked.

That is why people now prefer mulberry wood to cook turtle broth.

The Long-Beard Kingdom

In the early days of Dazu reign of the Tang Dynasty, a scholar of the Confucian school went along with an envoy to Silla. A storm carried their ship to a strange place where people all grew long beards, from which the country acquired its name. The kingdom seemed prosperous and the people there spoke the same language as on the mainland, though the style of their attire and buildings was slightly different. The scholar was well received wherever he visited, and one day a train of carriages came to pick him up, announcing that the king was inviting him to the palace.

After two days of traveling he arrived at a large walled city with armored soldiers at the gates. He was led to a magnificent palace attended by a splendidly decorated honor guard. He kowtowed to the king, who rose from his throne in acknowledgment and dubbed him the Minister of Winds. The king also married him to the princess who was quite beautiful except for her long beards. Now a royal son-in-law, he enjoyed high social status and became rich in pearls and coral, but he hated to go home to see his wife.

It was a custom of the king to throw a monthly banquet on the night of the full moon. On his first attendance at such an occasion, he quickly discovered that all the noble ladies and courtesans had beards, for which he wrote this doggerel:

> Leaves make the blossoms red;
> Beards make the beauties dread.
> Dad fails to have it gone,
> So better have it on.

The king laughed aloud when he heard the verse and said

soothingly, "Why let a few hair on the chin and cheeks stand in your way to happiness?" A decade thus passed and a son and two daughters were born.

Then one day, a cloud of gloom seemed to fall over the Court. The scholar, annoyed, eagerly inquired about the cause.

"My country is in imminent danger," said the king with tears welling up in his eyes, "and our lives hang upon your help."

Taken aback, the scholar promised that if he could be of any help, he was ready to sacrifice even his life.

"We are most grateful to you then," said the king. "May we beg you to go and pay our respects to the Dragon King? Please tell him that the seventh island in the third trench of the East Sea is at peril and is imploring his mercy. Our country, however, is trivial, and could be easily overlooked. Only your perseverance will save us."

A boat was already prepared, and they parted in tears.

In less time than he had imagined his boat reached shore. The beach was a field of pearls and gems, and the people there were tall and well dressed. He hastily sought an audience with the Dragon King.

The palace shone like that in paradise as depicted on the temple murals. The Dragon King descended the marble steps to extend his welcome.

He explained his mission and the king decreed an immediate investigation. After a long while, someone reported that there was no such country within the king's territory. The scholar pleaded once more and specified the exact location. The king demanded a more careful search. After what might be the time for a meal, the officer returned to say that the shrimps of that island were rationed to be the king's food for the month, and they were just brought in yesterday.

"Sir," the king chuckled, "you have been bewitched by those shrimps. You must understand that although I'm the king of the ocean, what I eat is pre-arranged by heaven. I don't have much choice, but I can manage to eat less this month for your sake."

Then he led the scholar to the kitchen storage. There stood rows of huge room-size iron pots full of shrimps. Five or six of the shrimps were crimson and as large as a man's arm. They hopped about when they saw the scholar as if bowing and begging for life. A chef said those were the shrimp king and his family. The scholar couldn't help shedding tears.

The Dragon King ordered the shrimps in that particular pot be released into the sea, and appointed two attendants to send the scholar back to the mainland. Next day, the scholar was on the shore of Deng Prefecture. He looked back and saw two dragons on the waves.

The Mother Bear

In Shengping reign of the Jin Dynasty, there was a man who stumbled into a deep pit during a deer hunt in the mountains. Down in the murky recesses he found himself not alone, but in the company of several bear cubs.

His plight soon worsened when the mother bear returned. Her inimical gaze made him shudder. At long last she looked away, and retrieved from some secret nook a hoard of fruit and nuts. Separating them into small piles, she gave each cub its share, and, after a deliberative pause, pushed the last pile over to the man. His craving for food had been so sharp that he grabbed and ate, dismissing all thoughts of consequences.

As days passed, familiarity developed between the man and beasts. Every morning, the mother would go out to collect food and return to share her harvest. In that way, the man managed to survive.

The cubs grew slowly but steadily bigger. Then came the day when, instead of going out to seek food herself, she carried the cubs, one at a time, out of the pit. Pretty soon, only the man was left at the bottom. Trapped as he was, he despaired. However, the mother returned and sat beside him in such a way that made him catch the idea. He seized one of her legs and, with one mighty jump, she carried him out.

He thus lived to tell of his adventure.

The Hunter and the White Elephant

People living on the southern frontiers gained a livelihood by hunting and they put poison on arrowheads to ensure that every hit would be deadly.

In mid Kaiyuan reign, a hunter ventured into the remote mountains alone. He was taking a nap under a tree when he felt a push. He jerked open his eyes to see a white elephant, several times the size of an ordinary one, nudging him with its trunk. It was the kind that hunters called "the leader."

Seeing him awake, the leader wrapped him in his trunk and carefully lifted him onto its back. Then one by one it picked up his arrows, bow and poison pouch, placed them in his hands, and stumped off in haste. After many many miles, they entered a ravine. On both sides ancient trees as thick as towers blocked out the sun. Before long, they came into sight of an enormous table rock in the middle of the valley. The hunter could feel his mount trembling beneath him as it approached the rock, its eyes wandering in all directions. It finally halted beside a giant tree overlooking the rock and gestured upward with its trunk. In a gleam of comprehension, the man climbed up the tree with his bow and quiver. He stopped halfway to look down. The animal was gazing at him intently, its trunk raised straight up as if commanding him to go even higher. Nearing the top, he peered down again. This time the elephant seemed satisfied and trudged away, leaving him alone to spend an uneasy night in the tree.

By the first rays of dawn, he perceived two glossy eyes on the rock. Gradually he was able to make out the body of a massive jet-black shaggy beast. It must be over 100 feet long. As the mist rose he saw in the distance the white elephant leading a herd of hundreds filing into the ravine toward the rock. They went down on their knees before the beast, which snatched two out of the herd and tossed them into its mouth. Satiated, it seemed ready to leave. At that moment it suddenly occurred to him why the leader had carried him all the way to this place. He dipped his arrows in the pouch, drew his bow to full length, and let the arrows fly. Two hit the beast, prompting deafening roars, probably more out of anger than out of pain, that made the trees vibrate. He yelled back in an attempt to lure the beast to his side, which did turn around to face him. Clinging to a stout bough, he waited patiently till the beast opened its mouth, and shot right down its throat. The beast rolled onto its sides, moaned and kicked, and finally lay still.

When all was quiet, the leader reappeared. It hesitantly made its way toward the beast, pushed it with its head, and when it was absolutely sure that the beast was dead, it raised its head and trumpeted a prolonged cry. All of a sudden the whole valley reverberated in a chorus of bellows.

The leader came to kneel by the tree and beckoned with its trunk for the man to descend. With the hunter mounted, it marched off with the whole herd in procession. They reached a wooded mound and the leader used its trunk to push aside the dead leaves and dirt. The herd bent their heads to do the same. By the time the sun declined toward the west the top earth was cleared, revealing thousands upon thousands of tusks.

The leader carried the hunter off again. Every hundred steps or so it would snap off a branch as if blazing a trail. At last, they arrived at the spot where the man was found napping the day before. The leader bent down on its knees once again as if kneeling and bowing in gratitude, and left.

The hunter returned to town to tell the garrison commander of his adventure. A task force was assigned to him to bring back the tusks. Because of such a stockpile, ivory depreciated in the south.

As a souvenir for the commander, a bone of the beast was removed from the skeleton. It took 10 hefty soldiers to lift and carry it. The bone had a hole in it, through which a man could easily pass.

The White Ape

In the Liang Dynasty, troops were once sent to the barbarian south to subdue rebellions there. During that operation, Ouyang He, captain of a small detachment, led his men into the virgin mountains and successfully brought the cave-dwelling tribes to their knees.

When the aboriginals saw his pretty, fair-skinned wife in camp, they were very much disturbed. "How can Your Excellency bring such a beauty into this region?" they muttered their concern. "This is a dangerous place for young women. There is a woman-chaser at large. He steals them from their homes, especially those with good looks. Your Excellency must look out."

Half alarmed and half convinced, he intensified security, and at night had a special squad patrol the bungalow in which he hid his wife. As a further precaution he had her accompanied by a dozen slave girls.

It was a murky and wet night, yet it seemed to be passing peacefully for it was almost daybreak. Suddenly, the tired sentries were alerted by a slight stir. They checked and were surprised to find that the captain's wife was already gone though the doors and windows were as tightly locked as before. It was a mystery how anyone could have gotten through without being noticed. The morning fog was dense in that craggy area, obscuring everything. Search teams were withheld until there was light enough, and they didn't even find a trace.

The extremely grieved captain vowed that he would not withdraw from that area until he found his wife. He stationed his troops there on the excuse of illness. Day after day he

would go out in every direction and search high and low for his wife.

A month thus passed when one day he found an embroidered shoe in the bush some 30 miles from camp. Though it had been exposed to harsh weather, he had no difficulty in recognizing it was his wife's. The shoe brought him renewed pain and yet made him more determined than ever. To penetrate deeper into the uninhabited mountains, he selected a team of 30 tough soldiers and carried provisions for longer trips.

Ten days later, they were about 60 miles from base when they saw a luxuriant peak to the south. Reaching its foot, they found it was moated by a rushing stream. They had to build a raft. Landing on the opposite bank, they spotted flickers of red among the verdant bamboo growth atop the looming cliffs and caught floating notes of light-hearted laughter. With the help of ropes and vines they climbed up. Different from the surrounding area, the trees atop seemed to have been planted by hand and there were many beautiful and rare flowers. The grass was as well kept as a lawn. It was a kind of exotic solitude. A stone gate faced east. Dozens of brightly dressed women moved in and out, singing and playing. They didn't seem to be embarrassed by strangers, and when the captain approached them, they simply asked, "What brought you here?" Hearing his explanation, they glanced at each other and sighed. "Your wife has been here for more than a month," they told him. "She is sick in bed."

They led him through a wicker door into a cave. There were three large chambers with beds lining the walls and the bedding was either silk or wool. His wife was lying on layers of plushy mattresses on a stone bed. Delicious dishes were laid out within her reach. As he bent over her, she gave him a quick glance and urgently waved him away.

"This is the home of a superman," the women put in. "We and your wife are all in his hands. Some of us were caught 10 years ago. He has enormous strength and can easily break a man's neck. A hundred soldiers with all their weapons would not be his match. You're lucky he's not back yet. Better leave right away. If you want to rescue your wife, come again with two jars of the best wine, 10 fat dogs and several dozen pounds of hemp. We'll help you kill him. But don't be here too early. Noontime will be all right. Now you have 10 days to get things ready." So saying, they hurried him away.

He went back to collect those things and returned on the 10th day.

"He loves good wine, and every time he drinks he gets drunk," an older woman told him. "That makes his body go limp. Even so, if we try to tie his hands and feet to the bedposts with lengths of silk, he might still break it. We must twist it with hemp. Perhaps that is the only way we can tie him down. His body is as hard as cast iron. Knives cannot hurt him, but he often takes care to shield a spot several inches below the navel. That must be his soft spot." She pointed to a rock and said, "That's where he keeps his food. You can hide there and wait quietly until I call for you. We'll place the wine by the flowers and set the dogs free in the woods." The captain held his breath and waited.

The sun declined toward the west. Suddenly, something white cascaded from the heights and flowed right into the cave. Presently, a man over six feet tall with a flowing beard emerged from the cave. He was clad in white, with a stick in one hand and the other hand on the shoulder of one of the women. The dogs gave him a pleasant surprise. He leapt and grabbed, tore off a leg, sank his teeth into the juicy meat and sucked. The women vied with one another to fill his jade cup. He seemed most content and stumbled back into the cave, leaning on the shoulders of the women. Sounds of billing and cooing poured out from the cave among chuckles and gurgles. After a long while, the woman appeared at the door, beckoning the captain in.

A giant white ape lay sprawled out on a bed, his four limbs tied down. He frowned when he saw the captain, his eyes flaring like thunderbolts, though he could not break free. The captain's sword seemed to be hitting iron and rock. Then he remembered and stabbed below the navel. The blade sank in and blood spouted from the wound.

"It's heaven that kills me, not you!" he bellowed. "Anyway, your wife is pregnant. Don't kill the child. He'll bring glory to his ancestors." And that was his last breath.

The captain studied the place. There were hoards of jewelry and treasure that filled tables. What humans treasured, he had more than plenty. There were more than 30 women and all could be called beautiful without exaggeration. The longest held captive had been there 10 years. They said that when one's beauty faded he would carry her away to where no one knew. He did all the hunting and collecting by himself. It seemed he was the only one of his kind. In the morning, he would wash his face and put on clothes like a human being, always wearing a hat and a white lined-robe. Seasonal changes didn't seem to affect him. His body was covered with thick white hair several inches long. When at home, he would often read books inscribed on wood strips, the words of which were illegible. He kept his books under a flagstone. On fine days, he might practice his paired swords for a change. He could whirl them into a solid patch of glistening light. His diet included a variety of things, mostly fruits and nuts. Dog meat was his favorite, however. As soon as it passed high noon he would disappear like a flash of light and used to return before sunset, often traveling over hundreds of miles during those few hours. He could always get what he needed. At night, he would make love from bed to bed. He hardly slept. Though he could speak our language fairly well, he looked more like an ape than a human. In early fall this year, for no reason at all he let out a deep sigh, saying that he was charged by the mountain god and could be punished by death. To elude that fate he said he had to solicit the help of divine spirits. On the day of the past new moon he built a fire on the flagstone and burned his books, murmuring as if in a trance that he had lived 1,000 years without having a son, and now that he was about to have one he was going to die. He gazed long at us, from one face to another, with choked sobs. At last he spoke out, "This mountain peak is most inaccessible to outsiders. You haven't even seen a woodcutter, have you? Anyone that can reach this place must have been sent by heaven."

The captain returned to camp with the treasures and the women. Some of them still had a home waiting for them.

A year later, his wife gave birth to a boy who seemed to have taken after the ape. The captain was later killed by the new emperor of the Chen Dynasty. His son, however, grew up to be a famous literary figure of his time.*

---

* The son refers to Ouyang Xun (557-641), one of the most celebrated calligraphers of the early Tang Dynasty. He is said to have had the face of a monkey and an extremely quick wit. Such characteristics may have fostered the details of this story.

Mount Raven
(abridged*)

Taoist priest Xu Zhongshan had been dreaming of becoming an immortal ever since his youth, and as his years advanced he was increasingly obsessed with the idea.

Once, traveling along the trails in a mountain some 30 miles west of the county seat of Jian'an, he was caught in a heavy downpour. Driven by the shifting winds and blinded by the sheets of rain, he soon lost his way. Suddenly, by a flash of lightning, he saw a grand mansion ahead where he ran for cover. He was greeted by a man in splendid feathered livery at the gate. After a brief introduction and an explanation of his obvious plight, he was invited in.

"How come I didn't know there was such a mansion around here?" he wondered aloud.

"You're at the abode of immortals," said the man in livery. "My humble self is their janitor."

A girl appeared at the second gate wearing a spotted aqua blouse and an auburn skirt. In her left hand she held a gold-handled deer-tail whisk. "Who are you talking to out there?" she demanded. "Why didn't you report we are having a guest?"

"This is Mr. Xu Zhongshan, the local Taoist priest," the janitor replied.

Presently, a voice announced from within, "His Excellency invites Mr. Xu in." The girl he had seen came to lead him through a maze of verandahs to a small yard in the south.

---

* A description of the priest's moral cultivation is deleted from the first paragraph.

There stood a handsome man in his fifties, his hair and beard all silvery, his skin cream-pale, with a snow white cloak wrapped around his shoulders and a plumed crest on his head. "We hear you've been practicing Taoism for many years," he said, "and have raised yourself well above the ordinary folk. My young daughter is quite interested in Taoism, too. By the consequences of karma she is to be your wife, and today just happens to be an auspicious day for a wedding."

Xu stepped forth and bowed his gratitude. Out of politeness, he asked for permission to pay his respects to his future mother-in-law.

"My dear wife died seven years ago," said the lordly man, "leaving me three sons and six daughters. Your bride is the youngest."

At his order a nuptial banquet was laid out in the inner court. The brisk clinks of bracelets and fragrance of perfumed bodies floated in with the deepening night air and he was ushered into the bridal chamber by a train of candle lights.

On the third day, he emerged from the chamber to take a look around the place. In a shed facing west he saw many feathered cloaks hanging on bamboo racks. Fourteen were of kingfishers, the others, with the exception of a white one, were of black ravens. He rambled southwest and discovered in another shed an additional 49 such cloaks on the racks. But this time all were of owl feathers. He returned to his room with puzzled eyes.

"What took my lord so long?" his wife asked. "Did you find anything interesting?" As he made no response, she continued, "Celestial beings can travel in heaven and cover great distances in a wink, can't they? How do you think they can make it without wings and feather?"

"Then, who wears the white raven cloak?" he made bold to ask.

"That's my father's."

"Who wears the kingfishers'?"

"The maids."

"Who are the other raven cloaks for?"

"They are for me and my brothers and sisters."

"How about the owl cloaks?"

"They are the livery of the nightmen and guardsmen like the janitor you met at the gate."

Just then, the whole household broke out in a commotion. "What's up?" he questioned.

"The villagers are coming to hunt. They've set fire to the mountain," she explained.

"Oh, my! We didn't have time to make a cloak for the bridegroom!" he heard chirpings outside.

"It seems fate has brought us together only for a transitory tryst. Farewell, my lord," his bride said.

They each grabbed their feathered cloaks and flew off. The entire mansion disappeared before his eyes.

The mountain thus acquired its name of Mount Raven.

Translator's note:

The ability of birds to soar freely in the sky always stirs up man's imagination, to say nothing of a priest's lifelong obsession that may become an immortality complex. However, it is interesting to note that the imagined immortals in this story are not exempt from death, as we learn from the host that his wife died seven years before.

MAN AND LIFE

The Wrestler
(abridged*)

In Guangqi reign, General Wang Bian was appointed commander-in-chief of the garrison force stationed in Zhenwu Region and a reception party was held in his honor. When the singing and dancing were through, wrestlers were called in to perform. Among them was a bulky fellow from a neighboring prefecture on a traveling tournament. He had thrown down more than a dozen of the strongest men from the garrison force. Even the new commander cheered for him. Then another three muscular soldiers were picked out from the ranks and told to fight the bulky wrestler one after another in succession. The bulky man defeated them all, winning prolonged praise from Wang and all present.

Just then, a pale young scholar stood up from among the guests and claimed that he could throw the man off his feet. The commander-in-chief could hardly believe his ears, but since the scholar was insistent, he agreed to give him a chance.

The scholar stepped down from the raised platform where the guests were feasting and headed, not for the ring, but for the kitchen. He reappeared in a moment, his robe tightened around his waist and his left fist clenched and raised.

"I can push you off with one little finger," the bulky man laughed as he saw the scholar.

As they accosted each other, the scholar suddenly spread out his left palm. The bulky fellow staggered and collapsed as if hit directly on the head. The audience burst out with roars of laughter. The scholar strolled off quietly to wash his hands

---

* The postscript has been deleted.

and then went back to his seat at the table.

The commander-in-chief was fascinated. "How did you do that?" he kept asking.

"In recent years," the scholar replied, "I traveled a lot. I met that fellow once at a roadside inn and I saw him stumble and fall as he walked up to the food counter. His friends said he has an instinctive dread of the pasty brown sauce made from soy beans, and swoons at the very sight of it. Because of its extraordinary nature, I remember the incident well. So, just now I first went to the kitchen and asked the chef to put a little of that sauce in my palm. It did work, didn't it? Good cheer for the banquet."

Translator's note:

This story serves as an outstanding example of suspense—the climax is carefully built and the secret is surprisingly simple.

The Stutterer

Y ang Su, a cabinet member during the Sui Dynasty, would often call in a stutterer for a witty chat when he was free from his office duties.

One day near the end of the year, Yang and the stutterer sat facing each other.

"Suppose you were placed in a steep pit a dozen feet deep and a dozen across," Yang teased, "how are you going to get out?"

The man dropped his head to think. After a long moment he asked, "Can I...I have a ladder?"

"Say no, or why should I have asked?"

The man bent his head again. After another extended while, he asked, "Day...day...daytime or...or ni...night?"

"Never mind if it's day or night. As long as you can get out, what does that matter?"

"If...if it were not p...pitch dark, and I...I were not b...blind, how...how could I...I've fallen into that pit?"

Yang burst out laughing and came up with another question. "Say, one day you were made a general to defend a tiny town with less than 1,000 soldiers and provisions that would last you no more than a few days. The enemy besieging the town is 10 times your number. What strategy would you adopt?"

"A...are there re...reinforcements a...coming?" the man stammered out after a prolonged deliberation.

"I'm afraid not. That's why I asked you," Yang replied.

The man brooded over the problem. Finally, he raised his head and looked Yang in the eye. "If...if it rea...lly were as you said, the town is finished."

Yang almost split his sides. "It seems you have a way out of every difficult situation. Now, we're sitting here chatting. What if a snake should bite someone's foot? How would you treat the bite?"

"F...fetch May fifth snow from the f...foot of the sun... sunny side of the wall, and a...apply it to the bite," the man answered without a moment's hesitation.

"How can there be snow in May?" Yang retorted.

"If snow doesn't fall in May, how can a snake strike in this deep winter?"

Yang had a good laugh and sent the stutterer home.

The Princess' Stolen Treasures

Empress Wu once bestowed upon Princess Taiping two coffers of antiques and jewelry worth tens of thousands of ounces in gold. The princess locked them up in a secure storeroom in her palace, but when she came to pick out some a year or so later, she was appalled to find all the treasures stolen.

Infuriated by her daughter's report, the Empress summoned the assistant mayor in charge of the East Capital's security and told him that if he did not have the case solved within three days he would be punished. The terrified assistant mayor in turn summoned the county sheriff and ordered him to get the treasures back within two days, or he would die. The sheriff sent for the sergeant and allowed him one day either to catch the thief or be the first to die. The petrified sergeant dashed out into the street without the least idea how to start.

Wandering through the streets, the sergeant happened upon Su Wuming, deputy prefect of Hu Prefecture, and led him to the sheriff's office. "I've got the man!" he announced excitedly to the sheriff.

Su was already at the hall steps when the sheriff came out and asked in confusion, "Who are you?"

"I'm the deputy prefect of Hu. I'm in the capital on business."

"How dare you joke about His Excellency!" the embarrassed sheriff growled at the poor sergeant.

"Don't blame him, sir," said Su with a soothing smile. "He has his reason to say that, for at the various posts I held through my career, I've won a reputation for being a shrewd detective. No criminal can escape my eyes. Sergeants like him must have heard of my name. I think he brought me here to help him out of his predicament."

"How shall we go about it?" asked the overjoyed sheriff eagerly.

"Let's go and see the assistant mayor first. Say, why don't you go ahead and request an interview?"

The assistant mayor was exhilarated at the news and descended the hall steps to welcome Su. Clasping Su's hand tightly, he said, "You must have been sent here by heaven to save my life. I would appreciate your advice."

"I would like to have an audience with Her Majesty," replied Su succinctly.

At the assistant mayor's request, an audience was arranged. "So you can capture the thieves and recover the stolen treasures, can't you?" the Empress came right to the point.

"If Your Majesty trusts me with the case," replied Su, "I shall beg Your Majesty to grant me two requests. First, no deadlines, and relieve the municipal and county officials of their responsibility regarding this case. Second, I will need to have the local agents at my disposal. Then, I'll hand Your Majesty the thieves. It shouldn't take more than a couple of months."

The Empress granted him his requests.

"Don't take any action," Su instructed the agents, "and clues will appear in time."

A month thus passed and then it was the Cold Food Festival.*

Su gathered all the agents and divided them into teams of five or 10. He told them to position themselves at the eastern and northern city gates and look out for a party of Persians

---

* The Cold Food Festival, a festival in memory of the dead, occurs in early April, about the time of Easter. On that day and the following two days, people do not light a fire to cook hot meals but eat cold food instead.

in mourning gowns. If they were seen going in the direction of the public cemetery in the Northern Hills, tail them and report back.

Before long word came that a group thus described was discovered. Su set out immediately. He asked the agents how the Persians behaved. "They stopped at a new grave," reported one, "and held a memorial service. They wept a lot, but their cries didn't sound very sad. Also, they didn't leave the site after the service was over, but lingered around the grave and looked at each other with knowing smiles."

"We've got them!" exclaimed Su cheerfully. He ordered his men out of their hiding to arrest every one of the group. The coffin was dug up and pried open. Instead of containing a corpse it was filled with the stolen treasures.

The Empress praised Su for his exceptional ingenuity and was curious to know how he figured out the case.

"Your Majesty's humble servant is no wiser than others," Su replied. "My only advantage is that I can tell who is a thief by intuition. The day I arrived in the capital I happened to pass by those Persians in a funeral procession. As soon as I saw them, I knew they were thieves. What I didn't know was where they buried their stolen goods. At the Cold Food Festival, as people go to sweep their ancestor's tombs, I reckoned they would take that opportunity to get out of town among the crowds to check their cache. We only needed to follow them to find the place. Their unemotional crying only proved that what was buried down there was not a corpse. They strolled about the grave after the service and grinned at each other because they were glad to find the grave intact. If we had pressed the case, they would have been forced to take action and risk fleeing with their booty. But since we slackened up our search, they would most probably abide their time and wait for the heat to cool off entirely."

The Empress was pleased. She loaded him with gold and silk, and promoted him two ranks.

The Rope Acrobat

Emperor Xuanzong of the Tang Dynasty often ordained special county fairs and feasts. On one such occasion the administration of Jiaxing County was going to hold an acrobatic contest with the penitentiary. The warden was very enthusiastic about the event. "If we let the administration outdo us in every performance," he told the prison guards, "we will no doubt be ridiculed, but if we can present something striking, even if it was only one item, we might be able to win donations and benefactions." Reflecting upon his men's incompetence in acrobatic skills, he let out a deep sigh.

The guards talked this over among themselves and in front of the prisoners, ready to recommend anyone who was able to do a trick or two, such as juggling balls or climbing tall poles.

Overhearing their discussion, one of the prisoners laughed and boasted to a guard of having learned a trick. But, he said, since he was a convict, he was not in a position to perform it.

Pleasantly surprised, the guard asked him what kind of trick this was.

"I know how to perform on the rope," the prisoner answered.

"If that is true, I'll make a report to the warden," said the guard.

The warden asked for what crime the man was punished, and was told that this prisoner was involved in a case of defaulting on taxes, and nothing more.

"Rope tricks are quite common. I don't think there is much to brag about," said the warden when the prisoner was brought before him.

"What I do," answered the prisoner, "is a little different

154

from ordinary ways."

"How's that?"

"Well, usually, a performer would have both ends of the rope secured to posts and then walk on it and perhaps turn a few somersaults. All I need is no more than a length of finger-thick rope about 50 feet long. I don't need to tie the ends to anything. I'll just throw it into the air and then do all kinds of acrobatic tricks on it."

The warden was delighted, and entered the prisoner's name in the contest.

The next day, the prisoner was escorted by the guards to the fairground. It was really a scene of bustling excitement. Then, it was the prisoner's turn to perform.

The prisoner entered the arena with a coil of rope about 100 feet long, which he placed on the ground. He picked up one end and threw it into the air. The rope stood erect like a pencil, reaching a height of some 30 feet. The next throw sent the rope up to about 50 feet, straight as if being pulled by someone at the other end. The audience was awe-struck. When the whole length was thrown up into the air, the upper end was lost from sight, no matter how one might crane his neck and strain his eyes.

The man started to climb up the rope, his feet now off the ground. He kept climbing and casting the rope further up. Like a bird on wings, he fluttered away into the depth of the firmament.

What an ingenious way to escape from jail!

Translator's note:

Meticulously conceived plans by modern prisoners for breaking out of jail by helicopter loses its novelty when compared with this artful prisoner 12 centuries ago. He contrived his escape at a time when flying machines were unknown, and managed it without outside assistance.

The Corpse on the Coffin

The young son of the Lius was a daring tough who had spent most of his adulthood in Huaiyin County, associating with the town thugs. Once, he took a fancy to the daughter of the Wangs, his next-door neighbor. But when he asked for her hand he was flatly turned down.

Things went on uneventfully for a few years. Then famine struck the land, forcing him to enlist in the army in order to get daily rations. When he was demobilized several years later he returned to Huaiyin County to seek out his old pals. Together, they roamed the country, hunting during the day and carousing through the night.

It was a warm summer night and a storm had just rolled past. As the gang sat drinking, someone casually suggested a bet on anyone who dared to go at that late hour to the nameless grave which they had come across during the day's hunting. It was a dilapidated tomb three or four miles out of town and part of the coffin was exposed.

Emboldened by wine, Liu offered to go. The gang hoorayed and promised to throw a banquet in his honor if he had the guts to do it. To prove his accomplishment, he had to place a brick on the coffin on which each of them carved his name. Liu strode out into the night as the group went on with their drinking.

It was near midnight when he reached the tomb. The moon had just risen over the horizon revealing the silhouette of a figure crouching on the coffin. He rubbed his eyes and looked again. It was a woman corpse. He slapped the brick on the lid, picked up the body, and carried it on his back.

The gang was still in a noisy revel when they heard a

heavy thump against the door. The door flew open and Liu came straight into the lamplight and stood the corpse upright. There she stood, her face powdered pale and her hair hanging loose. The throng was stunned, some even dashed for cover. "She shall be my wife," Liu announced as he carried the corpse over to the bed and lay down beside it. The mob was glued to the ground.

When the cock crowed, Liu imagined that the corpse was breathing faintly. Taking her pulse, he realized that she was coming to. Soon she was able to talk and he learned that she was none other than the daughter of the Wangs. She seemed confused to find herself in such company. For all she remembered, she died of a sudden attack of illness. Liu fetched water to wash her face and helped her make up her hair and soon she was fully recovered.

It was now broad daylight outside. People in the streets were excitedly talking about the missing corpse of Wang's daughter who had died of a sudden illness on the verge of her marriage. The corpse, laid out on the bier for final services, was lost during last night's thunderstorm.

Liu went over to tell the Wangs about what had happened. The news swept away their sorrows and they ungrudgingly allowed him to marry their daughter.

If that was not a predestined marriage bond, it must have been a reward for his bravery.

Prince Ning

Prince Ning, elder brother of Emperor Xuanzong of the Tang Dynasty, often went hunting in the suburbs of the capital. One day as he and his men were searching through the woods they came upon a tightly locked chest hidden in tall grass. The prince ordered it opened, and in it lay a young girl.

When asked, she said she was the daughter of the Mo family. Her father had been an official. She was kidnapped in the previous night by a gang of bandits, among whom were two Buddhist monks. It was they who locked her up in this chest. Her woes, as she poured them out, in no way effaced her grace and charm, which the prince did not fail to notice with surprised delight. He offered her a seat in the back of his carriage. Having caught a bear that day, he told his men to lock in the bear instead, and leave the chest exactly where it had been found.

It happened then that the emperor was looking for beautiful girls. Since Miss Mo was from a decent family, the prince decided that she would be a strong candidate. So that very day he sent her to the palace together with a memorandum relating her story. She was accepted and was given the title of "talented girl."

Three days later, the municipal government sent in a report. Two monks, the report said, paid an unusually high price of 10,000 to rent all the rooms of a certain inn for one night. They claimed they were going to hold a Buddhist ritual there. A witness saw them carry in a heavy chest and neighbors said they heard brawls in the stillness of the night before all went quiet. The morning sun was high, but there was neither movement nor sound within, and the doors and windows remained shut up. When the mystified owner of the inn forced open the door, a bear dashed past him. The two monks were found sprawled out on the floor, white bones protruding from their dead bodies.

The report gave the emperor a hearty laugh. "Elder Brother," he wrote to Prince Ning, "you really had a way to deal with those monks."

The girl had a real talent for composing new tunes, which became popularly known as the tunes of Mo.

The Blacksmith's Money

Toward the end of the Sui Dynasty, there was a poor scholar in Taiyuan City, who managed a meager living by teaching a handful of private students. As his house happened to be next to a government warehouse, he hit upon the idea of digging an underground tunnel into the storeroom, which he did, and found himself amidst millions upon millions of copper coins. He was about to take some when he was stopped by an iron-armored guard with a spear. "If you want to take any money out of this room," said the guard, "you must have a payment note from Lord Yuchi Jingde. This is his money."

The scholar had no idea who Lord Yuchi was. As he inquired about town, he came upon a blacksmith's shop whose owner answered to the name of Yuchi Jingde. The blacksmith was working bare-chested by the furnace, his face smudged with sweat and his hair disheveled. The scholar waited till he took a break and stepped forth with a bow.

"What can I do for you?" the blacksmith asked, somewhat tickled by the undue respect.

"I'm impoverished and you're wealthy. I just wonder if you could help me with 500,000 coins."

"Are you insulting me?" the man snarled. "I am a blacksmith. Where do I get that money?"

"If you care to show some compassion for my embarrassed conditions, you only need to write me a payment note. You'll understand some day."

It was such a simple request that no one could refuse. So he told the scholar to write: "Give 500,000 coins to the person who bares this note," and signed his name.

The scholar made a grateful bow and marched off with the

note. As soon as he was out of hearing, the blacksmith and his apprentices slapped their thighs with laughter. They had seen the biggest fool in the world.

Meanwhile, the scholar went straight to the warehouse and handed the note to the iron-armored guard.

"That's it," the guard grinned, and pinned it onto a beam. The scholar went away with 500,000.

Many years later, Yuchi became the right-hand man of Emperor Taizong of the Tang Dynasty in conquering the land. When he petitioned for retirement back to his native place, the emperor awarded him a whole storeroom of money. Checking the accounts with the stock he found that 500,000 coins were missing. In his anger, he was going to punish the keeper when he caught sight of a note pinned to the beam. He had it taken down and was surprised to find that it was the note he signed when he was still a blacksmith. Discreet confidants were sent out to look for the scholar, while he kept wondering over the matter for days.

The scholar was found, and he related his tunnel experience. Yuchi sent him home with lavish gifts, and distributed the money among his friends and subordinates.

Translator's note:
Yuchi Jingde was a famous general under Emperor Taizong, founder of the Tang Dynasty, and was later made a duke. This story is under the category of "Fate" in Records of the Taiping Era. Like "Li Jing the Demigod," a person's rise from the ranks to become a general is seen as the predestined arrangement of life.

Li Jing the Demigod

When Li Jing, a celebrated general and strategist in the early days of the Tang Dynasty, was still an unknown figure living in obscurity, hunting trips into Mount Ling was his favorite pastime. On such trips he used to put up at a certain mountain village. His elderly host, who seemed to have perceived something unusual in him, treated Li with great respect, and that respect grew as their acquaintance developed.

Once, Li spotted a herd of deer which he chased and traced until he lost both the herd and his way in the thickening darkness. Dispirited, he gave the reins to his horse and wondered where he might spend the night.

A light appeared in the distance. He spurred his steed and came into sight of a grand mansion enclosed with high walls and broad, red double gates. He knocked and a long while passed before someone answered. Li explained that he was lost and asked for permission to stay the night. It might be improper, the servant said, for his masters were out and only Her Ladyship, the dowager, and womenfolk were home. Li begged him to convey his appeal to the dowager and see what she would say.

Presently, the servant returned. She didn't like to have strangers in the house, especially at night, but considering his situation, she thought it better to host him.

Li was shown into the reception hall. A maid came in to announce the presence of the dowager. The lady was in her fifties, wearing a cloud-white blouse over a sea-blue gown. She carried an air of nobility as if she were not a village dame but a lady of aristocratic birth. Li stepped forth and bowed.

She curtsied in return. "You must understand, sir, that it's inadvisable to invite a man in while my sons are away. But as you've strayed to our place at this late hour, it is inappropriate to deny you shelter. Hope you won't mind the coarseness of our mountain life. If you do hear some commotion at night, don't be alarmed. That will be my sons coming home."

Dinner was served. The food was excellent, with many fish courses. It was quite unusual for alpine fare.

After dinner, the dowager retired to her quarters and Li was led by two maids to a guest room. The room was stately and the bedding clean. Having made the bed, they withdrew and shut the door behind them.

Li, however, was unable to sleep. In this remote mountain village, who would make a fanfare returning home at night? He sat bolt upright with ears pricked.

Approaching midnight, urgent knocks were heard at the gate and someone responded. "Heavenly mandate!" another voice blared. "Big son, immediately produce rain in the two hundred mile area around this mountain till five o'clock in the morn. No delay, no deluge!"

A servant must have passed on the billet, for Li heard the dowager say, "It couldn't have come at a worse moment. Neither son is home yet. Even if messengers were dispatched right away, they would not be able to return in time. Any negligence of duty or delay of action would be reprimanded, and it certainly is inappropriate to have a servant execute the heavenly mandate by proxy. What shall we do now?"

"The guest we entertained this evening seemed to have some extraordinary traits. Perhaps we can ask him to do it." It sounded like a maid's voice.

It seemed that the idea appealed to the dowager, for she came in person and tapped on his door. "Are you awake, sir? Can I have a word with you?"

Li responded and came out.

"You might have realized that ours is not a human abode. As a matter of fact, you are in a dragon palace. My elder son has gone to the East China Sea to attend a wedding ceremony and my younger son is escorting his sister to her husband's. Just now we received a heavenly mandate to produce rain. As both sons are thousands of air-miles away, it's impossible to call them back in time, and what's more, I can't find a gentleman surrogate. I wonder if I can enlist your immediate assistance."

"I'm just an ordinary man. I can't ride the clouds. How can I produce rain? But, if Your Ladyship can teach me how, I'm at your service."

"I'll tell you what to do. It's not as difficult as you think." She ordered the groom to saddle the piebald horse and fetch the rain-producer, which turned out to be a fairly small bottle. Hanging the bottle on the pommel, she said, "Ride this horse. Just give it a free rein. When it paws and neighs, pour out a drop from the bottle onto its mane. Remember, one drop is enough."

He mounted and the piebald cantered off. Not realizing that he was already on the clouds, he wondered at the smoothness of the ride. High winds whistled like arrows; thunderbolts flashed from beneath the hoofs. He poured out a drop wherever the horse indicated. All of a sudden, the clouds split apart and he saw right below him the village where he used to sojourn. For years, the villagers there had been very nice to him and he had been torn by the thought that he was not in a position to repay their hospitality. Now that he was in charge of rain, and their crops were scorched by a severe drought, why should he grudge giving them a little extra? What is one tiny drop of water to such thirst? So he sprinkled out 20 drops.

In a while his job was done and he trotted back triumphantly.

The dowager met him at the hall with teary eyes. "Why did you let me down? I told you one drop would be enough. How could you have acted on your own and meted out 20!

One drop from this bottle means a foot of rain on the ground. You made a flood of 20 feet in the dead of the night. Do you think anyone can survive that? I've already been punished. Look, 80 lashes across my back!" Blood was oozing through the back of her blouse. "My sons were punished, too," she sighed.

He was too ashamed to mumble out a reply.

"You are only mortal and have no idea how heavenly things work. I don't blame you, but I'm afraid my sons won't be so happy to see you here. Better leave now. However, since I have requested your service, I'm not going to send you away empty-handed. Though we don't have treasures hoarded in this mountain residence, I may offer you two slaves. You can take both, or pick one as you please."

At her beckoning, two slaves emerged. One stepped forth from the east chamber, beaming amiably; the other stalked out from the west chamber, his face dark with anger. To take both is certainly impolite, he reasoned with himself. I'm a hunter and take pride in physical strength. If I should choose the amiable one, people would laugh behind my back, ridiculing me as chicken-hearted. So he said, "Thank you, ma'am. One will be enough. If I can choose, I'll take the angry fellow."

"He is yours," said the dowager with an elusive smile.

He made his farewell and left with the slave. Several steps out of the gate, he glanced back. The mansion and walls were all gone. He swirled round to question the slave, and the slave had vanished too.

By dawn, he managed his way back to where the village once stood. A vast expanse of water greeted his eyes, only the tops of a few big trees remained above the surface. No one could have survived.

Later, Li became a seasoned general and helped the new emperor quell many revolts and border incidents. His feats were unsurpassed, and yet, he never reached the position of prime minister. Isn't it because he didn't pick the right slave?

A popular saying has it that prime ministers are born in the more cultured east, while great generals arise from the rougher west. Isn't that what the chambers imply? "Slave," too, can be suggestive, symbolizing loyal service to His Majesty. What if he had taken both slaves? Could his career have been reshaped?

A Powerful Sneeze

Fu Huangzhong, magistrate of Zhuji County in the Tang Dynasty, recounted a true story that happened to one of his former subordinates.

The man was quite drunk after a party, but he insisted on walking home alone through the night. Following a familiar mountain path, he dropped asleep on the brink of a precipice.

A tiger came sniffing at the smell of man. Its whiskers somehow poked into the man's nostrils, setting off such a violent sneeze that the big cat jumped with a start and fell off the cliff. It sprained its waist and was caught by the drunkard.

Translator's note:
This story illustrates the conciseness of classical written Chinese. Many stories in Records of the Taiping Era *are similarly short.*

The Scarred Monk

During Yuanhe reign of the Tang Dynasty, a Mr. Du was visiting a Buddhist temple in Bianzhou City when he noticed a monk with a long horizontal scar across his face between the nose and the brow, as if severing the face into upper and lower halves. Upon his inquiry, the monk sank into a dreamy retrospection and slowly related his story.

He said: I'm a native of the town, and I lived with my parents and a married elder brother. My brother was a merchant, trading between Bianzhou and the Yangtze valley. Later, he expanded his business to the south. On his first trip, he gained a double profit. Next year, he set off again, but this time he did not return. In the year that followed a fellow merchant came back to announce that my brother had drowned when his ship capsized. Our whole family went into mourning. However, before the mourning period was over, yet another merchant from Hannan came asking for my father. He chanced upon me at the temple, and when I told him I was the son of the man he was seeking, he said he was carrying a message from my brother. Somewhat shocked, but anxious for any good tidings, I led him home to see my parents.

My brother's business, according to this messenger, suffered heavy losses in the south. He went broke and somehow wandered to Hannan, where an army officer took pity on him and recruited him with permission from the garrison commander. Though penniless, for the moment at least he did not have to worry about food and clothing. Being too poor and ashamed to return in person, he had beseeched the man to bring his parents his well-wishes.

The news made my parents and sister-in-law cry with

renewed grief and hope. The very next day they sent me off to Hannan to look up my brother.

Seven or eight days of trekking brought me into Nanyang. Late one afternoon, I found myself deep in a boundless swampland. As far as the eye could stretch there were no human beings, no houses, no farmland, and no traces whatever of human activities except for the faint trail beneath my feet. Dark clouds were closing in. At sunset, I finally reached a hamlet of two or three huts. I begged for shelter for the night. My presence, however, seemed to have alarmed the villagers. They told me to move on because a murder had just happened the night before and officials were hunting for the fugitive. They added that there was a temple a mile or so to the south where I might stay for the night. So there I headed. A chilly wind rose, sprinkling cold raindrops. The swamp became wilder with every step and I soon lost my way. Wandering aimlessly, I suddenly perceived a candle light ahead, which didn't seem far away, but I must have covered a couple of miles before I saw a cottage. As the wind and rain were gaining momentum, I dashed right into the room without stopping to knock, only to find a room of dead bodies, not a breath of life. Just at that moment thunder cracked. A woman corpse leapt to her feet, her hair electrified. She flung herself toward me, chasing me out of the room into the rain. I fled headlong for probably another couple of miles until I caught sight of a compound. The rain had stopped and the moon was peering out from behind the dispersing clouds. I entered the parlor in the outer yard and was content to find a couch in the room. I dropped myself onto the couch, and was going to stretch my weary legs when I beheld a man over seven feet tall entering from the gate with a shining broadsword in his hand. As there was no way for me to escape unnoticed, I hastily slid into a dark corner, standing bolt upright against the walls, holding my breath.

The tall man sat on the couch for quite a while as if

expecting someone. Then he stood up and went outside. Against the wall separating the outer and inner yards was a heap of manure, standing on which one could easily survey the living quarters. Three or four women's hushed voices effused from the other side of the wall and in a while the tall man reappeared with a bundle in his other hand, followed by a woman. They must be eloping. The tall man must have had a hunch, for he muttered to himself whether there was someone hiding in the room. He held out his broadsword at arm's length, swiveled around on his heels, and dragged the tip of the blade along the walls. The blade scratched past my face. Luckily, he didn't seem to sense any difference and left with the bundle and the woman.

Realizing that it was unwise to stay any longer, I set out again. I couldn't have gone half a mile when I stumbled and fell into a dry well. To my surprise, I found I was not alone, for lying at the bottom of the well was a corpse, its body still warm. Day finally broke over a long and troubled night. The master of the compound must have noticed a girl missing, for he and his men traced the footprints to the well. A torch was lowered and I was discovered with the corpse.

I was brought before the county magistrate who appeared to be a reasonable man. I showed him the sword mark and told him what I overheard. An aunt of the family was found to be involved. Her confession cleared me of all suspicion and I was free to continue my southbound trip.

Approaching Hannan, I came upon an old man sitting under a big juniper tree by the roadside. He asked me where I was from, which I told him, and he offered to read my fortune, claiming that he was an expert in the art. I prayed to a bunch of yarrow grass stems and let them fall. After some calculation of their positioning, he sighed and pronounced that I'd had two wives in my previous life, and I had mistreated them both. The woman corpse that chased me at the cottage was my first wife, and the one I lay with in the dry well was my second. The sympathetic county magistrate was none other than my former mother, and he himself my former father. The brother I was looking for lived no more. These revelations brought blurring tears to my eyes. When they cleared, the old man had vanished.

Despite his prophecy, I went on to Hannan, but could by no means find my brother.

Ah! How weirdly retribution strikes!

The Man with a Dark Countenance

In Baoying reign the governor of Yue Prefecture was a Huangfu Zheng. His wife, known as Madame Lu, was very beautiful, but was sterile.

The prefecture boasted a Buddhist temple named Treasure Forest in which there was a shrine consecrated to the Magic Mother. Women from all over the prefecture who wished for children would come and pray before her statue. It was said that not one of those prayers had been left unanswered. So one holiday Huangfu brought his wife to the temple where they went directly to the shrine to offer incense.

"Give me a son," Huangfu prayed, "and I'll dedicate a million coins out of my salary for a new hall for Your Ladyship."

"If you do give us a son," his wife added, "I'll chip in a million out of my powder and rouge allowance to paint you a new portrait." Then they visited the other halls of the temple. Twilight was coming on when they returned home.

In two months the wife became pregnant and a boy was duly born. Huangfu was overjoyed. He kept his promise and built a three-purlin-wide new hall, luxuriously decorated. In the yard his wife heaped a million coins inviting a painter to fresco the walls. As the news spread, painters from near or distant neighborhoods and even from remote corners of the country converged at the temple, but though the reward was unusually high, they all hesitated to undertake the task.

Among them was a man who refused to disclose his name and origin except to say that he was a master painter from Shu. He had loitered in the temple for more than a month when one day he stared fixedly at the blank walls of the newly built hall and gave several confident nods.

"Why not bring this business to a quick end?" suggested the abbot tentatively.

"Please have plenty of oil lamps ready," the man smiled. "I'll do it tonight."

The abbot did as bidden.

When day broke in the east, the painting was done, resplendent and magnificent. But the painter was nowhere to be found.

Huangfu held a grand vegetarian feast at the temple, attracting hordes of merchants and wealthy men. He then picked another auspicious day on which the prefectural functionaries, local gentry, and the secular were all invited to attend the consecration ceremony. Music and dancing were in abundance. At noon, a man wearing a lotus-leave hat and a straw cloak came to the temple with a hoe in hand. He was over eight feet tall and had a very unpleasant dark countenance. The guards stopped him at the gate, but Huangfu ordered him to be let in. The man walked straight up to the front, raised his hoe, and scraped out the face of the Magic Mother. The plaster of the wall crumbled; the congregation seethed; and the guards moved in to catch and kill, but the man showed no fear.

"Are you out of your mind?" Huangfu asked.

"No," replied the man.

"Do you consider yourself a better painter?"

"No."

"Then why did you destroy the mural?"

"Because I hate to see the painter cheat you. Your Excellency and Your Ladyship donated two million for a portrait of a goddess, yet that fellow left you a portrait with plainer looks than an ordinary dame!" Huangfu's reprimand only made the man laugh. Rubbing his palms, he said, "You're incredulous? Go and have a look at my ordinary woman and you'll believe me."

173

"Where is she?" demanded Huangfu.

"At home right now. That's only a mile or so south of the lake."

At Huangfu's order, a team of 10 soldiers escorted the man home to fetch his wife. From a hut of reeds and sticks the man called out a woman of about 16, slightly powdered. Her clothes were cheap but her features were beyond description, her looks most appealing. Before long, they were back at the temple. The multitude stretched their necks for a glimpse. Everyone agreed that the painted goddess was not her match. Compared to her, Madame Lu looked pale and plain.

"How can a man as low born as you," rebuked Huangfu, "horde such a wife. She must be presented to the emperor!"

"All right, but please let her go home and say good-bye to her relatives and friends," said the man.

Huangfu consented and dispatched 10 waiting women and 50 soldiers to escort her home. Reaching the lake, they boarded a big boat while the dark man got on a small yacht alone. Midstream, the man's wife suddenly jumped overboard into the yacht. The soldiers were taken aback and rowed hard in pursuit. The couple had reached shore and walked hand in hand while the soldiers followed at their heels. The two then turned into a pair of white cranes and soared up into the sky.

Translator's note:

"She must be presented to the emperor!" If we compare this with the fate of Miss Mo in "Prince Ning" and the women in "A Dandy's Pleasure Trip," etc., we may be able to piece together a general view of women's predicaments in ancient times.

Mr. Xiao

When Mr. Xiao retired from office in the government of Yangzhou Prefecture, he decided to take that opportunity to visit the south before going back to his native place in the north.

On the ferry crossing the Yangtze River he sensed that two youngsters were studying and talking about him. "That man looks rather like the Prince of Poyang," he caught their whispering. Being the great-grandson of the prince, he was intrigued by their perceptiveness. He accosted them and introduced himself.

"We've known your great-grandfather for many years," they said.

As he was aware that on such a packed boat it would be out of place to ask private questions, he chose to wait till they got ashore. But as soon as the ferry docked, even before he had a chance to open his mouth, the two young men clutched their shoulder poles and baskets and whirled off, leaving him to think that his luck had brought him across some celestial beings or immortals. He bowed in their wake and prayed.

Next year, passing through Xuyi County while returning to his home town in the north, he was having a chat with a town head when a constable reported that six grave-robbers had been caught.

At the town head's command, the six were led into the courtyard and securely tied up. Xiao was astonished to see among the gang the two young men he had met on the ferry. He related that strange incident to the town head, who ordered the two to be interrogated first.

Before long, the two confessed that they had been in the

175

grave-robbing business for years. They had dug into Prince Poyang's tomb and reaped a harvest of jade and goldware. There, facing the entrance on a marble bier lay the owner of the grave, his colors fresh as if alive, hoary-headed, about 50 years of age. And then they ran into a gentleman on a ferry who just seemed to be molded out of the corpse. Since he introduced himself as a Xiao, they were pretty sure he was an offspring of the prince.

So, they were neither celestial beings nor immortals.

Ms. Wei's Dragon Ride
(abridged*)

Ms. Wei was married into the Meng family. Toward the end of Dali reign, her husband and her brother qualified in the same round of imperial selection, and both were assigned to official positions.

Her husband was appointed chief secretary of Lang Prefecture in the southwest, her brother lieutenant of Yangtze County in the southeast. So they parted and Ms. Wei went along with her husband.

The southwestern regions were mountainous. Roads soon became too narrow and steep for carriages, compelling her to continue on horseback. They were passing through a craggy valley when her horse shied and threw her down the ledge. Peeping down the fathomless cliff, one could only see shadows of darkness, and there was no way down. All her husband could do was cry and moan, and offer her a quick libation before the column had to move on.

In the meantime, Ms. Wei had fallen on a cushion of dead leaves dozens of feet thick. The impact knocked her out, but she was unhurt and soon regained her consciousness.

A day elapsed and hunger seized her. She rolled up some leaves with snow and ate them, thus giving herself a little strength to look around. Beside her was a fissure in the rocks. There was no telling how deep it might be. Above, only a patch of sky could be seen, as if one were gazing up from the bottom of a well, no hope of climbing out. Suddenly, she seemed to see a faint candle light in the depth of the crevice.

---

* The postscript has been omitted.

177

The light kept growing, and soon she was able to descry two separate lights instead of one. They continued to move in her direction. They were the eyes of a dragon! Terrified, she pressed her back against the rock wall to make way for the dragon. It gradually emerged from the crack and shot up into the sky, its body stretching 50 to 60 feet long. Then, she saw another pair of eyes coming. She would rather fall prey to a dragon than die a protracted death in this abyss, she convinced herself. So when the second dragon was pulling itself out of the crevice, she flung her arms around its neck and mounted it. The dragon soared up without bothering to pause. Too frightened to open her eyes, she held tightly onto the dragon, resigning herself to its wishes.

Hours seemed to pass until she sensed the dragon descending. She ventured to open her eyes and take a look. Beneath her, trees and watercourses could be clearly distinguished. Now, she couldn't be more than 50 feet above the ground. Fearing the dragon was going to plunge into the river, she let go of it and fell into the tall grass along the bank.

She came to after a long while. Weak from three or four days of living on leaves, she could barely walk. Then, she came upon a fisherman, from whom she learned that she was in Yangtze County. What luck! She congratulated herself. Furthermore, it was only six miles from the county seat. She told the fisherman of her extraordinary experience and begged for food. However strange her story might have sounded, the fisherman offered her some porridge without raising a question.

"Has the new county lieutenant, a Mr. Wei, assumed office yet?" she asked.

"Sorry ma'am, I don't know."

"I'm his sister. If you ferry me to town, I promise you a fortune."

So the fisherman paddled up to the town gate. The new lieutenant had been in office for several days already, she was informed.

"How on earth can my sister be here? She is with her husband in Lang Prefecture in the southwest!" her brother exclaimed when the bailiff announced her presence at the gate. Though very much suspicious of her identity, he decided to receive her.

Except for her pale face and haggard appearance she otherwise looked exactly like his sister, but, her tears and her account of the miraculous deliverance did not have him thoroughly convinced. It was not until a few days later when the obituary of his sister's death arrived from his brother-in-law that his doubts were swept away and the happiness of their reunion was fully savored. He looked up the fisherman and rewarded him with 20,000 coins.

Later on, he had his sister safely escorted to her husband's side.

The Golden Berry

One day, a herdsman in India discovered that a cow was missing from his pasture, and when it rejoined the herd at dusk it looked rather spirited, even its mooing sounded somewhat different.

His curiosity aroused, the herdsman kept a close eye on the cow the next day, and saw it stray off again. He traced it into a deep cave. After a couple of miles in, the tunnel suddenly brightened up and a world of exotic trees and flowers greeted his eyes. The cow was grazing on a patch of unnamable grass bearing golden berries. He plucked some to bring home, but before he was able to leave the cave they were snatched away by some invisible demon.

On another trip to get berries, the demon sprang for them again. In the flurry of the moment the herdsman threw one into his mouth and swallowed it. Instantly he felt his body expanding so fast that he only had time to get his head out of the cave before his body choked the tunnel. In just a few days, he turned into stone.

Translator's note:
The expansion of commerce and travel into distant lands brought back many outlandish stories such as this one and "The Kingdom of Silla." Some stories were so domesticated through the centuries that their foreign origins became obscure. For instance, "A Ride in a Goose Cage" is believed by some scholars to have its roots in India.

Stories from the Kingdom of Silla

Kim is the noblest family name in Silla. Its earliest ancestor can be traced back to Pangyi.

Pangyi had a younger brother who was quite affluent, while Pangyi himself was poor and without a livelihood. Someone gave him a small piece of deserted land and he begged his prosperous brother for wheat seeds and silkworm eggs.

Unknown to Pangyi, his brother steamed the seeds and eggs before he gave them to him. So when spring arrived, only one silkworm hatched. However, it gained several inches a day, and in a fortnight grew to the size of a calf. Leaves from a grove of mulberry trees were not enough to feed it. Envious of its fabulous growth, his rich brother took the first opportunity to have it killed. Within days, silkworms from the surrounding areas thronged to Pangyi's house. The whole neighborhood came to help reel silk from the cocoons. People believed that the giant silkworm was a king.

As for the wheat seeds, only one survived to sprout. Its ear was heavy and more than a foot long. Pangyi watched it closely, but one day it was snapped and carried off by a bird. Pangyi chased the bird into the mountains, but the bird disappeared into a crack in the rocks. The sun had set behind the hills and the trails along which he had come were shrouded in darkness, so he decided to spend the night by the crack.

By midnight, a full moon had risen to cast its light on the slopes. Pangyi was awakened to see a group of children, all clad in red, amusing themselves in the moonlight. One said, "What do you want?" Another answered, "Wine." The first boy then took out a gold hammer and knocked on a rock. Wine and drinking vessels appeared. Still another asked for food. The first boy knocked again, and pancakes, roast meat and soup surfaced on a table rock, around which the children sat and feasted themselves. Then they stowed away the hammer in the crack and left.

Delighted, Pangyi took the hammer home. With it he could get whatever he desired, and before long he became as rich as a king and from time to time he would share his pearls and jade with his brother.

His brother, however, was not satisfied and wished to acquire a magic gold hammer for himself. Although Pangyi knew it was a silly scheme, he could in no way dissuade him. So he did as his brother had done to him—giving him steamed seeds and eggs. Just as before, only one silkworm hatched, but it was nothing more than an ordinary worm. And only one wheat seed sprouted. When it was almost ripe, a bird came to snatch it off. The brother was exhilarated. He followed it into the mountain to the crack, but what he met was a host of demons.

"This is the one who stole our gold hammer!" they shrieked. "Which punishment do you prefer, to stew three caldrons of sugar syrup for us,* or to have a nose 10 feet long?"

The brother chose the former, yet on the third day he was too exhausted and hungry to carry on. In spite of his pleading, the demons pulled at his nose till it looked somewhat like the trunk of an elephant. People crowded the streets to have a peep at his long nose. Their ridicule was too much to bear and he soon died of shame.

Generations passed. One frivolous descendent of Pangyi's used the hammer to strike for wolf's droppings. A loud thunder cracked and the hammer was forever lost.

---

* History records that an envoy was sent to India in the year 647 by Emperor Taizong to learn the skills of stewing sugar. So it must have been novel and laborious work at that time.

In the early years of Tianbao reign, Lord Wei was appointed special envoy to Silla to crown the new king. Old and unused to ocean voyages as he was, he anxiously inquired about the place and heard the following story from a recent traveler to that country.

In mid Yonghui reign when China was on good terms with Silla and Japan, there was an imperial envoy who had completed his mission in Silla and was going across the sea to Japan when he and his fleet were caught in a severe storm. The waves were high and the wind was strong. For more than 10 days they drifted with the currents and soon lost their bearings. Then one day at sunset the wind suddenly dropped and he and his crew found themselves near land. They anchored and went ashore, about 100 of them. The bank consisted mostly of sheer cliffs rising nearly 30 rods, but as houses were spied atop, they climbed up eagerly.

They were met by a man about 20 feet tall who, though properly clothed, spoke an unknown language. He seemed more than pleased to see the Tangmen* and ushered them into a big house. When they entered, he rolled over a huge rock to block the gate, and left. Presently, he returned with 100 more of his like. They examined the Tangmen and picked out those who looked plump and soft. About 50 of the captives were thus selected whom they cooked and ate with wine and music. Late into the night, they were all stone drunk, so the remaining Tangmen were able to probe around the house.

In a backyard room they found some 30 women. The women, too, as they soon learned, were victims of storms, and had fallen captives to the tall men. Their menfolk were eaten while they were kept alive to make clothes.

"Now that they are drunk," the women said, "it might be our only chance to escape. We know the way about."

The men favored the idea and they set to work. The

---

* Tangmen, people of the Tang Dynasty.

women collected the cloth they had woven and tied it onto their backs; the men found knives and cut the throats of the drunken giants. They ran out from the courtyard toward the shore.

The shore was craggy and the sky was dark, obscuring the trails. They twisted the cloth into ropes and lowered themselves down the cliff. When they finally reached their ships, the east was pale. Terrifying roars could be heard atop the cliff. They looked back to see hundreds of tall men following them, some already on their way down. Soon the tall men reached the waterside. They yelled and jumped angrily up and down the beach, but the ships had set sail and were off the shore. The envoy with his attendants and the women safely returned to the mainland.

The Pearl

In Xianyang City there was a temple built to commemorate Emperor Wudi of the Northern Zhou Dynasty. Inlaid in the crown on a statue's head was a pearl the size and shape of a spring plum. Generations of visitors had seen it there but no one seemed to have given it much thought.

During the reign of Empress Wu, a passing merchant dropped in at the temple. Taken by a whim, he plucked the pearl off the crown. As the day was growing warmer, he removed some clothes and, wrapping them around the pearl, he tucked the bundle beneath the huge foot of one of the four warrior statues at the gate. By the time he was leaving the temple he had clean forgotten the bundle, and the pearl as well. The very next day he went on to Yangzhou to collect some overdue debts.

Spending a night at an inn in a small town called Chenliu, he overheard a group of Persians next door bragging about the rare treasures they had seen in their life. Intrigued, he slipped on his clothes and went over to join them. For his part, he boasted of the plum-shaped pearl in Emperor Wudi's crown. The mere mention of the pearl silenced the group. They had long heard China harbored such a treasure, they told him, and as a matter of fact, had come to hunt for it. That he had lost it made them sigh and fret. If he could recover it, they said earnestly, they would load him with gold and silk. How much did he say those people in Yangzhou owed him? Five hundred thousand? They immediately counted out the coins for him and asked him to go back right away to find the pearl.

The pearl was still safely tucked beneath the statue's foot. So happy were the Persians to lay their eyes on the pearl that they danced and drank for a whole fortnight before they asked the man to name a price.

"One million," the merchant said offhandedly, which he thought, though impossibly high, would gain him a good bargaining position.

The Persians almost split their sides with laughter. "You're insulting this pearl," they whooped. After a brief discussion among themselves, they offered him 50 million, which they pooled and handed over on the spot.

Then they invited the man to go with them to the sea, and see for himself how much the pearl was actually worth.

They sailed out into the East Sea. A senior Persian, who seemed to be their leader, set up a silver pot on the deck, built a fire under it, and filled it with a creamy substance. Next he placed the pearl in a gold bottle and steeped the bottle in the simmering cream.

On the seventh day, two venerable-looking elders appeared with hundreds of attendants carrying a myriad of treasures which they laid before the Persians to ransom the pearl, but their offer was flatly rejected.

Several days later, they arrived again, this time with mountains of jewelry which the Persians ignored as before.

The stalemate lasted more than 30 days, and the treasure bearers finally withdrew themselves. Then, out of the sea emerged two charming white dragon virgins, who threw themselves into the gold bottle. Together with the pearl they melted into an ointment.

"Why were they so anxious to ransom the pearl?" asked the merchant in amazement.

"This pearl is the treasure of all treasures," replied the senior Persian, "and it is guarded by the two dragon virgins you've just seen. The dragon king is so fond of his daughters that he would pay any price. But to me, worldly treasures are of little value. What I'm after is immortality." So saying, he applied the ointment to the soles of his feet and jumped overboard. To everyone's surprise, he walked away on the waves.

"We shared the price of the pearl," the other Persians exploded in protest. "How can you reap all the benefit! Now that you're leaving, what is to become of us?"

"Apply the cream to the hull of the boat," the senior Persian shouted back, "and a favorable wind will send you all the way home."

It turned out as he had said, but where he was heading remains a mystery.

The Blood-Stained Coat

Chen Yishuang and Zhou Maofang, both natives of Fuchang County southwest of the East Capital, Luoyang, were
classmates at a local school in the small town of Sanxiang. As
it turned out, Yishuang succeeded in the imperial examination
and came home in glory to marry a girl from the Guo family,
while Maofang failed both in the exam and in getting himself
a wife. They remained good friends, however.

In mid Tianbao reign, Yishuang was appointed to an
official position as magistrate of Yilong County in Shu. As was
the custom, his family was to follow him to his new job. His
mother, however, was reluctant to leave her birthplace and
preferred to stay behind.

The date for their departure was drawing near. As part of
the hectic preparations for leaving, Yishuang's wife wove and
dyed a bolt of silk to make her mother-in-law a new coat. But
while she was cutting out the garment, the scissors slipped and
cut her finger, leaving a blood stain on the coat.

"Mother," she said as she presented the coat to her
mother-in-law, "we've lived happily together for seven or eight
years and I hate to leave you alone at home, but I must go
with my lord. Since I can no longer wait on your daily needs,
here is a new coat I just made for you. It's a pity this blood
stain can't be washed off. Anyway, it may remind you of me
whenever you see it." She broke down in tears and her
mother-in-law wept too.

At Yishuang's insistence, Maofang was going with them.
Maofang was very fond of Yishuang's son, who was then two
years old.

Over mountains and rivers they traveled to within 200

miles of Yilong County. The mountain path wound along the edge of steep cliffs overhanging a turbulent river. It was thrilling to see the pounding torrents plow its way through the bedrock of the virgin mountains right under one's feet. Often, despite the dangers, Yishuang and Maofang would cling to the vines for a better view. A vicious idea suddenly sprang up in Maofang's mind and seized him. He told the servants to go ahead and wait for them at the next post with a meal ready, for they would linger awhile at this magnificent sight. So, leading their horses by the reins, he and Yishuang took a leisurely walk along the path. At a sheer drop, Maofang suddenly pulled out a copper hammer, thwacked Yishuang hard on the back of the head, and pushed the body down into the raging torrents below. Then he wailed his way into the post house to announce that his friend's mount shied and threw its master over the precipice into the stream. He said that he went stooling in the bush and when he was about to rejoin his friend he saw the terrible thing happen.

A memorial was held that evening. Yishuang's widow and the servants wept and moaned over the death of the master. "What has happened has happened," Maofang said to the widow. "What is important is what we are going to do next. Since nobody else knows about this incident except the servants and us, we probably can go on if you let me assume office in your husband's name. In that way, we at least can collect his official stipend through the following three years, and save enough to go home. Then we can formally announce his death and hold the proper services." As she did not know the truth, the widow agreed to the plan. Maofang promised hefty rewards to all the servants if they kept their mouth shut.

So Maofang became the magistrate of Yilong County. In less than a year the servants were made submissive, and he was bold enough to come up to the widow and claim, "Now I have achieved my ambitions. Don't you try to betray me!" As he kept a close eye on her, she could find no chance to get her revenge. She had to bury the hatred deep in her heart.

The three-year tenure soon expired. Instead of retiring, Maofang managed to be transferred to Changjiang County as magistrate. And at the end of another term he was even promoted to department chief in the prefectural government. Seventeen years thus passed and the son, Yilang, was now 19 and well read. Thinking that the long years should have obliterated anyone's memory of the past, and as his present term of office was expiring, Maofang judged it time for him to take Yilang to the capital for the imperial examination, which was to be held in the East Capital that year.

He, however, decided to take the northern route while sending Yilang along the southern one, which led right through Sanxiang Town. By that way, he figured he might be able to learn how things stood at home without risk.

At Sanxiang Town, Yilang stopped for a meal at an old woman's food stall. Throughout the meal, the old woman kept glancing at him, and when he was paying for the food she refused to take his money. "You look so much like my son when he was young. This is my treat," she muttered as she fumbled in a trunk and took out the blood-stained coat her daughter-in-law had made for her, which she gave to the young man with watery eyes but without further explanation. Though he couldn't understand why she was so upset and didn't suspect anything related to his father, he kept the coat at the bottom of his bundle. He, however, failed to win himself a name in the exam and returned to Changjiang County the following year.

His mother, putting away his clothes upon his return, was astonished to see the coat. She asked how he had come into possession of such a coat, and he told her about the old woman he met in Sanxiang Town. Inquiries about the age and looks of the old woman assured her that it could be none other than her mother-in-law. She pulled her son into a vacant room, shut the door, and told him amidst bitter sobs that his so-called father was not his father but his father's murderer. "I had wished to tell you all this long ago," she said, "but I was afraid you were too young to handle it. I am a woman, and you are our only hope. If your move should miscarry, there'll be no one else to avenge your father. I've lived to this day, not because I fear death. And now it could only be a sign from heaven to have this blood-stained coat sent back to me!"

Yilang secretly sharpened a knife. He waited till Maofang was fast asleep and slashed the throat of the usurper. With the head, he surrendered himself to the governor, who pardoned him for his righteous revenge.

The widow and her son later returned to Sanxiang. The reunion of three generations was a mixture of joy and sorrow. She died after caring for her mother-in-law three more years.

The Two Friends
(abridged*)

In late Dali reign, living in the Wisdom Woods Temple in the East Capital of Luoyang was the monk Yuanguan, a versatile man. Besides being a scholar of the Buddhist scriptures, he was also versed in music and farming. The practicality of the latter yielded much grain and silk and earned him the nickname "rich monk." Nevertheless, nobody really knew where he was from.

Also living in the temple was a layman named Li Yuan, son of a Court official. In his youth he was known as a man-about-town, wallowing through drinking bouts and all-night parties. But after his father was taken prisoner by the An Lushan-Shi Siming Rebellion army while defending the East Capital, he swore off silk and delicacies for rough cloth and plain food, and, as an assertion of will, donated his entire family property to the temple in return for mere shelter and board. Like a recluse, he severed himself from all contact with the outside world, keeping no servants, not even a handmaid. Yuanguan was his only friend, and they would chat through the day over a cup of tea. Though to many it seemed an unlikely mixture, their friendship stretched over three decades.

Then one day they decided to make a journey to Shu.

Together, they visited the sacred religious sites in the Qingcheng and Emei Mountains in quest of the ultimate Way and the magic art of refining immortality pills. After that, Yuanguan intended to travel north via the Xiagu Pass to the

---

* The postscript and two poems have been omitted from the end of the text.

192

West Capital Chang'an, while Li suggested going east down the Yangtze River through the Three Gorges to Jingzhou. Half a year passed and they still could not agree on which route to take.

"After shunning official circles for so many years, I don't feel like going to the capital again," Li insisted.

"All right, one's way is always predestined," Yuanguan finally gave in with a sigh. "Let's take the Three Gorges."

Down through the Gorges they sailed. Mooring at the foot of a mountain one evening, they saw a group of women with tinkling bracelets and earrings filling their water jars at the riverside.

"I told you I didn't want to come this way, because I don't want to meet these women," Yuanguan mumbled with trickling tears.

Startled by his friend's sudden burst of emotion, Li asked in concern, "What's the matter? On our way through the Gorges we've encountered many women like this. What's so special about this group that makes you cry?"

"Among them is a pregnant one of the Wang family. The baby in her stomach is my soul's next residence. She has been in a family way for three years now without giving birth. You know why? Because I haven't arrived. Once I see her, my present life is ended. That's what we call the transmigration of the soul. Better pray for me and wish me an easy and quick passage. You may also do me a favor by staying here a few days longer and see to it that my discarded body is properly buried, won't you? Three days after the child is born, you can pay the family a visit. If the newborn should give you a big smile, that would be me showing recognition. Twelve years from now, on the full-moon night of the Mid-Autumn Festival, we shall have a chance to cross paths in front of the Tianzhu Temple in Hangzhou City."

Choked with remorse for having been so insistent, Li bade his friend a tearful farewell. Then he called the pregnant woman over and gave her a prescription for smooth delivery.

She held it to her bosom and went joyfully home. Shortly, her whole family gathered at the riverside to offer an oblation of dried fish and wine.

Yuanguan bathed and changed into new clothes. That very night, he passed away and the pregnant woman gave birth.

Three days later Li went to visit the family. Holding the infant to the window, he saw the baby smile at him. Tears welled up in his eyes as he told the Wangs of Yuanguan's reincarnation. The family then provided for a decent burial.

Next day, Li started on a return trip to the Wisdom Woods Temple. When he announced Yuanguan's death he learned that Yuanguan had written a will in which the circumstances of his death were accurately predicted.

It was the eighth lunar month 12 years later. Li had traveled over half the country to Hangzhou to fulfill his appointment. A shower had washed the hills and a full autumn moon was shedding its silvery light over the Tianzhu Temple and the slopes. He was just wondering where he could find Yuanguan when he caught a soft tune floating over from the dale. A buffalo appeared around the hill and a boy in a short coat whose hair was combed into double buns was singing on its back, beating time on the horns. As the boy approached, Li thought he could distinguish certain features of Yuanguan. He stepped forth and greeted, "How have you been doing, Master?"

"What a faithful man!" remarked the buffalo boy, avoiding a direct answer. "Don't come too close to me, for we now live in different realms and your mortal life is not yet over. Keep cultivating your moral character and never let it slip. In that way, the day will come when we can meet again, person to person."

Seeing it was impossible to strike up a conversation, Li saluted his former friend with tearful eyes. The boy picked up his song as he turned round the bend of the hill, his tune trailing in the crystal air.

The Lis' Youngest Daughter

The humid lowlands north of Mount Yong were once occupied by a gigantic python about three feet thick and 70 or 80 feet long. Its presence scared away the natives from the vicinity and caused unexpected deaths among local functionaries. Cows and lambs were sacrificed to no avail.

Then it was revealed through dreams and the prophecy of witches that virgin girls of about 12 years old were most desired. The authorities had no choice but to scrounge around for girls to please the python. They would usually opt for girls from criminal families or those who were born household slaves. Early in the eighth lunar month, the designated girl would be sent to the temple built outside the python's cave where the sacrificial rites were held. The python used to come out at night and devour the poor girl. It went on like this year after year, until a total of nine girls had been sacrificed.

The eighth lunar month was approaching again, but this year officials had not yet been able to find a girl for the occasion.

In Jiangle County there was a Li family with six daughters and no son. The youngest one, named Ji, resolved to offer herself, but her parents fought against the idea.

"There's no sense in keeping me," she argued with her parents. "What's the use of having six daughters when you don't have a son? Daughters are always married into other families. They can neither carry on the family line nor provide for you when you are old. It's just a waste of food and money to raise daughters, and it doesn't make much difference with one less. If I sell myself, at least I can get you some money. Isn't that reasonable?"

Though her parents would not hear of it, she was persistent and finally had her way.

She asked the authorities for a sharp sword, a snake hound, honey, glutinous rice and wheat flour. She steamed the rice and baked the flour, and mixed them with honey into a huge sticky rice ball.

The day came. She and her huge rice ball were carried to the python's cave. She placed the ball right outside the cave mouth and sat waiting in the temple with the sword on her lap and the hound beside her feet.

Deep into the night, the python emerged from its cave, its head as big as a fodder silo, its two eyes like king-size bronze mirrors. It caught the sweet smell of the rice ball and swallowed it at one gulp. Instantly, she let go of the leash. The hound pounced at the python while she hacked it from behind. The python squirmed out of the cave and lay dead.

She went into the cave and collected nine skeletons. "What a shame!" she said contemptuously. "You died because you didn't have the guts to fight." Then she strolled back to her village.

Her story reached the King of Yue who made her Queen, appointed her father magistrate of Jiangle County, and bestowed many gifts upon her mother and sisters.

Her story was passed down in song.

Red Strand
(abridged*)

General Xue Song, garrison commander of Fuyang Prefecture, had a house maid called Red Strand. She was very good at playing the lute and was also well-read and intelligent. As he often asked her to draft his communications and reports, she won the nickname Domestic Secretary.

Here is just one story showing how talented she was.

Once during an army banquet she called Xue's attention to the music, saying that the drummer must have something weighing on his mind for the drums sounded rather melancholy. Xue, cultured in music himself, listened and agreed. Upon his query, the drummer disclosed that his wife had passed away the previous night, and since there was this banquet going on, he didn't dare ask for leave. Xue granted him immediate permission to go home.

This was just after the An Lushan-Shi Siming Rebellion. The eastern plains were still in the turbulent aftermath of war, the population was sparse and the administrative system shattered. Located near the southern tip of the Taihang Mountain Range where the Yellow River pours out onto the plains, Fuyang was a place of strategic importance, and Xue's troops were deployed there to deter the eastern provinces. To further ensure regional stability, the Court had ordered him to marry his daughter to the son of General Tian Chengsi, garrison commander of Wei Prefecture, and to marry his son to the daughter of the garrison commander of Hua Prefecture. As the three prefectures in that triangle area of 100 miles were

---

* A poem is omitted from the second to last paragraph.

198

thus related by marriage, traffic and trade flourished.

Tian was suffering from a severe case of pulmonary emphysema, which worsened when the days grew hot. "If only I could be re-stationed in Fuyang and enjoy the summer coolness of its higher altitude," he said many times, "I might have more years to live."

With that in mind, he hand-picked 3,000 soldiers from his bravest troops to form an elite force which he called his Private Braves. Every night, 300 of them took turns guarding his official residence. Then a date was set to attack and annex Fuyang.

Xue was greatly upset by this news. Day and night he was lost in thought but could not come up with a satisfactory counter plan.

Night had fallen again, the gates were locked and he silently paced the courtyard. Only Red Strand followed. "My lord," she broke the silence, "in the past month you've lost both appetite and sleep. There must be something worrying you. Is it because of our neighbor?"

"It's a matter of life and death. You girls don't understand."

"I know I'm not in a position to discuss this, but I think I can be of some help."

Surprised by her confidence, he said, "I had a hunch you are not an ordinary chamber maid, but I didn't expect you to have exceptional prowess." He told her of the imminent threat and continued, "If I should lose any territory in my care to some defiant general, the several hundred years of glory attached to my family name would be tarnished at my hands. How shall I face my ancestors and His Majesty!"

"Don't worry, my lord. This is but a trifle. With your leave, I'll make a trip to Wei Prefecture right away to size up the situation there and see what I can do. Meanwhile, please draw up a complimentary letter to General Tian, and have a dispatch rider on stand-by. I'll come back before daybreak."

"What if you are caught? Wouldn't that make things worse?"

"Everything will turn out well. There's nothing to worry about, my lord." So she went back to her room to prepare herself.

She twisted up her hair into a snug bun and secured it with a gold pin, changed into a tight-fitting dark-blue jacket, put on a pair of light, black cloth shoes, fastened a carved dragon dagger to her belt, and wrote the magic name of the polestar god on her forehead. All done, she knelt down and bowed to the god's statue, and whisked out of the room.

Xue also retired to his room and shut the door behind. With his back to the candle, he tried to relieve his anxiety by drinking. He was not a big drinker, and at ordinary times a few cups would send him reeling, but on that particular night his head remained especially clear, though he had poured down more than a dozen cups. Suddenly, he heard a breeze brushing a flag and dew drops shaken off a leaf. He sprang to his feet and whispered, "Is it you, Red Strand?"

It was.

A smile of relief cracked on his face as he asked how things stood.

"You know, I couldn't afford to fail my mission," she replied.

"Hope you didn't have to hurt anyone."

"No, that wasn't necessary. I only took this gold box from beside General Tian's pillow. That was enough of a warning."

"I reached Wei's capital town well before midnight," she went on with a fuller account. "There were sentries and patrols everywhere, demanding passwords, but I had no trouble passing through gates and barricades. Outside his official residence, I could hear those Private Braves snoring as loud as thunder on the verandahs. I pushed open the left plank of his bedroom door and there I stood right beside his curtained bed. My lord's in-law was lying on his back in a sound sleep, his legs crossed, his hair tied up with a piece of yellow gauze. The gem-studded handle of a sword was protruding from beneath his rhino-skin pillow. Beside it was a gold box, its lid open. Inside was a piece of silk inscribed with his Eight Characters of life and the symbol of the Wain, overlaid with pearls and rich spices. He imagined himself secure on his curtained bed, yet he didn't realize his heart was lying exposed; he slept peacefully in his protected room, yet he didn't know his life was hanging by a thread. He was not even worth my catching. I only pitied him.

"By that time, the candles had burned out and the fireplace was in cinders. There were soldiers all about the place, their weapons tangled up. Some leaned their heads against the wall snoring, some stretched out on the floor with towels and fans still in their hands. I plucked the pins from their hair and tied the tails of their coats together while they slept like the dead. I left with this gold box without encountering any trouble. When the moon touched the distant tree tops and the first rooster began to crow, I had already reached our border. I was so happy to have completed my mission that exhaustion was swept away. So, by covering 200 miles in a night and through half a dozen fortified towns, I at last am able to repay your kindness to me over the years."

Thereupon, Xue sent a messenger on his way with the gold box and a letter to Tian. "Last night," the letter reads, "I had a guest from Wei. He offered me a gold box which he said he had taken from the side of Your Excellency's pillow. I dare not keep such a precious thing as this, and I am sending it back to you by special carrier."

The rider galloped through villages and towns without taking a rest. It was nearly midnight when he arrived at Wei. The whole town was in chaos. Soldiers swarmed the streets and were making a house-to-house search. He went straight up to the commander's mansion and knocked on the gate with the butt of his whip. Tian received him in person, though it was an unusual hour for an audience, and he all but swooned when the messenger produced the box. He feasted the man and piled him with gifts.

The very next morning, he dispatched an envoy with 30,000 bolts of silk, 200 thoroughbreds, and myriads of jewelry to Xue. In an accompanying letter he wrote:

"I am most grateful to Your Excellency for not taking my head. Guilt loads my heart and I shall mend my ways. Now I pledge complete loyalty to Your Excellency and shall forever remain your humble servant and obey your orders. The so-called Private Braves were for no other purpose than a precaution against burglars. They shall be demobilized and sent home at once."

In the months that followed, ambassadors from many neighboring army chiefs converged at Fuyang to pay their respects and tribute.

One day, however, Red Strand announced her intention to leave.

"This is your home," Xue said. "Where are you planning to go? You know how much I need you. How can you leave me at this moment?"

"In my previous life," she replied, "I was a man, studying medicine with an ambition to relieve people of their sufferings. There was a pregnant woman with a parasitic disease. I treated her with an alcohol extract of lilac daphne to purge the worms, but killed her instead with the twins in her womb. Because of that, the nether force reincarnated me into a woman of inferior status. It was very fortunate indeed for me to be born in Your Excellency's household. During my 19 years of life, I was clad in silk and fed with delicacies. And it is also good fortune to see law and order prevail again. People should be allowed to live in peace. That I took it upon myself to abort a traitor's undertaking was first to do my lord a service, and second to prevent a confrontation that could have taken thousands of innocent lives. As one of the fair sex, such a feat is enough to atone for my previous sin and clear me of any worldly obligations. No more shall I be bound by this material world. I'm going to seek the immortality of a pure existence."

"What do you say if I build you a temple in the nearby mountains?" Xue suggested.

"Thanks, but one's afterlife cannot be pre-set."

Seeing that she was determined to go, Xue held a grand farewell party in her honor. Guests arrived from near and far. He sang her a toast, only to break down in sobs. With tears welling up, she bowed her gratitude and excused herself for feeling tipsy.

She was never seen again.

Translator's note:
Weakened by eight years of civil war, the central government of the Tang Dynasty was not able to eradicate the separatist forces in what was roughly present Hebei Province. Quite a number of warlords who nominally submitted themselves to the throne after the main force of the rebellion was crushed retained their power, and were even appointed local garrison commanders as a means of appeasement. Both Xue Song and Tian Chengsi were such rebel generals.

The Assassin

A scholar once served as county lieutenant in charge of public security in the capital's suburbs. Held in custody was a suspect in connection with a burglary case waiting to be tried. The lieutenant was sitting alone in the hall when the suspect suddenly said, "I am no burglar, neither am I any ordinary peasant. If Your Highness can have me acquitted, I may one day render you a service in return."

Though he shouted down the request as nonsense, he did notice that the man had some unusual traits and sounded well-educated. In his heart, he had already decided to pardon him.

After nightfall, he secretly summoned the jailer on duty and instructed him to set the suspect free, and then flee town himself.

The jailbreak was discovered in the morning, but since the jailer on the night shift was also gone, the case seemed self-evident. The lieutenant only received a mild reprimand from his superior.

After his term of office, the scholar took to traveling. He arrived in a county where the magistrate, as he found out, bore the same name as the suspect he acquitted. So he went to the magistrate's official mansion to pay him a visit.

The magistrate, who was indeed the former suspect, was startled to see the scholar's card. He hurried to the gate in person to accord him a cordial welcome. The scholar was put up in the official mansion, and the magistrate himself accompanied him night after day, sharing the same room. For nearly a fortnight, he didn't even go home.

The magistrate did go home one day. The scholar went to

the outhouse, which happened to be separated from the magistrate's private residence by a low wall. In the privy, the scholar heard the magistrate's wife ask, "What important guest has kept you at your office for these 10 days?"

"He is my benefactor," the magistrate replied. "He once saved my life! Now that he is here, I really don't know how to repay him."

"Haven't you heard the saying: A debt too big to repay is not paid at all?"

There was a long silence, then he heard the magistrate say, "You are right."

The scholar rushed to the stable to get his horse. "No time to pack up. Just follow me!" he shouted to his puzzled servants and galloped away. By sundown they had covered some 20 miles and were out of the county when they stopped at a village inn.

His servants finally had a chance to ask why he fled in such haste. When his panting subsided, he told them how ungrateful the magistrate was. He sighed and sighed, and the servants wiped their impassioned tears from their eyes. At that moment, a man sprang out from beneath the bed with a dagger in hand, scaring the scholar out of his wits.

"Don't be afraid," the man said. "I'm a man of honor. The magistrate hired me to take your head, but from what you said, I now realize what an ungrateful scoundrel he is. He almost made me kill a good man. Such a scoundrel shouldn't live. Wait for me here. I'll be back in a moment with his head. The wrong must be redressed."

The scholar thanked him for sparing his life and the assassin dashed out with the speed of a whirlwind. He returned before midnight. "Here he is," he shouted. By torch light, they could see it was the head of the magistrate.

The assassin excused himself and disappeared into the night.

The Dark Slave
(abridged*)

During Dali reign there was a Mr. Cui holding an honorary position in the imperial guards as an officer. He was a quiet young man with a soft white face. Though he was one of few words, his conversation was intelligent.

His father was a high official and the friend of a very powerful cabinet celebrity. On one occasion, his old man sent him over to pay a courtesy visit to the bigwig, who happened to be afflicted with an indisposition.

A maid lifted the bamboo door-drape and ushered him into the big shot's bedroom. He kowtowed and conveyed his father's best wishes. The bigwig took an immediate liking to him and asked him to sit down for a friendly chat.

Three pleasure-girls came forth with fresh cherries in gold bowls. It would be no exaggeration to say that they were the beauties of beauties. With their gentle fingers they removed the kernels and steeped the pulp in sweet cream. One of the girls wearing a red silk blouse knelt and held up the bowl for him. Unused to the service of pleasure-girls, Cui shied away from the cherries. The bigwig told the girl to feed him with a spoon, so he had to take mouthfuls. His innocence made the girl chuckle.

He stood up to take leave. "Do drop in when you have time. I hope you haven't been bored by the company of an old man," the bigwig said as he motioned the girl in red to see Cui to the gate.

Out of the gate, he glanced back to see the girl raise three fingers. Then, flapping her hand round three times, she

---

* Two poems have been omitted from the sixth and 17th paragraphs.

pointed to the little round mirror hanging from her neck and muttered, "Don't forget." And that was all she said.

He returned home to report his mission to his father, then buried himself in his study. His usual light-heartedness gave way to moody thoughts, so much so that he forgot his meals and indulged in dream-talking to himself. Even his immediate servants couldn't figure out what was wrong with him.

There was a dark slave working in his house. "What's worrying my master?" he asked, studying his face. "Why not share your concerns with your old servant?"

"What do you know?" he snapped. "Can one like you relieve my heart?"

"Just tell me what it is. Maybe I can help you work it out, no matter where it might take me."

Taken aback by his self-assurance, he poured out his story.

"Trifling matter," the slave said lightly. "You should have told me earlier. Why let that worry you so much?"

Cui then described the girl's gestures.

"That's not difficult to figure out. That bigwig keeps 10 pleasure-girls in his backyard. She raised three fingers to tell you she is the third. Turning her hand round three times means 15. The mirror stands for the full moon. So she is asking you to come on the 15th of the month."

He could hardly contain his joy. "But how can I get there?" he asked.

"The day after tomorrow is the 15th. May I ask you for two bolts of dark blue silk? I need to make you a tight-fitting suit. The bigwig has the courtyard guarded by a pack of bloodhounds. No one can enter without his permission. If an intruder tries to break in, the hounds will tear him to pieces. They are as fierce as tigers and as vigilant as gods. Nobody in this world can beat them, nobody except me. I'll go first and have them killed to clear the way for you."

Cui bought him a good meal of wine and meat. At midnight of the 15th, the slave set off with a sling hammer.

One couldn't have finished a meal before he was back to announce that the dogs were dead, so now the only obstacle was overcome. He helped Cui into the dark blue suit and carried him on his back. They scaled a dozen high walls and arrived at the third door in the backyard.

The door was unbolted, shedding a strip of yellow light into the yard. They could see her sitting on the bed sighing, her hairpins and jewels removed. The guards were all asleep and the night was deadly quiet. Cui cautiously lifted the curtain and entered the room. It seemed that she could hardly believe her eyes when she beheld him. She jumped off her bed and grasped his hands. "I knew at first sight you are intelligent and could understand my gestures. But how on earth have you managed to reach my room?"

He told her about the dark slave.

"Where's he now?"

"Right outside your door."

She invited him in and offered him wine in a gold goblet. "I was born in a well-off family in the north," she told Cui, "but unfortunately, the governor had his eyes on me and I was forced to work as a servant in his house. I hate myself for having lived so long. Every day, though I put on powder and a smile, my heart is cold and congealed. Though I eat with jade chopsticks, wear silk and satin, sleep in an embroidered bed behind pearl curtains and live in scented rooms among utensils of gold, I hate this life. It's no less than serving an endless prison term. Since your servant has such magic powers, why don't you let him take me away from this dungeon. If only I can escape from this kind of life, I don't care what may befall me. I'd like to be your serving maid, and attend upon your needs. It's all up to you."

Cui made no response.

"If you're that determined," the dark slave put in, "it won't be difficult to take you out."

Exhilarated, the girl packed up frantically. It took the dark man three trips to carry her belongings. "The sun will soon be up," he finally said, "we must leave now or never." So he carried both of them on his back and scaled the walls back to Cui's study, where they hid the girl.

None of the guards sensed anything until broad daylight. The governor was horrified to see his dogs dead and the girl missing. "Up till now," he said, "my house has been safe and secure, and well-guarded. It's strange nobody heard anything. It must have been the work of someone who has mastered the art of weightlessness. That man is a potential threat. Don't let this incident leak out," he warned his servants.

For two years, the girl lived safely in Cui's house. Then one spring she took an outing to a scenic bend of the river where she was recognized by a servant of the bigwig, who was surprised by the report. He then summoned Cui to ask about the girl. Since it was useless to lie, the young man revealed every detail of what had happened. She was carried out by his family slave, he confessed.

"That girl deserves serious punishment," the bigwig said, "but since she has been yours for more than a year, I won't press charges. Nevertheless, I must stamp out the potential danger to our society."

He dispatched 50 soldiers to surround Cui's house and catch the slave. All of a sudden, the dark man rose from behind the high walls with a dagger in hand and fluttered away as swiftly as a falcon. The soldiers shot, but their arrows missed. In a blink he had disappeared. The whole Cui household looked on in utter disbelief.

The slave's escape filled the bigwig with dread that the man might seek revenge. He reproached himself for having acted so tactlessly. Every night after he had his servants bear arms to guard the house. This lasted for a full year before he slacked off.

A decade later, a member of the Cui family spotted the dark man in the East Capital peddling herbs. In spite of all the years, he didn't look a day older.

The Magic Bottle

Sometime during Zhenyuan reign of the Tang Dynasty, a woman vagrant became a phenomenon in the streets of Yangzhou City. Nobody knew where she came from or who she was, except that her name was Hu Meir. Anyway, that was how she introduced herself. She made a living by performing magic arts, and her arts were rather outlandish. In a fortnight, as her name spread, a permanent crowd gathered around her. In that way she earned tens of thousands a day.

One morning, she retrieved from the folds of her garment a glass bottle. It was transparent and one could clearly see through it. She placed it on the straw mat and announced that if someone could fill it she would not need to beg any more. It was not a big bottle, about the size of a half-liter jar with a neck no thicker than a reed stem. Someone offered 100 coins. One could hear the coins clinking to the bottom, but once inside the bottle they looked as small as grains of rice. The audience was fascinated. Another came up with 1,000 coins, and still another dropped in 10,000. Then one dude jingled in 100,000 coins and the bottle was no fuller than it had been. Horses and donkeys were driven in, and they shrank to the size of bugs, but still plodding along as if nothing had happened.

Before long, a high official from the revenue department came along with a caravan of several dozen wagons loaded with local produce on their way to the capital. The official stopped to watch. She could by no means carry off the heavily guarded caravan under his nose, he thought, not to say that this was royal property. "Can you transport my whole caravan into your bottle?" he challenged.

"With your permission," she replied succinctly, and he gave his consent.

Tilting the bottle slightly, she let out a loud hoot. The whole caravan rumbled ahead into the bottle like a line of crawling ants. Slowly, the wagons faded from sight. Before the astonished official realized what was happening, she herself jumped into the bottle. He grabbed the bottle and smashed it on the ground. There was nothing in it.

A month later, someone saw Meir in Qinghe County, hundreds of miles to the north of Yangzhou, leading a wagon-train in the direction of Dongping, the capital of warlord Li Shidao.

Translator's note:

Magic bottles are common in fairy tales, but what lies behind this story is a successful hijack of a government caravan by rebellious forces. The heroine of the story, Hu Meir, is probably the mastermind of the operation.

In the Tang Dynasty, regional army commanders sometimes grew so powerful that they not only became semi-autonomous but even were a threat to the central government. Li Shidao and his forefathers had been governing what is roughly present-day Shandong Province for three generations, until his open rebellion was crushed in 819.

From this story we may gain an insight into the evolution of legends from historical events.

Two Humorous Stories

a) The Woman's First Mirror

A peasant bought a mirror at the market and gave it as a present to his wife, who had never seen a mirror before. At her first glance, his wife cried out in alarm, "My lord has brought home a new wife!" Her mother came running in, grabbed the mirror, looked, and burst out indignantly, "Not only a new wife, but the mother-in-law as well!"

b) The Bitten Nose

Two men had a fight, and one bit off the other's nose. Before the magistrate, the offender asserted that the nose was bitten off by the victim himself.

"Nonsense!" shouted the magistrate. "The nose is above the mouth. How can his mouth reach his nose?"

"That's easy enough," the offender replied. "He could have stood on a stool."

The Muddlehead

Guo Wujing, a county official of Nanpi, was a muddle-headed man. Staying at an inn one night, he bragged to his colleague Liu Sizhuang that it was most adventurous to serve in His Majesty's train, which honor he had when he was younger. During that episode he lost his family for three whole days. He searched high and low, and finally found them at a lieutenant's place.

"Do you mean your wife was missing, too?" asked Liu.

"Sure she was, what is so unusual about it?"

After a while, he spoke again, saying that these days thieves were running riot. For instance, when he returned home around 10 o'clock last night, he saw a thief sneaking out from his bedroom.

"Lost anything?" Liu asked in concern.

"No, nothing."

"Then, how do you know it was a thief?"

"Well, I had that hunch because I saw the man fleeing in panic."

Translator's note:

A Chinese proverb says: "To accompany the emperor is like associating yourself with the tiger." It is hard to tell whether this Mr. Guo deliberately shut his eyes to his superior's desires or was really so muddle-headed as not to recognize adultery.

A Potential Rapist?

Jian Yong, one of the chief counselors to Liu Bei, king of Shu in the Three Kingdoms period, had followed the king faithfully through wars and hardships since his youth.

One year, the Kingdom of Shu was hit by a severe drought, and wine-making was therefore strictly prohibited. Anyone who dared to violate the prohibition was unrelentingly punished.

During a search, wine-making equipment was discovered in a farmer's cottage. The magistrate judged the possession of the equipment as bad a crime as producing wine.

Jian was accompanying the king on an inspection tour when the case was brought before the king. Jian suddenly pointed at a man walking down the street and exclaimed, "Why don't you arrest that man! He's going to rape!"

"How do you know?" asked the king incredulously.

"He possesses sex organs!" Jian asserted. "Isn't having the organs the same as having the equipment?"

The king burst out in laughter and ordered the farmer released.

An Old Man in the Han Dynasty

In the Han Dynasty there was an heirless old man. He was rich but stingy. What he wore was rags; what he ate was coarse rice and vegetables. He rose with the sun and worked till it was too dark to see. To him money could never be too much, yet he would never spend a coin on his own comfort. If a beggar could not be driven off, sometimes he might go inside and count out 10 coins. Caressing them in his palm, he would put away a coin every few steps on his slow return. By the time he reached the counter, only half of the coins would remain in his hand. Always shutting his eyes to the painful sight as he placed them in the beggar's hand, he would repeatedly say, "I'm ruining my business to assist you. Don't let others know, lest they follow you here."

Before long, the old man died. His house and land were confiscated by the government; his store and money went into the imperial coffer.

The Fox Tail

In Bing Prefecture there was a man who took pleasure in playing practical jokes. Thinking that he could take advantage of people's belief in the fox's ability to bewitch and change shapes, he procured a fox tail while he was out of town. He pinned the tail inside the back of his coat in such a way that when he sat down the tip of it would be dangling out. Thus he went home to his wife.

His wife spotted his tail and suspected he was a fox vampire in her husband's guise. She returned to the room with a hidden ax, and swung it down on him. Dodging and bowing, he proclaimed that he was no fox, but his wife couldn't be convinced. He fled to a neighbor's. They, too, drove him out with swords and sticks. Scared out of his wits, he confessed his silly trick and said he never expected his jokes could almost cause him his life.

Aren't evil spirits created by man himself?

The Lucky Stones

In the early days of the Sui Dynasty, Hou Yu, a young scholar of the Confucian school, set out from his native place in Shu to Chang'an, the capital. As he drew near a mountain pass called Sword Gate, he saw four lovely stones by the roadside, each the size of one's head. Being fascinated, he picked them up and placed them in his rattan bookcase on the donkey's back.

The first thing he thought of at his next stop was to take out the stones for further inspection. To his surprise, the stones had turned into gold ingots. He sold them in the capital for a good price. With that money he bought a dozen pretty girls, built a grand mansion and purchased rich farmlands in the suburbs.

One pleasant spring day he took all his mistresses and a train of servants with him for a picnic in the country. Food and wine were laid out when an elderly man with a big willow box seated himself at the other end of the rug. Enraged by this rudeness, he reproached the man and ordered the servants to drag him away. The old man did not budge, neither did he appear to be annoyed at all. He poured out wine for himself and grabbed thick slices of the roasted meat.

"I came," he laughed, "to collect the debt you owe me. You haven't forgotten about the gold ingots you took from me, have you?"

Thus speaking, he seized Hou's mistresses and threw them all into his box, which seemed to have an infinite capacity. Carrying the box on his back, he scudded away as swiftly as a bird. The servants gave chase, but soon lost track of him.

After that, Hou's business declined till he became as poor

as he had been before his acquisition of the lovely stones. After some 10 years, he finally decided to return to his hometown. At Sword Gate, he was just in time to catch sight of the elderly man parading through the street with his former mistresses and a multitude of servants. They all laughed at him, and none answered his questions. When he tried to stop them, they simply vanished.

In spite of his dogged search in and around the area, no one seemed to have ever heard of such an old man.

Translator's note:

Brief as this story is, the rise and fall of a parvenu was vividly portrayed through his gain and loss of four roadside stones.

The Lunar Goddess

Lu Qi was poor when he was young and for a time lived in a miserable hut in the East Capital. Among his neighbors sharing the compound was a lonely dame nicknamed Pocked Granny. When he was struck down with a serious illness for a month, every day she would come over to help him cook some porridge. It was due to her care that he managed to pull through.

One day coming home he was surprised to see a gold-foiled ox carriage parked at Granny's door. He peeped in and beheld a girl of 14 or 15 years old. "A fairy beauty!" his heart exclaimed.

The next day he strolled over to strike up a bush-beating chat with Pocked Granny about the girl.

"Would you like her to be your wife?" Granny asked. "I can talk it over with her."

"Oh, no! Poor as I am, I wouldn't even dream of that!"

"No harm in asking," she said.

That night she dropped in and announced, "All is settled. I've arranged an appointment with her in the deserted Taoist temple outside the east gate of town, but you must first hold a three-day fast."

Only wild grass and eerie trees distorted by the years greeted them on the former temple ground. Just then, a thunder crack brought forth a violent storm and a palace in all the splendor of jade and gold emerged before their eyes. A carriage landed from the sky and a young lady stepped out to meet him. It was the girl he had seen the other day.

"I am a celestial being," she stated. "By permission of His Almighty, I may pick myself a spouse from the human world.

Since you have the extraordinary features of divinity, I have asked Pocked Granny to convey my inclination to you. Please fast another seven days and we'll meet again." She beckoned Granny over and handed her two pills.

Dark clouds and thunder closed in and she disappeared. The grand palace once again gave way to the unruly grass and ancient trees.

On the seventh day of Lu's fast, Pocked Granny dug a couple of holes in the earth and planted the two pills. They sprouted almost instantly. Vines grew and two gourds were borne which swiftly swelled to the size of giant water-vats. She scooped out the pulp, and handing him three oilskin coats, told him to get into one of the gourds while she took the other. A wind rose, and his ears were filled with the booming of waves as he rocketed up into the firmament. Gradually, he started to feel cold. Granny told him to put on an oilskin. It seemed they were traveling through ice and snow. He was instructed to put on another coat, and when he had all three layers on he felt rather warm.

"We are already 30,000 miles from the East Capital," he heard Granny say.

After what seemed a long while, the gourd finally stopped. Before his eyes were palaces and pavilions built of luminous crystal, and hundreds of spear-bearing guards in shining armor. Granny led him into a purple palace where the young lady was waiting with her train of maids. He was offered a seat and a feast was laid out. Pocked Granny retreated to the side of the hall.

"Sir," the young lady said, "you have three possibilities before you, and now you must decide on one. First, you may choose to stay in this palace forever and live as long as heaven itself; second, you may choose to be an immortal living on earth and enjoy occasional visits to this place; third, you may choose to be the prime minister of China."

"Of course my first choice is to live here forever," Lu

replied.

"That's a wise decision," the lady beamed. "You know, this is the crystal palace and I am the Lunar Goddess, quite a high position in heaven. That you can live here is no less an accomplishment than realizing a daydream. But you must make sure you won't change your mind, or you'll not only mar your own fortune but mine as well." She then wrote a petition on a sheet of aqua-blue paper and, with full ceremony, sent it to the Almighty.

Presently, a voice was heard in the northeastern direction, "Here comes His Almighty's special envoy."

The goddess and other celestial beings descended the palace steps to extend their welcome. Amidst a cloud of banners and fragrant smoke, a youth in red arrived at the steps. "Lu Qi," he pronounced from a scroll, "we received a petition from Her Ladyship the Lunar Goddess that you wish to live forever in the crystal palace. Is that your true wish?"

Lu made no reply. Despite the goddess' urges, he just held his tongue. The goddess and those present were horrified. She hurried in and brought out five bolts of "dragon gauze" to bribe the envoy for time. After a brief intermission, the envoy spoke again, "Lu Qi, you must decide right now whether you wish to live in the crystal palace, be an immortal on earth, or become a prime minister."

"I want to be prime minister!" Lu burst out.

The youth whisked off, leaving the goddess ashen with shock. "You, Pocked Granny, have failed me! Take him away!"

He was pushed back into the gourd and the sound of rolling waves filled the space. When he opened his eyes, he found himself lying on his crumpled bed in his filthy room. Nothing had changed, except that it was past midnight. There was no gourd, no Pocked Granny.

Translator's note:

Lu Qi is an historical figure who served as prime minister during Jianzhong reign and is remembered in history as vicious. He was later banished from Court.

This story also demonstrates that more than a millennium ago people already had distinct ideas about space travel and flying off the ground like birds, as represented by "Mount Raven" and "The Carpenter and His Wooden Cranes." Wings, as it was correctly perceived, are not sufficient to carry one to the moon, so that spaceships (in this case, the gourds) are needed, as well as protective coats. The temperature drop at higher altitudes and the booming sound of rockets tearing through the air are also accurate speculations.

The Meditator

For more than 30 years Ming Siyuan, a Taoist priest on Mount Hua, had been practicing the magic arts of Tao. He delighted in giving lectures on alchemy and meditation, and his disciples were many.

In Yongtai reign, Mount Hua was infested with tigers. Ming assured his audience that there was nothing to fear. If only one knew how to regulate his breathing and concentrate his thoughts, he would be able to produce a lion from each fingertip and drive the herd forth with his will power. That alone would frighten away any man-eater.

At sunset one day, he and a group of his disciples came face to face with a tiger at the mouth of a ravine. His followers took to their heels, while he held his ground and plunged into meditation.

His disciples ventured to return the next morning. All they found was his torn shoes in the bushes.

Translator's note:
If you do not believe in the magic powers of the Taoist priests as presented in the first part of this book, you might like to know that even in the Tang Dynasty there were people as unimpressed as you are.

The Erudite Gentlemen in the Capital

A group of erudite gentlemen in the capital were holding a party when one of them touched upon the topic of courage. "Whether a person is brave or timid," one argued, "solely depends on the physical qualities of his gallbladder. If it is positively built, then he will be fearless and, consequently, a true gentleman."

One of the guests chipped in, "Speaking of one with a positively built gallbladder, to be honest with you, I am that person."

The group roared with laughter. "All right, but it must be tested first."

Someone suggested an old house owned by a relative. Having been the stage of many dreadful incidents, it was locked up and vacant. If he could spend just one night in that house by himself without being frightened, they would throw a banquet in his honor.

"It's agreed," replied the brave one.

There they gathered the next afternoon. The house was actually an ordinary old house—it was simply unoccupied at the moment. Having arranged for wine, food, lamps and candles, the group asked whether he would need anything else.

"Nothing," answered the man firmly. "My sword is sufficient to defend me. Put your heart at ease and have a good night's sleep." The group left the house and locked the yard gate behind them.

He tied his riding donkey in a wing room and retired into the bedroom. Night soon descended. He blew out the lamps but, being a coward at heart, he didn't dare to close his eyes.

Apprehensive and panicky, he sat on the couch clutching his sword to his chest. It was midnight when the moon rose up outside the window, illuminating an owl-shaped figure perching on the coat-hanger, flapping its wings. The man plucked up his courage and swung his sword. At this stroke, the creature fell down onto the floor with a loud thud. Then there was absolute silence. The effort had drained him of whatever courage he might have had to go over and inspect his kill. He sat stiffly with his sword in hand.

In the pre-dawn quiet something slowly ascended the doorsteps and pushed against the door. As the door held, it squeezed its head through the dog's entrance. Its heavy breathing could be heard distinctly. The terrified man made a desperate swing with his sword. The violence threw him off his feet and he lost hold of the sword, but with a monster in immediate proximity, he felt it unwise to grope for it. He kept to the ground and slithered beneath the couch, where he huddled motionlessly. Sleep, however, overcame him.

At sunrise, the group returned to open the gate. At the bedroom door they were surprised to find the dog's entrance smeared with fresh blood. Their alarmed calls awakened the man, who crept out to unbolt the door. He described to the dumbfounded group the war he went through during the night, his legs still trembling in retrospect. Together they searched the floor by the window and found only a cleft straw hat. That must have been the bird-shaped figure—the breeze made the battered old hat flutter. His sword was found beside the dog flap. The blood drops led them to his donkey. Its lips were gashed and a front tooth was knocked out. It must have managed to get loose near daybreak and received that cut as it poked its head through the hole, probably looking for fodder.

The group clung to one another in convulsive fits and laughed all their way home. A fortnight passed before the brave man recovered from the shock.

The Tiger at the Yangtze Gorges

During Kaiyuan reign, the Yangtze Gorges were infested by tigers. Passengers going either upstream or downstream often fell prey to the man-eaters. Then it began—nobody knew when—that each passing boat would leave one passenger on shore for the tiger before it sailed through the Gorges. That practice would guarantee a safe voyage, otherwise more than one life might be lost. And this became an implicit rule among the boats.

So once there came a boat of rich passengers, all rich except one, who was unanimously elected to be the tiger's next meal. Aware that one tongue could not argue against so many, the poor guy agreed to go ashore.

"As a poor fellow," he said, "I understand I must sacrifice myself for you gentlemen. Each man's fate, however, is on the books. Just in case I'm not destined to die in the tiger's jaws, I hope you gentlemen will grant me one, and only one, request."

Somewhat touched, the group asked what his last wish was.

"Now I'm going ashore to look for the tiger. I know full well what I'm doing. Yet, I beg you to wait here for me till noon. If I don't return by then, you may set sail and go on your way."

"We'll do more than that," the group chorused. "We'll stay here throughout the day and spend the night here as well. We'll wait for you till tomorrow morning."

The boat moored and the poor man went ashore with a long-handled ax.

He went into the mountains. There were no trails made

by man but there were sporadic traces of a tiger. The woods grew denser when he came upon a well-tramped beat. He followed it to a mountain pass. The ground was wet and tiger paws could be clearly discerned. Further on, he spotted a cave in the rocks. Peeping in, he saw a Taoist priest sleeping soundly on a couch-shaped flagstone, a tiger skin hung beside him on a dead branch. This must be the lair, where the priest used the skin to change himself into a tiger, he thought to himself. He tiptoed over, grabbed the skin and draped it over his shoulders. He stood beside the couch with a ready ax.

The priest woke up suddenly, only to find the man in possession of the skin.

"You're ordained to be my prey," said the priest. "Why steal my skin?"

"You're fated to fall prey to me," contended the man. "Why call me a thief?"

They argued on and on, and the priest finally gave up. "Well," he sighed, "I had offended god and was banished to the Gorges to be a tiger. I've got to eat 1,000 people just to redeem myself and so far I've finished off 999. You are the 1,000th. Bad luck for me today to have you steal my skin. If you don't give it back to me, I'll have to start all over again and devour another 1,000 people. Listen, I've got an idea that could save both of us. Do you want to hear it?"

"Go ahead."

"Now, you take my skin back to your boat. Cut off some of your hair, beard and finger nails. Wrap them up with two or three pieces of your old clothes and then smear them with blood from your face, arms, legs and other parts of your body. When you see me on the bank tomorrow, throw me my skin so that I can change back into a tiger. Next, toss me that bloody bundle. That'll be as good as having you to eat."

The man agreed and returned to the boat with the tiger skin and ax.

The passengers aboard were more than surprised to behold

him alive. He explained what had happened and prepared a bundle as the priest had told him to. As day broke, the priest was seen on the bank. The man tossed the skin ashore. The moment the priest put it on, he turned into a roaring man-eater. The man then hurled the bloody roll onto the bank, which the tiger gripped in its teeth and bounced away.

Ever since, the Gorges have been free of tigers. It is assumed that having eaten its destined share, it must have returned to heaven.

Translator's note:
What kind of god is it that punishes by demanding the offender to take 1,000 lives? Isn't this god a reflection of a cruel oppressor on earth?

The Disciplinarian

Empress Wu, a believer in Buddhism, forbade the butchering of life. So her courtiers had to keep to a vegetarian diet.

Lou Shide, then head of the Disciplinary Department, once went on an inspection tour to Shan Prefecture where the chef served mutton.

"Her Majesty forbids butchering. How can you have mutton?" demanded Lou sternly.

"The sheep was killed by a jackal, Your Excellency," replied the chef.

"What an intelligent jackal!" remarked Lou, and he savored the mutton.

The next course was fish.

"How is it you killed the fish?" questioned Lou again.

"The jackal killed it as well."

"What a fool you are!" shouted Lou. "Why didn't you say it was killed by an otter!"

"It was indeed killed by an otter, Your Excellency," echoed the chef.

Lou finished off the fish with no qualms.

The Two Brothers

Two brothers of the Xue family lived in Yique, south of Luoyang, the East Capital. Their ancestor had been a high official governing a large jurisdiction, so the family was quite affluent.

One fine day in early summer, a venerable Taoist priest with a flowing silvery beard and wearing a pair of straw sandals appeared at their gate, begging for a cup of water to quench his burning thirst. He had been traveling far, he said.

The two brothers invited him into the reception hall where he talked volubly and vehemently about the Way of Tao. He didn't drop in just to seek a random drink, he confided, but was captivated by the geomantic omens of this place. "Aren't there five twisted pine trees to the southeast of your mansion," the Taoist priest said, "in about 100 steps?" "Indeed there are," responded the brothers, "right in the middle of our best farm land."

The priest seemed excited. He requested a private conversation, and when the servants had withdrawn he lowered his voice to a whisper and told the brothers that buried under the pines were thousands of ounces of gold and a pair of priceless swords. He had been treasure hunting for years and espied an ethereal aura hovering above this area. The bearer of the swords would rise to become a top official. The brothers could keep one, and he would like to have the other to facilitate his magic arts in eliminating evil spirits. As for the gold, they might pass it out to their poorer relatives.

The two brothers were greatly intrigued.

"Tell your servants to get their spades and pickaxes ready. We'll choose an auspicious day to break earth. Then you can see for yourself if what I said is true. But, the slightest disturbance could make the treasures dissipate into the earth and vanish completely if we lack the power to confine them there. So, on that very night we must build an altar on the spot. I'll ascend it to cast a magic spell over the area so that the treasures do not escape. Meanwhile, you must warn your servants against divulging our secret."

"What would Your Reverence need to build the altar?" the brothers inquired.

"Three hundred feet of pure black rope and lots of silk and satin of the five colors for the five positions, that is, green for the east, white for the west, red for the south, black for the north, and yellow for the center, and of course incense burners, joss sticks, tables and chairs, cushions and other necessities. Don't think I covet material goods," he added. "These are for the magic arts. Also, prepare 10 tables of dishes for the gods, complete with wine and fragrant tea. The utensils must all be gold."

The two brothers frantically went about their preparations. It was a demanding task at such short notice, and they were forced to borrow from friends and relatives.

"I'm versed in alchemy," the priest mentioned casually. "To me gold and silver are as cheap as dirt. It's only a means for me to help the needy. And I have trunks of them stored in a temple. Do you mind if I have them transferred here and placed in your trust?"

The brothers were only too pleased to consent.

Without delay, the priest called for his men. They carried in four enormous trunks, heavy beyond measure and securely locked and sealed.

In due course the selected day arrived. A grand ceremonial ritual was held amidst the five pines. The brothers were asked to prostrate themselves before the gods, and then told to go home and wait. "Lock the gate and do not try to peep out," the priest emphasized. "If I am spied on while performing magic arts, immediate disaster will strike me, and you as well. When the spell is cast, I'll raise a torch. Then you can bring in your servants with spades and baskets to do the digging. We can have it done before daybreak. You can't imagine what you'll behold!"

The brothers sat through the night craning their necks toward the distant darkness, but no torch light was seen. Morning came and they threw open the gate. It was very quiet outside, nothing stirred. They walked to the pines. Wine goblets, empty bowls and used plates littered the ground. The gold ceremonial utensils, the colored silk and satin were all gone. Tracks of cart wheels and hoofprints crisscrossed the site. It seemed that even the dark ropes were exploited to fasten the spoils onto the carts.

The two brothers rushed home to pry open the trunks, and what they found was nothing but stones and crumbled bricks.

The brothers were weighed down by self-reproach and debt, and in spite of their being derided as swindlers by their creditors, they were too ashamed to explain. The family had been in decline ever since.

Love-Knot Inn

Wei Gu, orphaned in infancy, had a wish to marry early and have a family, but he was always turned down whenever he proposed.

In the second year of Zhenguan reign, while he was traveling to Qinghe County, he stopped at a small inn south of Songcheng City. A fellow lodger offered to introduce him to the daughter of a retired official in Qinghe County, and arranged for them to meet the very next morning at the gate of the Dragon Rising Temple, west of the inn.

Anxious and excited, Wei was up while the moon was still hanging in the sky, and went straight to the temple. An old man resting against a cloth bag was sitting on the steps, studying a book by the moonlight. Wei leaned forward to have a look, but found the characters in the book altogether unintelligible.

"What's this book you're reading?" he asked with curiosity. "I've devoted myself to books ever since school age and, no bragging, I can read any kind of writing, including writings in Sanskrit. How come I've never seen characters like these?"

"This book isn't intended for humans," the old man smiled in reply. "Little chance that you have come across it."

"But please tell me, what book is it?" Wei persisted.

"This is our book in the nether world."

"If you mean you belong to the nether world, how is it you're out here?"

"Don't accuse me of being out here. Just ask yourself why you're up and about at this hour. Since it's we nether officials who are in charge of the life and death of you humans, do you think it possible for us to avoid mingling ourselves with

234

you? Look, of all those walking creatures in the streets, probably half are humans and half are ghosts. It's a pity your mortal eyes can't tell who is which."

"If that be the case, what are you responsible for?"

"I arrange all the marriage contracts under the moon."

"Gee!" Wei beamed with joy. "You know, I grew up an orphan and have looked forward to an early marriage to extend my family line. However, for the past 10 years at least, all my wooing efforts have come to naught. Today, a friend is going to introduce me to the daughter of an ex-official. Will I succeed this time?"

"I'm afraid not. Your destined wife is only three years old at this moment. She'll not become your bride until she reaches 17."

"What do you carry in your bag?" Wei shifted the topic.

"Some red thread. I use it to tie up a man with his predestined wife by each's ankle. They won't even notice it, but once they're thus connected, there's no way for them to escape their fate, no matter whether they are from opposite sides of a bitter feud or their families sharply differ in wealth and status, and no matter how far apart they may be living at the moment. Your foot has been tied to that girl's. It's no use trying to court anyone else."

"In that case, do you mind telling me where my future wife lives? What's her family?"

"She's the daughter of a greengrocer woman. They live just to the north of the inn."

"Is it possible for me to steal a look at her?"

"The woman often carries her to the market place. If you come with me, I'll point her out."

The sun rose out of the east but the people Wei was expecting didn't show up. The old man placed his book into the bag and set off for the market, and Wei followed. From the other side came a woman blind in one eye, carrying a child about three years old, both raggedly dressed.

"She will be your wife," the old man pointed.

"Can she be killed by some means?" growled Wei, humiliated by the sight.

"No, that's unlikely. As humble as she may seem, this girl has a bright future in store for her, and by virtue of her son, she is to become an entitled lady. How can she be prematurely killed!" So saying, the old man faded from sight.

Wei went back to the inn to sharpen a dagger, which he handed to his servant. "You've never let me down," he said. "Now, go and get rid of that girl for me and I'll give you 10,000 coins!"

"I will," said the servant.

Next morning, the servant went to the market with the dagger hidden in his sleeve. He spotted the girl in the crowd, stabbed, and fled amidst the chaos.

"Did you make it?" Wei asked eagerly.

"I aimed at her heart, but somehow the knife landed between the brows."

Fourteen years went by, during which time Wei made many more matrimonial attempts, but, as always, his efforts didn't lead to marriage. Then, as a posthumous honor to his diseased father, a position was opened for him in the Xiang Prefecture garrison force. Wang Tai, the prefect, appointed him a deputy chief of the law department. His abilities soon won Wang's favors and he decided to give Wei the hand of his beautiful 17-year-old daughter.

Wei was gratified to have a wife but, strange to say, she always wore a flower sticker between her brows. She would not remove it even when they were home alone, not even when she was taking a bath.

After a year of dogged questioning, Wei finally managed to draw out his wife's unhappy past. She, in fact, was a niece of the prefect, not his daughter, she confided. Her father had been the mayor of Songcheng City and had died at his post when she was a baby. Then her mother and brother passed away too. All that was left was a farm house south of the town, where she and her wet nurse took shelter. The nurse grew vegetables and sold them at a nearby market to make a living. Reluctant to leave her alone at home, the wet nurse would often take her along. Then one day in the market place, when she was about three, a scoundrel struck her with a knife and left her a permanent scar, which she had been trying to hide with a flower sticker. Seven or eight years after that, her uncle was transferred to Lulong. He found her and raised her as his own child.

"Was your wet nurse blind in one eye?" Wei asked.

"She was! How do you know?"

"It was me who had you stabbed!" Wei confessed, and told her the whole story. They marveled at their fate, and their marriage seemed all the sweeter to them after all those misadventures.

A son was born who later became the prefect of Yanmen, and his mother consequently had a ladyship conferred upon her. How life is predestined!

When the new mayor of Songcheng City heard this story, he renamed the inn Love-Knot Inn.

The Blushing Cheeks

Cui Hu, a handsome young scholar who had just succeeded in the imperial examination, was a quiet man, not the type that enjoyed a rowdy association with friends and peers.

On the Day of Qingming, a spring holiday in memory of the dead, he went on a lone excursion out of the capital into the southern suburbs. His roving led him to a village where he saw among the spring blossoms a little cottage. It was all quiet as if unoccupied. He knocked at the gate. After a long pause, a girl peeped out. "Who's it?" she asked.

He gave his name. "I came out of town alone," he explained, "to have a look at spring. I'm thirsty. May I have some water?"

The girl went back into the house and returned with a cup of water. She opened the gate and offered him a stool. Then she leaned against an extended bough of a blooming peach tree to watch him. She was rather good-looking, more charming perhaps than he had expected of a village girl. Her eyes twinkled with eloquence. He tried to strike up a conversation without success. Nevertheless, that didn't make them avoid each other's gaze.

Now it was time to leave. She saw him to the gate and suddenly dashed back into the room as if her emotions might burst at any moment. With each step he took, he glanced back over his shoulder.

He didn't visit that village again until Qingming in the following year. The festival reminded him of the girl and the urge to see her was so strong that he could not help going in that direction.

The cottage stood silently as it had before, but a lock was

239

hanging on the gate. Disappointed, he wrote a poem on the left plank of the double door.

> This day last year behind the double door
> Peach blooms contended with her rosy cheeks.
> Where are those blushing cheeks that smile no more?
> Alone the blossoms face the vernal breeze.

Several days later, business happened to take him to the southern suburbs, so he made a detour to the village. Wails and moans issued from the courtyard. He knocked to inquire. An elder answered the door. "You are Cui Hu, aren't you?" he asked.

"That's me."

"You killed my daughter!" the old man burst out in tears. Taken by surprise, he didn't know what to say.

"She was 15 and had learned to read and write. Starting from about this time last year, I found she was often lost in a trance. Several days ago when we returned home, there was a poem on the left plank of the gate. She read it and went straight to bed, down and ill. She ate not a grain after that, and now she's dead! She was my only child. I am old and had hoped to engage her to a gentleman. In that way I wouldn't have to worry about my remaining years. That's why I didn't hurry to marry her off. But she should not have died so young. Isn't it you who killed her?" He threw himself on Cui's shoulders and sobbed bitterly. Cui was touched to the quick. He asked for permission to go inside to pay his last respects.

She was lying on her bed as if in a sound sleep. He lifted her head onto his lap and wailed, "It's me! It's me!" Suddenly her eyes jerked open, and after a while she regained her senses. The old man was happy beyond words. He approved their marriage right away.

Re-matching the Broken Mirror

Xu Deyan was a counselor to the crown prince of the Chen Dynasty. His wife was the beautiful and gifted sister of the emperor. This was during a chaotic time.

Realizing that the fall of the empire was but a matter of days, he said to his wife, "Because of your charm and talent, I'm afraid you can't escape the fate of being seized and concubined by some enemy general when the city is occupied. We shall never be able to meet again. If you then still have a place for me in your heart and hope to see me, here is a token of faith." So saying, he broke a bronze mirror in half and gave his wife one piece.

"Try to sell this piece at a major market on the first full-moon day of the year. If I am alive, I'll search for it in the markets on that very day," he said as a farewell promise.

The Chen Dynasty was overthrown, and as he had predicted, the princess was taken by Yang Su, commander-in-chief of the triumphant army. Yang didn't hesitate to lavish money and affection on her.

Meanwhile, Xu fled town and wandered from place to place in utter distress. He finally managed to reach the capital of Sui.

On the full-moon day of the first lunar month, he went to the town market. There he saw a man-servant hawking a half mirror for a forbidding price, which drew taunts and jeers from the passers-by.

Xu hurried the servant to his quarters and offered him food. While disclosing his story, he took out the other half of the mirror. The two pieces matched perfectly. On the mirror he wrote:

241

> Gone is she whom it once portrayed;
> It now returns to reunite,
> Without the image it relayed—
> Blank as the full moon's aimless light.

The princess shed night-long tears over the poem and refused to eat any more. Yang was moved when he learned of the reason. He sent for Xu. At the banquet, Yang asked the princess to compose a poem in response. She wrote:

> Is fate again to flip a latch,
> To make my new lord face my old?
> Neither should I be glad or sad,
> For life as always holds a catch.

The banquet being over, Yang handed back the princess to Xu, together with a handsome endowment. Xu and his wife returned to the south and lived happily ever after.

Translator's note:

The often-quoted Chinese idiom "broken mirror re-matched" originated from this story, symbolizing the happy reunion of a broken marriage or of a long-separated couple. Ancient Chinese mirrors were highly polished bronze disks.

The Departed Soul
(abridged*)

In the third year of Tianshou reign, an official named Zhang
Yi was transferred to Heng Prefecture. As a prudent man, he
didn't have a wide circle of friends. He had no sons but two
daughters. The elder one died early; the younger one was
called Qianniang, beautiful beyond compare. He also had a
nephew with him, his sister's son Wang Zhou, who was a
bright, handsome lad. Zhang thought highly of his nephew
and remarked more than once that the two youngsters would
be a perfect couple when they came of age.

The two grew up admiring each other and wished the time
would come for them to be man and wife. Yet, because of
etiquette, that wish was kept their secret.

Then one day a colleague asked Zhang for Qianniang's
hand, and Zhang consented. Qianniang was grieved by the
news and Wang was deeply hurt and dejected. Arguing that
it was time for him to seek an official career, he asked his
uncle for permission to leave for the capital. Since he was so
determined, Zhang sent him on his way with an ample purse.

The young man boarded a boat and departed with a
bleeding heart. At sunset his boat moored at the foot of a
mountain. Midnight came and passed, yet tormented by his
unfortunate love he could not sleep a wink. Suddenly, he
heard rapid footsteps scudding along the bank. In no time he
saw a figure approaching the boat. Who could it be but
Qianniang coming barefoot! He grasped her hands in ecstasy
and asked how she managed to follow him.

---

* A postscript has been deleted.

"For so many years," she sobbed, "we've been together. Our mutual feelings run deep. Now that I know you still hold me dear in your heart even when I'm to be married off to someone else, I'd rather die for you than let my will be violated. I've made up my mind to elope with you, come what may!"

This unexpected bliss made Wang's heart pound with joy. He hid her in the boat which immediately set sail. Traveling nights as well as days, in a few months they arrived in Shu.

Five years rolled by and two sons were born. Throughout this period they remained out of touch with Zhang and their relatives. A sense of homesickness had gradually developed in Qianniang till one day she poured out her mind to her husband, "That day when I deserted my parents to come after you, I went against a maiden's behavior code. For five years I wasn't able to attend to them. If anything should happen to them, what face do I have to live on alone?" Touched by her fidelity, Wang promised to take her and the children home.

Arriving in Heng Prefecture, Wang left Qianniang and his sons in the boat and went ahead alone to see his uncle and apologize for their elopement.

"Qianniang is in her boudoir!" Zhang exclaimed as Wang tried to explain. "She has been in bed ill for years. How can you fabricate such a ridiculous story!"

"She is now in a boat outside town," Wang insisted.

In utter bewilderment, Zhang dispatched a servant, who saw Qianniang on the boat, alive and exuberant. She even asked the servant about her parents. The puzzled servant rushed back to make a report. As soon as the girl in bed heard of it, her face lit up and she jumped out of bed to make up and dress. All this she did with a contented smile, but without a word. Then she came out to meet the other girl. There they merged into one—even their clothes blended perfectly.

Translator's note:
In the feudal times, young men and women did not have the freedom to choose a spouse. Their marriages were literally "arranged" by their

parents. On their part, they could only obey. It was in this stifling atmosphere that many fascinating stories were created to express suppressed yearnings for the freedom to love, such as marriage after death or in a dream. This story is outstanding in that one's wish can be fulfilled by the separation of the soul from the body. A behavior code can chain down a listless body, but cannot shackle the soul.

Mr. Shentu's Wife

In the ninth year of Zhenyuan reign, Shentu Cheng, a commoner, was appointed lieutenant of Shifang County in Shu. On his way to assume office he encountered a heavy snowstorm several miles east of Zhenfu, so heavy that his horse could not plow through. Not far from the road he saw a thatched hut which seemed to be full of life and warmth, so he made for it.

An aged couple and a girl about 14 or 15 years old were sitting around a fire. Her shabby clothes and uncombed hair did not eclipse her soft alabaster skin, petal-like cheeks, and the kindling fire in her eyes. The old couple hurried to their feet as they saw him enter. "Please come in and warm yourself by the fire," they said. "It's harsh weather for traveling."

The afternoon waned but the storm showed no sign of letting up. "Town is still far off to the west. May I put up here for the night?" he asked since he saw little hope of resuming his travel.

"If you don't mind the simplicity of our place, we would be honored to have you stay with us," said the old couple. He thus unsaddled his horse and took in his baggage.

Seeing that he would stay, the daughter went in to put on powder and rouge. When she returned from behind the corn-stalk screen, he found that she was much more beautiful than he had imagined.

The old woman came in from somewhere with a flask of wine and warmed it up over the fire. "Traveling through snow can be freezing," she said. "Please have a drink to drive off the cold."

"It's most kind of you," he said with a bow. "Mr. Host first, please."

The old man picked up the flask and took a sip, then

passed it on. When it was his turn, Shentu said, "Why isn't the young lady joining us?"

"Country girls are unaccustomed to having guests," smiled the old couple.

"Why grudge a cup of wine?" the girl flashed her eyes defiantly. "If you think I'm not entitled to a drink, just say so." Her mother tugged at her skirt and motioned her to take a seat beside her.

Curious to sound out the depth of this country lass, he suggested they play a drinkers' word game. "We shall quote from the poems to describe our present situation." Holding up his cup, he took the lead:

> On such a tedious night,
> Leave not until you're tight.

Lowering her eyes, the girl smiled and carried on,

> Weather and night forbid.
> Where go you, had you wished?

Now it was her turn to lead.

> Though cloud and storm aggress,
> Cocks crow nevertheless.

The quote took him by surprise.* "You're unbelievably talented!" he exclaimed. "Thank heaven that I am not married yet." Turning to the old man he asked, "Would you accept it if I should propose to her on my own behalf without first sending over a match-maker?"

"Humble as we are," replied the old man, "we do treasure her. To be frank, quite a few passers-by have offered gold and silk for her hand. We turned them down because we were reluctant to part with her. Now that you are proposing, I don't think we can hold her back any longer. She is yours." With that permission, Shentu knelt and performed the initial cere-

---

* The quote took him by surprise because the next lines are: *Now that my man has come, / My joy is maximum.*

monies of a son-in-law, and gave them as a betrothal gift all
he had with him.

"It's enough of a solace to know that you don't mind our
low and impoverished conditions," said the old woman, declining his offer. "We have no desire for gifts or money."

The next day, the old woman said to him, "This is a
desolate place, and our house is very inconvenient, so we are
not going to retain you for long. Since she is now married to
you, take her away." With lots of tears and good wishes the
young couple set off the following morning, the bride on
horseback, the bridegroom leading the reins.

His salary as a county official was meager, but his wife
managed quite well. Within weeks she had acquired many
new friends and a good reputation. They lived in ever-
increasing happiness. Her kindness was also extended to
relatives and to servants. Everyone liked her.

By the end of his third year in office, they had a son and
a daughter. Very lovely kids. He was all praises for her, and
to her he dedicated a poem:

> As modest as my status be,
> Your management has made us free.
> To what shall I compare our love?
> A couple of mandarin ducks.

His wife savored the poem. Her lips mumbled thoughtfully
every time she read it to herself, but she never came up with
a corresponding one. "To be the wife of a gentleman," as she
had often put it, "one can't be ignorant of books. But if one
should overdo her part by starting to write poems, she would
be degrading herself like a courtesan."

At the expiration of his tenure Shentu decided to bring
his whole family back to his hometown. Through Lizhou
Prefecture, they came to the Jialing River. Resting on the grass
by the river, his wife suddenly let out a heavy sigh. "On the
day you presented that poem to me," she admitted, "I impro-
vised one in response to yours. I had intended to keep it to

myself. Today's scene, however, makes it too hard for me to hold it back any longer. Here it goes:

> Though we're attuned like lute to harp,
> I can't reject the mountains sharp.
> What if there comes a change of fate
> That shall our bright future negate?"

Having thus declaimed it to the accompaniment of trickling tears, she sat motionless for a long while, as if her soul had wandered off.

"A good poem indeed," he remarked, "but mountain life does not seem fit for one so delicate as you. If it is because you miss your parents, why those tears? You should be happy rather than sad. We are approaching your native place. One's fate is always predestined. Don't let that worry you."

In another 20 days they reached his wife's maiden home. The thatched hut was still there as it had been, but it was deserted. They unpacked and put up in the hut. His wife became lost in thought, weeping from dawn to dusk. Beneath a pile of worn clothes in one corner of the room they found a dust-covered tiger skin. At the sight of it, his wife burst into laughter. "I really didn't expect to see this skin again!" she exclaimed. As soon as she wrapped it around her shoulders, she changed into a tigress. Roaring and pouncing, she dashed out of the door, leaving Shentu stupefied with fright.

Carrying the two children, he traced her in vain into the mountain depth. They wept and cried for days through the trackless forest, but she did not return.

Translator's note:
Love is universal, and these ancient love stories are not confined to relations between man and woman, but also between man and animal, man and nature ("The Conch Girl"), man and a portrait ("The Maiden on the Painted Screen"), man and a goddess ("Charcoal Valley"), and even across different realms of existence ("Zhang's Daughter").

The Conch Girl

Wu Kan, a submissive and kind-hearted clerk of the government of Yixing County, was a bachelor. As he was orphaned in early childhood, he had no brothers or relatives. He lived alone by a spring, and loved the stream so much that he built a low fence along that stretch of flow to prevent the water from being contaminated. Every day when he came home from the office he would watch it ripple and murmur along. He felt deep respect and attachment for it.

Years passed, and one morning he discovered a white conch in the shallows of the stream. He brought it home and kept it in a water-vat. That day when he returned from work he found that dinner was waiting for him on the table, and he sat down to eat. Things went on like that for nearly a fortnight. He guessed that it was a kindness from the old woman living next door, who often took pity on his lonely condition. She must have dropped by to help him with the cooking. So he went over to express his gratitude.

"You don't need to be shy," the old woman said. "I know you've recently got a nice girl. As for me, I didn't do anything that deserves your thanks."

"Don't kid me, ma'am. You know I'm too poor to marry."

"Me, kidding? Everyday after you've left for your office, I see a charming girl of 17 or 18 years old coming out of your house. Her clothes are bright and flimsy. And she retires into the house when she finishes cooking."

Suspecting that it was the white conch, he arranged with the old woman that the next day he would pretend to go to the office as usual, but would sneak back instead and hide in her house to see for himself.

As he peeped out through a chink next morning, he saw a girl emerge from his cottage and enter the kitchen* to prepare food. He slipped home and barred the door. Blocking the girl's way into the house, he made a deep bow.

"Heaven appreciates your efforts to protect the water source. You've done your share. Heaven is also aware of your loneliness, so I am sent here to be your wife. Hope you can accept my sincerity without suspicion."

He was more than pleased.

They became the most happy couple, and their story quickly spread throughout the neighborhood. Of course, not without some exaggeration.

In no time their story reached the ear of the county magistrate, and the rumored beauty of Wu's wife brewed his lustful dreams. But Wu had always been a cautious man, betraying no convenient excuse for a penalty.

One day the magistrate said to Wu, "You're a veteran on my staff, and a competent one. Now, go and get me some frog hair and a ghost arm. If you fail to hand them in by the end of the day, you shall be severely punished!"

Wu didn't dare object, though he clearly knew those things did not exist on earth. Depressed and worried, he went home to impart the bad news to his wife. "Darling," he sighed, "I am done for."

"If he had asked for something else, I might not be able to procure them, but these two things won't cause a problem," his wife smiled reassuringly.

Though he couldn't help being skeptical, his wife's confidence somewhat relieved his mind. She excused herself from

---

* In rural areas, the kitchen is often a hut outside the house. Barring the door was to prevent the girl from reaching her shell, in case she should change back into a conch. The shell here functions as the tiger skin to the priest in "The Tiger at the Yangtze Gorges" or to the girl in "Mr. Shentu's Wife." Props like these sometimes were instrumental to the transformation of shape.

253

the room and presently returned with the two articles, which he handed to the magistrate.

"Well done," the magistrate sneered. "You can leave now." Yet, in his mind he was still thinking of ways to have Wu killed.

Another day, he summoned Wu again. "I want a snail polliwog," he said. "Better hurry, or you'll be courting death."

Wu rushed home to tell his wife.

"That's not very difficult to obtain," his wife said calmly. "I happen to have one at home. Let me go and fetch it."

After what seemed an eternity, she returned with a dog-shaped animal and claimed it was a snail polliwog.

"What's so special about it?" Wu asked.

"It's a unique species. It can eat fire. I think you must run now."

"I asked for a snail polliwog, not a mongrel dog!" snarled the magistrate as soon as he saw the animal Wu led in. "Well, anything extraordinary about it?"

"Yes, sir, it eats fire and its droppings are fiery, too," Wu replied.

The magistrate wasted no time to send for burning charcoal. The animal devoured it and discharged burning excrement on the floor.

"What good is this damned animal!" raged the magistrate. "Choke the fire and sweep up the droppings!"

He was about to order Wu's execution when the footman's broom touched the droppings. Flames shot up to the ceiling; smoke shrouded the whole town; and the magistrate and his whole family were burned to ashes. Wu and his wife were never seen again. The town was consequently moved several rods west to its present site.

Translator's note:

Though environmental concerns seem to be new to modern times, its history in fact can be traced back thousands of years. One difference is that nowadays we protect our environment by law, while the ancients resorted to rewards and punishments from heaven.

Zhang's Daughter

Zhang Guo, chief of staff of Yi Prefecture in mid Kaiyuan reign, had a daughter who died of an illness at the age of 15.

It was the custom of the time to send one's remains back to the family burial ground but, as Zhang was reluctant to part with his daughter, he buried her by the summerhouse in the eastern courtyard of the official compound. Not long after, he was transferred to Zheng Prefecture. Citing the long distance and trouble for a reburial, he left the coffin buried in the eastern courtyard.

His position was soon filled by Liu Yi. Liu's son took a liking of the summerhouse and often spent the nights there.

One evening as the son was taking a stroll in the open, he saw a beautiful girl coming his way. Thinking that she might be escaping a forced marriage, he hailed her and invited her to come in. She stayed for the night. Her tender affections and refined manners won the young man's heart.

After that, the girl would come at dusk and stay till dawn. Things developed happily for months. Then one night she disclosed that she was the spirit of the former chief's daughter. She had suffered a premature death and was buried near the summerhouse. As she was not predestined to die so young she now had an opportunity to return to life and become his wife. If, on the third day from now, he would dig up her coffin and let her out, she would be able to regain her life. "Don't be frightened when you see a corpse arise from bed," she cautioned. She pointed to the site of her grave and vanished.

On the appointed night, the excited young Liu brought a confidential servant along to help him dig. Four or five feet down they hit a painted coffin. Carefully prying it open, they

255

saw the girl, her looks still fresh, her limbs soft and supple, and her clothes clean and intact. They lifted her onto the bed, and gradually she seemed to be breathing. Then her lips moved. They tried to feed her thin porridge, and she did swallow a little. By daybreak she was able to speak and sit up.

After his first excitement, young Liu soon began to worry that his parents might learn about the existence of the girl. Under the pretense of being preoccupied with his studies, he kept himself in the summerhouse and even ordered his meals to be sent there.

The father became suspicious. One day while his son was out seeing guests off, he took the chance to peep into the summerhouse and discovered the girl. Upon his inquiry, she told him the whole story and showed him the coffin boards hidden under the bed.

The parents were deeply touched by her sincerity and the wonders of the unknown world. She should have let them know earlier, they reproached kindly, and brought her to the main house where they offered her a room.

The son was stunned when he returned to find the girl missing.

"Why did you hide her away from us?" said the father. "Are you afraid we older people won't be appreciative of this inter-world relationship? A resurrection like this happens once in 1,000 years!"

They immediately dispatched a messenger to Zheng Prefecture to deliver the news to Zhang Guo, and asked for his blessing. Overcoming their first shock, the Zhangs erupted with tears and smiles. They hurried to Yi Prefecture to marry their daughter to young Liu.

So the couple enjoyed a long and happy life and had many children.

Translator's note:

This story can be regarded as the blueprint for the famous Ming Dynasty (1368-1644) play The Peony Pavilion *(1598).*

The Maiden on the Painted Screen

Zhao Yan, a scholar in the Tang Dynasty, bought a foldable cloth-screen from an artist on which was painted a maiden of unusual charms.

"It's a pity there isn't such a beauty on earth," he remarked. "If she could come to life, I would marry her!"

"Well," the artist replied, "my painting is no ordinary painting, for it has captured the spirit. This maiden I painted does have a name—she is called Zhenzhen. If one keeps calling her name for 100 days continuously, she will respond to his calls. What is vital then is he must immediately pour a cup of wine down her throat, and she'll come to life. The wine should be mixed with ashes of burnt multicolored silk collected from 100 households."

Zhao followed the artist's instructions and mounted a calling vigil. On the 100th day the maiden on the screen answered, "Fine." He poured down her throat a cup of ash-mixed wine and the figure stepped down from the screen. "Thank you for summoning me," she smiled. "I will gladly perform the duties of a faithful wife." She ate and talked in a perfectly human way. In a year, she gave birth to a boy.

Their son was one year old when a friend said to Zhao, "Your wife is a devil in human form. If you don't get rid of her, she'll bring you bad fortune. I can lend you my magic sword. It will do the job."

That evening, as was promised, his friend had the sword sent over to his place. Hardly had he brought the sword into the room when Zhenzhen started to weep. "Your humble wife is none other than the goddess of Mount Heng. I don't know how someone could have had my image sketched down, but since you called my name so earnestly, I felt obliged to comply with your wish. Now that you suspect me, I can no longer live with you." So saying, she led their son by the hand and both walked onto the screen. She spewed up the ash wine.

Except for the added boy by her side, the painting looked exactly as it had been two years before—a most lovely portrait on canvas.

Charcoal Valley

In the early years of Yuanhe reign, a man named Ma Shiliang committed an offense against the law. Under the administration of the mayor of the capital, a Mr. Wang who was renowned for favoring harsh punishments, a crime like that usually meant a death sentence. So Ma fled into the Southern Hills and huddled behind a big willow tree by a pond in Charcoal Valley.

At daybreak, he saw a fairy descending to the waterside on a puff of rosy cloud. She picked up a gold hammer and knocked several times on a jade slab. A bud stemmed from the lotus in the pond and gradually bloomed open, revealing a green seedpod in its hold. The fairy plucked three or four seeds from the pod and ate. Then she rode off on the cloud.

Seeing that the hammer and slab were left on the ground, he jumped out from his hiding place and knocked as the fairy had done. The lotus didn't fail to bud and bloom again. As he savored the dozen remaining seeds, he felt himself becoming weightless. So up the vines he climbed toward where the rosy cloud had disappeared. Once atop, he saw a complex of magnificent palaces. Among the celestial beings was the fairy he had seen. Surprised at the sight of a stranger, they rushed down the steps and hit him with their bamboo sticks. He fell down and down through the air, and landed beside a creek where he dozed off with exhaustion.

When he woke up he saw a girl sharpening a knife. Her hair was combed up in double curls. "I'm ordered to take your life, because you've stolen the forbidden pills," she said.

He dropped to his knees in a panic and begged for mercy. "There is no way to escape a fatal stab," she said. "Only the magic elixir can save you, but you must make me your wife."

Having his word of honor, she excused herself, and after a while returned with steamed rice in a small aqua-green porcelain bowl. No sooner had he finished off the rice than he fell into a slumber.

When he awoke the girl told him that the medicine was ready and produced, to his great admiration, seven sparkling translucent pills. Following her gaze, he looked down to see a faint scarlet cut in his chest as though done by a sharp blade. As she rubbed the pills over the wound it healed without even leaving a scar.

"Don't tell anyone of the secrets," she warned, "or the gash will burst. I'm the daughter of the Charcoal Valley god guarding the forbidden pills. That's why I am able to save your life."

They lived in the valley ever after, and up to the early years of Huichang reign people going there would chance upon them from time to time. If a disappointed angler should be going home empty-handed, he could drop a note into the pond. Fish of the exact weight he asked for would then be dangling on his hook.

Translator's note:
Readers might have noticed that in the love stories between a human being and a supernatural being, the supernatural being is usually the female, and it is almost always the female who takes the initiative. In the feudal days of China, men had relatively more freedom in choosing a spouse, while women had to wait to be chosen, or to be married off by her parents. The suppressed craving for the freedom to love on the part of a good woman finds antithetical expression in literary works. Even then, though, it is more often than not expressed metaphorically—the high-bred as goddesses, the low-bred as ghosts. For example, see "Mr. Tan's Bedmate."

Sea Giants

He Luguang, military commissioner of Canton Region, was born in a village by the South Sea. He said that in his life he had seen with his own eyes three mysterious things.

One was two islets about 200 miles offshore. On fine mornings they looked distinct and near, luxuriant with growth. In late Kaiyuan reign, a severe thunder storm broke out on the ocean. But instead of rain, what fell down was mud, a kind of light, foamy mud. For seven days the sky was darkened. Fishermen passing by the islets said that a giant fish, carried by the current, was caught between the two islets. Somehow one of its gills was hooked to a crag. The thunder was its roar; the mud rain was produced by its gasping; and the darkness was caused by the air it spurted out. On the seventh day, however, the crag collapsed and the fish escaped.

Another mystery was an immense patch of land in the sea, thousands of miles in circumference. Crouching on that "island" were several warty creatures shaped more or less like toads, only much larger. The bigger ones could be more than 100 miles around, and even the smaller ones were no less than scores of miles. On full moon nights, they would breathe out a kind of white luminous vapor into the sky, which virtually outshone the moon.

The third strange thing usually happened in early summer. Colossal snakes would appear by the mountain peaks in the sea. The snake could erect itself so high that its tail was often lost in the clouds. In late Kaiyuan reign, one of those snakes came to drink at the sea. It coiled itself around a peak and lowered its head to suck the sea water. It seemed to be extremely thirsty, for the sea level dropped for more than a dozen days straight. Subsequently, it looked as if it was being swallowed by an even larger creature in the sea. In half a day, the mountain crumbled and both the snake and mountain were engulfed. There was no way to imagine what kind of monster was hidden in that ocean.

Translator's note:

It is not difficult for modern readers to figure out that the strange creatures described in the stories are in fact three natural phenomena. The first story is a volcano eruption. The fish's gaping mouth is nothing but the crater of the volcano. The mysterious island in the second story could be an exceptionally large seaweed pad or plankton bloom—their size is certainly much exaggerated. Seaweed and plankton are usually phosphate-rich, and can give off phosphorescent light under certain conditions. The last is a description of a typhoon. Its cyclonic funnel does look like a coiling snake to an imaginative eye.

These three mystery tales are revealing in that they illustrate the origins of some mythical stories.

The Snake on the Shoulder-Pole

Once upon a time, a young scholar saw a small snake lying on the road. He picked it up and fed it. In a few months, it grew so big that he had to carry it in a basket on his shoulder-pole. He nicknamed it "my shoulder-pole baby." Gradually, it grew too heavy even to carry on his shoulder. So he released it into the vast swamp to the east of Fan County.

Forty years slipped by and the snake grew to the size of an overturned boat. People called it "the holy python." Anyone who ventured out into the swamp would be swallowed. It just happened that the scholar, now at a doddering age, once again traveled past that place. People warned, "Don't try to go through the swamp. A man-eating python lives there."

It was freezing winter then. The scholar replied, "Snakes hibernate in winter. They won't come out." So he went ahead. About six miles into the swamp, he suddenly noticed a snake chasing him. He thought he could still recognize the pattern and color of its coat. "Aren't you my shoulder-pole baby?" he cried out. The snake dropped its head. After a good while, it turned away.

The scholar reached Fan County, and so did his story of near escape. The magistrate conjectured that anyone who could have survived an encounter with the snake could not but be a sort of sorcerer. Upon that accusation the scholar was thrown into jail with a death sentence. In anger, he mumbled, "My shoulder-pole baby, I fed you and raised you, and you should cause me my death! Isn't that rather ironic?"

That night, the entire county was sunk by the snake and turned into a boundless lake. Only the prison was not engulfed. The scholar went free.

263

Toward the end of Tianbao reign, the magistrate of Fan County was an uncle of Mr. Dugu Xian. He and his family went boating on the lake on the third day of the third lunar month. The weather was fine but their boat capsized, drowning many.

Appended: A Granny in Qiongdu County

In Qiongdu County, Ye Prefecture, there was a poor granny living alone. Every time she had a meal, a small snake with tiny horns would crawl over to her feet to keep her company, and she would share her food with it. As years went by, it grew to a dozen feet.

One day, the county magistrate's horse was swallowed by the snake. The enraged magistrate had the granny arrested and interrogated.

"It lives under my bed," she said.

They dug very deep but found no snake. So the magistrate ordered her execution.

That night, he had a dream. The snake said to him, "Why kill my mom? She shall be avenged!"

After that, he often heard the rumbling of storms in his ears. In the late afternoon of the 30th day, people suddenly began a strange way of greeting. "Why are you wearing fish on your head?" one would say to another.

That night, the county town and the surrounding area for a dozen miles caved in and became a huge lake, which the locals later named Lake Qiong. Only granny's house remained above water. And its foundation is preserved to this day. Fishermen usually spend the nights there. People say they can see town walls and buildings in the clear waters.

Translator's note:

Obviously "The Snake on the Shoulder-Pole" and "A Granny in Qiongdu County" developed from the same source, though they were located far apart: The former on the eastern plains within the inundated area of the Yellow River, the latter in the remote mountainous region of the southwest. The cause of these disasters, and other similar stories in Records of the Taiping Era, could have been an earthquake, for the latter, which is probably closer to the origin, still bears a typical indication of a quake—the rumbling noise.

The Tumor

Entertainer Diao Junchao's wife, a native of eastern Shu, had a tumor on her neck. At first it was no bigger than an egg, but gradually it grew to the size of a gallon jar. And in five years it became as big as a huge water-vat, so heavy that she could hardly move. What was more frightening was that faint sounds like those made by a band of wind and stringed instruments could be heard within, and if one listened attentively, one could even recognize certain melodies.

Years later, millions of tiny pores appeared on the surface of the tumor, from which threads of white vapor would issue whenever it was about to rain. And when the opaque wisps gathered into a cloud, rain would fall.

Diao's relatives were so terrified that they implored him to send his wife away into the deep mountains. Though he was reluctant to part with his wife, he could no longer ignore the increasing social pressure.

"I can't hold out any longer however much I care for you," he said to his wife at last. "I have to find you a cave in the uninhabited mountains and send you there. You can understand, can't you?"

"I know this disease is disgusting," muttered his wife. "I'm dying anyway, whether you send me away or keep me here. So, why don't you cut it off for me and see what's in there?"

Diao went to sharpen a knife, and when he returned to his wife's bedside a loud commotion was heard within the tumor. It suddenly burst, and a simian jumped out and skipped away. All Diao could do was to dress the gaping wound with gauze. Although the tumor was now removed, his wife had slipped into a deep coma.

Next day, a Taoist priest knocked at the gate. "I am the simian from the tumor," he introduced himself. "To be frank, I'm a monkey spirit, and I can evoke winds and rain. To cut a long story short, I somehow got involved with the old dragon living in the Devil's Headache Gorge of the Han River. I would predict the approaching of vessels and he would have them capsized so I could collect the food on board for my offspring.

"The other day, God had the evil dragon executed and was searching for his accomplices. To save my life, I was forced to seek shelter in your wife's beautiful neck. Though that in no way impaired her fortune, I did cause her much discomfort over the years. So yesterday I paid the god of Mount Phoenix a visit and asked him for a little magic ointment. You may try it now. It should show immediate effects."

As soon as the medicine was applied, the wound healed. Diao was so happy that he killed chickens to make dinner for the priest. Satiated with food and drink, the priest started to sing, and accompanied himself with vocal mimicries of various kinds of musical instruments, which sounded as sweet as real ones. After that meal, no one ever saw him again.

This happened in Dading reign of the Northern Zhou Dynasty.

Translator's note:
Thyroid tumor was a common disease in the hinterlands, but a lack of scientific knowledge shrouded it in an aura of mystery. To some extent, it was by the brave experiments of people like Diao Junchao in this story that we gradually learned it can be surgically removed.

The Polyps

In the year of Yongzhen, there lived in the capital a literate businessman named Wang Bu. He was very rich, and his business relations spread far and wide.

He had a lovely daughter of about 15. She was talented and pretty, except for an inch-long polyp hanging out from each nostril on fine filaments, like pea pods dangling on a plant. An accidental touch would send a sharp pain down her spine. Millions were spent on it, but no doctor or medicine ever worked.

One day, a Buddhist monk came begging for alms at the gate. "I hear your daughter is affected with an unusual disease," he remarked to Wang. "May I see her? I might have a cure."

Wang was overjoyed and immediately sent for his daughter. The monk took out some white powder and blew it into the girl's nostrils. After a while, he plucked the polyps off. Except for the oozing of a little yellow fluid, the girl didn't even feel pain.

The monk declined the 100 ounces of gold Wang offered in reward, saying that monks had no need for money, but he begged for permission to keep the two polyps, which Wang ungrudgingly gave. Holding them dearly, the monk ran away as if escaping. Wang thought that this must be the way holy persons behave.

The monk couldn't have gone half a dozen blocks when a handsome lad with a face as white and smooth as alabaster came riding on a similarly white horse. He knocked at the gate and inquired whether they had seen a foreign monk. Wang invited him in and told him what had happened.

The lad sighed and groaned, "If only my horse hadn't hurt its hoof! How could I have let him get the better of me!"

Wang was puzzled, and asked why.

"I am a celestial being," the lad confided. "Two music gods are missing from heaven, and God just learned they were hiding in your daughter's polyps. He therefore ordered me to bring them back, but I let that monk take them first! I am doomed."

Wang bowed in respect. When he raised his head, the lad was already out of sight.

The Monk in Jiang Prefecture

This happened in Yonghui reign. A Buddhist monk in Jiang Prefecture was dying. For years he had suffered from a lump in his throat and could hardly eat solid food. At his final moments, he summoned his disciples to his bedside and told them that after he had breathed his last they should dissect his throat and chest to find out what had been choking him for so long. In that way they might be able to learn about the cause of his death.

His disciples did as bidden and discovered in his chest an alien object shaped like a fish, but with two heads and fleshy scales over its body. It jumped and flipped when it was thrown into a bowl. Out of curiosity, they placed many different kinds of food in the bowl. Though it did not actually eat any of the food, all the food was turned into water after a short while. Then they tried miscellaneous types of poison, and as before, everything was invariably resolved into watery transparency.

It was summer then, harvest time for the indigo plant. By the stream near the temple the other monks were busily making pigment out of this plant. One disciple happened to go there and returned with a little of the pigment which he dropped into the bowl.

The fish-shaped thing started to scud along the circumference of the bottom as if attempting to avoid the indigo. Before long, the fleshy lump was dissolved in the water.

People now believe that indigo pigment can cure esophageal tumors.

Translator's note:

In a manner of speaking, the monk dedicated his body to the development of medical science in which he, who lived nearly 1,400 years ago, still merits our respect. Early science was mostly a matter of trial and error.

The Ingenious Carpenter

Yang Wulian, the imperial carpenter, often came up with ingenious ideas.

Once at Qinzhou City he made a wooden monk which, holding a bowl in its hand, could go begging on it own. When the bowl was filled with copper coins, a switch would click on, and the monk would utter a prayer in gratitude for the alms.

People from all over the city flocked to see that wooden wonder. As they were eager to hear it speak, the bowl was frequently filled. In that way, the wooden monk could earn several thousand copper coins a day.

Translator's note:

For handicraft wonders see also "The Carpenter and His Wooden Cranes" and "The Pink Sleeve."

An Ancient Tomb

Li Miao, the governor's senior adjutant, had his manor house on a hill. His tenants were half a dozen years behind in their land rent, but being away from home, he did not have the time to deal with them till his term of office expired and he returned to his farm, ready to press for the delayed rent.

On arriving home, he was surprised to find that all his storerooms were richly filled, and yet the tenants were still carrying loads of produce into the yard. His curiosity aroused, he asked for an explanation.

"For years," a tenant told him, "we have lived by plundering. Not long ago we opened up an ancient tomb about three miles west of our village. It lies amidst a grove of pine trees about 400 yards across and has a magnificent mound. There is an inscribed stele by the mound, but having collapsed into the wild grass, the words on it are illegible. We started by digging a slant tunnel. About 100 yards down we came upon a stone door sealed with melted iron. For several days we kept it drenched with steaming-hot stool wastes until it was finally corroded.

"As it opened, arrows shot out like rain, killing several of my comrades on the spot. Frightened, those who survived thought of quitting. I fancied that it could not be the work of spirits but rather some mechanism. So I told them to throw stones into the open doorway. Every throw, at first, invited a shower of arrows, but after a dozen times no more arrows came out. With lighted torches we cautiously entered the grave. There was a second door. Upon its opening, scores of wooden figures goggled their eyes and brandished their swords, wounding some more of us. We fought them with

272

clubs and fended off their weapons. Only then were we able to look around. On all four sides the walls were painted with warriors as if they were the owner's honor guard. Against the southern wall lay a big lacquered coffin suspended on chains. Below the coffin were heaps of pearls, jadeware, and gold pieces. As we were not yet recovered from the shock we experienced, we hesitated. All of a sudden, a wind sprang up from the sides of the coffin, whirling sand into our faces. The wind rose with momentum, sand came down in sheets and in less than no time immersed our knees. We fled for dear life, and by the time we managed to get out, the doorway was clogged with sand. Another comrade was buried alive. To atone for our profanity, we made a libation and vowed that we would never again break into graves."

According to the book *Water Systems and Local Life*, the king of Yue once attempted to move his father's grave, but had to give up because of the wind-born sand. There are also written records from the Han Dynasty that when the civil engineers constructed a tomb, they would have such devices as arrows, bows, fire and sand built into the underground chambers. So, this was an ancient tradition.

Translator's note:

Because of their belief in the afterlife, the emperors, the nobles and the rich built elaborate tombs to preserve their corpses, and buried with them treasures of all kinds. As thick walls and strong doors were not enough to deter grave-robbers, they frequently resorted to intricate devices and mechanism. The well-known Ming Tombs in the suburbs of Beijing are said to have a bow system, and the unexcavated mausoleum of Emperor Qin Shi Huang near Xi'an is said to have underground rivers of quicksilver. Modern investigations testify to an abnormal concentration of mercury in this area.

Water Painting

Mr. Li had a friend called Hermit Fan who had been a guest at his house for half a year. Fan was versed in astronomy and in chanting incantations. He was also something of a prophet and his predictions were quite accurate. One day, he mentioned that he was leaving. To repay his host's hospitality, he said he would like to show him an art—what he called "water painting."

First, a ten-by-ten pool about a foot deep was dug out in the backyard. Next, the sides and bottom were carefully plastered and the pool filled with water. When the seeping had stopped, Fan laid out his brushpens, ink and pigment by the pool. He sat musing for quite a while, tapping his teeth with the shaft of his brushpen. Then, abruptly, he ran his pen over the surface of the water. Li looked into the pool but could distinguish nothing out of the turbid waters. Two days later, Fan told the servants to stretch four parallel lengths of white silk on the surface. After about the time it takes for a meal, he said they could lift the cloth from the pool. There, printed on the silk, were people and houses, trees and rocks, everything that was needed to be the greatest of paintings.

Astonished, Li begged him to tell how he did it.

"All I did," said Fan simply, "was concentrate the pigment in the water so that it wouldn't diffuse."

Translator's note:

Printing was invented at the turn of the Sui and Tang dynasties. The earliest xylographically printed material extant with a definite date is an illustrated scroll of Buddhist scripture. It was printed in the ninth year of Xiantong reign (868). Each printed sheet is 76.3 cm by 30.5 cm. Understandably, the art of printing must have been a fascinating novelty at the time of this story.

274

Into the Porcelain Pillow
(abridged*)

T his occurred in the 19th year of Kaiyuan reign. An elderly Taoist priest stopped at a roadside tavern on his way to Handan City. He took a table and laid down the bundle he was carrying.

Presently, a youth in a short peasant coat appeared along the road riding a black colt. He was the young master of the Lu family from a nearby village and was on his way to the fields. He jumped off at the tavern and took up a seat beside the priest. A casual conversation sprang up between the two, which went on merrily until the young man glanced down at his shabby coat and sighed, "See how miserable one can be if he is out of luck!"

"Your skin looks smooth and soft, your body seems in excellent condition, and your speech sounds intelligent. It doesn't seem befitting for one of your status to complain of ill luck," the priest commented.

"This life of mine is no better than a dog's. You can't call it a man's life, can you?"

"If this is not, then what is a man's life like?"

"A man in his life should fulfill high aims and make a name for himself. He should either rise to be a great military general or a cabinet member. His tongue should taste nothing but delicious dishes; his ears should hear the sweetest music; he should have a legion of offspring and be able to provide them with the luxuries of the world. That's a real man's life! As for me, starting from an early age, I studied hard at the books and

---

* The titles of the five sons and the text of the letters to and from the emperor have been deleted.

learned all the fine arts a man should acquire. In that way I thought I had secured a place in high society. But look at me now! Already beyond the prime of life, I'm still tilling the fields. If this isn't ill luck, what is?" With that, his spirits seemed to have plummeted and his eyes grew dreamy. Behind the counter, the proprietor was preparing lunch. Lu watched him put the millet rice into a grill-steamer on the stove.

The priest reached into his bundle and pulled out a pillow. "Place this under your head," he said as he handed it over, "and your wishes will come true."

It was a porcelain pillow, hollow and with a small hole at each end. Lu tucked it under his head and snoozed off. Soon he sensed the hole enlarge and effuse with light. He stepped in and found himself in his own house.

He had married a Miss Cui from a wealthy family in Qinghe County. She was quite a beauty and her dowry bountiful. Before long, his habits became extravagant. The following year he succeeded in the imperial examination and won a position in the imperial academy, thus being able to throw away his peasant coat for a robe. Then he took the selection tests for administrators, and was consequently assigned to Weinan County as county lieutenant. Later, he was elected to the Central Supervisory Commission, and not long after designated to the royal secretariat in charge of drafting His Majesty's edicts. In three years he was made a department chief and was nominated special commissioner to Tong Prefecture. Shortly after, he was transferred to Shan Prefecture. There, as the craving for grand projects had always been in him, he had a 30-mile-long canal cut through the rocky hills which greatly improved transportation and irrigation. People lauded this feat and erected steles in his honor. With that achievement, he was promoted to high commissioner of the region south of the Yellow River with his headquarters in Bianzhou City, and finally he returned to the capital as its mayor.

At that time, the country was at war with Tubo in the

southwest. Guazhou and Shazhou, important outposts in the western regions, had just fallen into enemy hands. Even Wang Junchuo, the famed general who had been successfully defending the region, was slain. His Majesty, in desperate need of an armed force commander to save the situation, raised him to deputy chief of the Central Supervisory Commission and placed him in command of all forces in the western regions. Under his masterful command, the imperial army not only destroyed 7,000 enemy troops but also pushed Tubo back 300 miles. At his orders, three fortified towns were built at strategic locations in the newly recovered territory. He was looked upon as the savior of the frontiers and monuments were raised in memory of his victories. Upon his return to Court, he was received with praise and honors. The emperor appointed him chief of the Central Supervisory Commission and concurrently deputy minister of the Personnel Ministry. His reputation and new fame won the jealousy of the prime minister, whose slanders had him condemned to the remotest south as prefect of Duan Prefecture.

At the end of his three-year tenure there he was recalled to Court and appointed minister of the Finance Ministry. Before long, he was further promoted to associate premier, sharing administrative power with Xiao Song and Pei Guangting for a decade. He gained the personal trust of His Majesty and implemented many highly received policies. He was known as the "good premier."

Jealousy stepped in again. His peers accused him of conspiring with frontier generals against the throne. An arrest warrant was duly issued and soldiers were soon knocking on his gate. In apprehension of the inevitable, he made a tearful farewell to his wife, saying, "I can't help thinking of my native place on the eastern plains where I had many acres of rich farmland. That was more than enough to keep us from hunger and cold, but I chose to come here to seek a fortune. Now that the dice are cast, gone are the carefree days when I could wear a short coat and take a casual ride on my black colt along the Handan Road." So saying he raised his sword to his neck, but was held back by his wife.

All those involved in that scandal were sentenced to death, all except him, for he still had a few powerful friends in Court to pull strings. Though he managed to elude a death sentence, he was again dismissed from Court and demoted to prefect of Huan Prefecture in the barbarian south. Years later, His Majesty realized that he was wronged, thereupon he was summoned back to Court to resume his office as premier. Royal bounties and favors showered down once more. To crown it all, he was given the title Duke of Zhao.

He had five sons, all high officials and wedded to powerful families. His grandsons grew to more than a dozen. In retrospect, his career was most miraculous. Rarely could one who had twice been banished to the remote areas be twice appointed premier. For over 30 years he had held various key positions both in regional governments and in Court. He certainly was the most celebrated and influential statesman of his time.

Now he was in his eighties, old and sick. He had thought of resigning and going back to his native place, but this was not permitted. On his deathbed, he wrote to the emperor expressing his gratitude and appreciation for the royal favors he had received. His Majesty sent his favorite eunuch to his bedside with a letter of praise. That night he died.

Just then, he stretched and yawned. Looking around he saw himself lying in the tavern. The elderly priest was sitting beside him. The millet rice was still steaming on the stove. Everything seemed unchanged. He sat up and asked, "Was I dreaming?"

"Life is a dream," the old man said.

He nodded thoughtfully, and said, "Thank you, sir, for having shown me the ups and downs of life, the turns of fortune and death itself. That cleared me of all desires. I do appreciate it." He made a deep bow and went down the road.

The Southern Bough
(abridged*)

A couple of miles to the east of Yangzhou City lived a celebrated gallant named Chunyu Fen. He was very much devoted to the bottle. Wine used to flame up his blood and loosen his mind, and that was how he offended his superior and was dismissed from the army. After that he remained at home, lavishing his immense family wealth on wine pals like him.

South of his house stood a massive locust-tree, its branches extending far and wide. Almost every day he would feast his friends in its verdant shade, and during one such spree on a fine autumn day in the seventh year of Zhenyuan reign he got drunk and sick. Two of his friends supported him back to the house and laid him on a couch on the east-wing verandah. "Lie down a little while," they said. "We'll feed the horses and wash our feet while waiting for you to recover. We won't leave till you feel better."

He untied his headwear and rested his swimming head on the pillow. His senses clouded as if falling into a dream. He saw two envoys in purple come and kneel before the couch, saying, "We are ambassadors from the Great Locust-Tree Kingdom. His Majesty invites Your Excellency for a visit." He felt himself getting off the couch and smoothing his crumpled clothes. He followed the two toward the gate, where he saw a coach painted in glossy black and attended by half a dozen liveried servants. They helped him aboard and the coach rolled out of the gate toward the ancient locust-tree. To his

---

* A postscript has been deleted.

surprise, it did not stop at the tree but drove right into a hole at its root. He ventured neither an objection nor a question. Peeping out of the window, he found that the entire view had changed: The road, the trees, the landscape were all different. After 10 miles or so a walled city came into sight and the road became crowded with traffic and people. He heard the servants shouting authoritatively, and the pedestrians jumped aside. Then there was a wide red gate and a magnificent gate-tower with words inscribed in shining gold above the arch: The Great Locust-Tree Kingdom. The guards at the gate bowed at the sight of the coach. A mounted messenger came galloping toward them and announced that at the king's order, the royal son-in-law was to be accommodated at the state guest house to refresh himself from the exhausting journey.

He was led to a big courtyard whose gates were thrown wide open and he stepped out and entered. The balustrades, pillars, window frames, and even the eaves were all delicately carved and brightly painted. Beautiful flowers and trees bearing rare fruits adorned the yard. The hall was richly furnished with writing desks and cushioned chairs, screens and curtains. He was basking in that rare delight of luxury when someone announced that the prime minister was at the gate. He hurried down the hall steps and waited respectfully. A man in a purple robe holding an elephant-tusk slab strode toward him. After an exchange of greetings, the prime minister said, "Notwithstanding the remoteness of our humble kingdom, His Majesty took the liberty to invite Your Excellency to join him. He wishes you will grant him the honor of establishing family relations by marrying one of his daughters."

"The honor should be mine!" he replied. "I'm but a rough man and never dreamed of relating myself to the royal family." He was then invited to the palace.

A hundred steps led him into a red gate. Ceremonial weapons of all kinds were arrayed in the courtyard. Hundreds of officers stood obediently on both sides of the paved path leading up to the hall. He was thrilled to see among the crowd the familiar face of Zhou Bian, one of his closest wine pals. But he checked the impulse to go over and speak to him.

The prime minister led him into a spacious audience-hall where guards stood in solemn silence. On the throne sat a tall man of regal dignity wearing a white robe and a crown studded with rubies. He lowered his eyes in awe while the guards shouted him down to his knees.

"Thanks to your father's recent proposal," he heard the king say, "His Excellency never belittled us, we are pleased that our second daughter, Scented Jade, will be your lady of the house."

Not knowing what to reply, he kept his head bent.

"Preparations for the wedding ceremony are underway," the king continued. "For the time being, please take a brief rest at the guest house. Mr. Prime Minister will conduct you there."

The incidental mentioning of his father baffled him. He had lost contact with his father ever since the frontier fell into the hands of barbarians. As a garrison officer, his father might have died on the battlefield or been captured. Had peace been negotiated that he now could make this arrangement?

That evening gifts of gold and silk, lambs and wild geese were sent to his quarters, as well as a guard of honor and banners, musicians, tablefuls of food graced with thick red candles, horses and carriages. Then came an assemblage of ladies with such names as Aunt Sunny, Aunt Brook, Fairy Itty, Fairy Bitty, and so on, each waited on by many servants. They wore emerald coronets, gold bracelets, and flimsy cloaks glistening like the morning rays of the sun that blazed the eye. Thus they entered the house in a hubbub of jolly noise. They poked fun at him, teasing him so coquettishly that he felt tongue-tied in defending himself.

"Remember that day at the Temple of Wisdom?" one of

them said. "It was the third day of the third lunar month. Lady Truffle and I went to the temple to watch a Brahman dance. We were sitting on a stone bench by the north window when you came riding by on a fine steed—you were much younger then. When you saw us, you dismounted and forced your presence on us, teasing us with your obscene jokes. Sister Ying and I tied a knotted pink handkerchief to a bamboo stem. Don't you remember? And on another occasion, that was the 16th of the seventh lunar month, Fairy Itty and I went to the Temple of Filiality to listen to Monk Metaphysics' lecture on the Bodhisattva Scriptures. I donated a pair of gold hairpins and Fairy Itty contributed a rhino-skin case to the altar. You were also among the audience. Do you remember you stepped forth and begged the monk for a look at those objects? You turned them round and round in your palm with the most eloquent admiration. You leered at us and said, 'Such rare handicrafts and such beautiful creatures cannot but belong to another world.' You asked our names and addresses. We didn't give you a chance, but you just wouldn't let up. Your eyes were riveted on me. Has all that slipped your mind?"

"In heart it buries; for e'er there tarries," he quoted two ancient lines from *The Book of Songs* in reply.

"Isn't it marvelous that we are now to be related?" they chorused.

Just then three exquisitely dressed men stepped forward and bowed to him, saying that they were chosen by the king to be his best men at the wedding. One of them looked rather familiar.

"Aren't you Mr. Tian Zihua from Pingyi?" he asked. Indeed he was.

"How come you are here?" he beamed, clasping Tian's hand eagerly in his.

"I rambled around and my talents happened to be recognized by Marquis Duan the prime minister, so here I stayed," Tian answered.

283

"Zhou Bian is also here. Do you know that?"

"Oh, yes. He is now a man of consequence. He is commander of the capital's garrison force. That's a very powerful position. He has exerted his influence to help me on several occasions."

And so they chatted and chatted.

Soon it was announced that it was time for the wedding. The three helped him put on a ceremonial robe, jade badges and ribbons, and a decorative sword.

"Lucky for me to be present at your great time," Tian said. "Hope you won't forget your old friends."

A large band of pretty girl-musicians appeared, playing soul-touching tunes, sweet and somewhat sentimental. Such tunes as he had never heard before. Dozens of attendants holding lanterns and candles led the way. Screens in a rainbow of colors lined the road. It was a splendid sight, and yet he sat bolt upright in the carriage nervous with anticipation and uncertainty. Tian spoke to him several times, trying to make him relax. The ladies who were to become his relatives were also in the procession in their respective carriages.

Then they arrived at a palace called Hall of Etiquette. The aunts and itties were waiting at the door. They conducted him through the ceremonial procedures, which were very much like those of the human world. When the bride was finally unveiled, he discovered a girl in her teens, more lovely than a fairy. She was addressed as Princess of Golden Bough.

It was a successful marriage. Their love grew with each passing day, as well as his wealth and popularity. His guard of honor when he set out, the extravagance of his banquets when he entertained his guests, were second to none but the king himself.

Not long after his wedding the king asked him and all the courtiers to join in a grand hunting game at the Tortoise Mountain west of the capital. It was a beautiful mountain, thick with vegetation and sprinkled with sapphire lakes. Game of many kind abounded and their carts were loaded with prey when they returned in the evening.

One day he asked the king, "On the day of my marriage, I remember Your Majesty mentioned that it was the wish of my father. The last I heard of him was that his troops were overwhelmed in a border conflict, and he was either trapped in enemy territory or killed. I've had no news from him in the past 17 or 18 years. Since Your Majesty knows his whereabouts, I beg for permission to go and see him."

"Your father is dutifully guarding the northern territory," the king emphasized quickly. "We were never out of contact with each other. You can send him a letter if you wish, but there is no need for you to go in person." So he asked his wife to pack a box of gifts as a filial offspring should do, and sent it along with his letter.

Several days later a reply came from his father. He checked the handwriting carefully. It was indeed his father's. As he read along, trembling tears spattered down on the paper. The fatherly care and advice were as warm as of old. In his letter, his father also inquired about family members and neighbors. He sounded melancholy and lonely when he mentioned the rough roads and insurmountable distance that made traveling impossible, yet he didn't seem eager to see him. "We will meet again in the year of Fire and Ox,* " he wrote in conclusion.

"Aren't you thinking of pursuing a political career?" his wife remarked casually one day.

"I'm sort of happy-go-lucky, and not used to politics," he replied.

"Don't worry. I'll help you," his wife assured him. So she went to speak to her father about it.

At an audience a few days later the king told him, "I have dismissed the prefect of Southern Bough from office because

---

* In ancient China, two sets of symbolic figures were combined to represent ordinal numbers.

he has been rather disappointing. I hope you will lend your talent to its administration by accepting that position. The princess will go with you."

He accepted graciously and a prefect's outfit was made ready. Gold and silk, trunks of various sizes, liveries and maids, and carts and carriages lined the thoroughfare waiting for the princess and the new governor. He had adored heroism in his youth, but never imagined himself becoming a public figure. And now he felt pleased with his new fortune. In that elated state of mind, he presented a memorial to the king. "Although I was born in an army officer's family," he wrote modestly, "I myself have neither military endowments nor governing qualities. I fear that my inability to hold such an important position as prefect might impair our national interests. Therefore I would like to recommend garrison commander Zhou Bian, who is most loyal to Your Majesty and a rigid law enforcer, to be head of the prefectural law department; and Tian Zihua, who is a master hand at politics and very diplomatic, to be head of the prefectural agriculture department. I have known both of them for over 10 years, and they have my trust. With their assistance, I believe I can exercise my duties faultlessly."

The king granted his request and ordered Zhou and Tian to accompany him to Southern Bough.

That very evening, the king and the queen held a grand farewell banquet outside the south town-gate. "Southern Bough is one of our biggest prefectures," the king told him. "It has a large population and vast resources, but these will not be advantages unless it is governed benevolently. Now that you have Mr. Zhou and Mr. Tian helping you, we look forward to your success."

"Mr. Chunyu is sometimes too fond of the cup," the queen at the same time imparted her private concerns to the princess, "and his youth makes his temper even more fiery. You need to be most tactful and dutiful as a good wife should be.

286

With you at his side, we can put our hearts at ease. However, I'll miss you a lot, though Southern Bough is not very far away. I don't know how I can bear that!"

They kowtowed to the king and queen, and the train of carriages and carts lumbered south among a legion of guards.

Having traveled several days in each other's happy company, they approached the City of Southern Bough. The local functionaries, together with the clergy and gentry, had been awaiting their arrival miles out of town. Musical bands and dramatic troupes lined the road to town. Bells chimed and drums boomed. The entire population seemed to have turned out. The gate-tower loomed high against the azure sky and flags fluttered over the battlements. A board hanging over the archway bore four larger words in gold: City of Southern Bough. In a while, their carriage pulled up before the first of a row of stately mansions. The entrance-hall was flanked with a whole set of ceremonial weapons. This was the prefect's official residence.

As soon as he assumed office, he set out to investigate the situation and relieved the peasants of their sufferings. Thereafter, he left all the daily administrative duties to Zhou and Tian. Thus he governed for 20 years, and Southern Bough became a happy and prosperous place. People extolled his benevolence. They raised steles eulogizing his achievements and built temples with his statue on the altar. The king also had a high opinion of him. A fiefdom and many titles were bestowed on him. His status rose as high as the prime minister. Zhou and Tian were also promoted several ranks for their managerial abilities. During those years, five sons and two daughters were born. His sons were born noblemen, and his daughters were married into the royal household. He had all the wealth and fame one could desire.

Then, the Red Sandalwood invaded his land. The king ordered him to organize a counter-attack. He named Zhou Bian commander-in-chief and placed a 30,000-man force under his command to meet the enemy at Nephrite Heights. Zhou, being overconfident of his personal valor, acted rashly and was so badly defeated that only he himself managed to escape back to town under the cover of night—in his underwear! The enemy returned to their country with loads of trophies.

He had to throw Zhou Bian in jail and sent a memorial of self-reproach to the king. Though the king pardoned them both, Zhou did not survive the month. He died of an infected ulcer on his back. As misfortunes never come singly, the princess also fell ill, and died in a fortnight. He offered his resignation to escort his wife's remains back to the capital, which the king accepted, and Tian Zihua replaced him.

The hearse set out among wailing crowds. His colleagues set up tents along the road offering memorial services, and ordinary folks poured into the streets in farewell tears. All along the way, peasants blocked his carriage trying to make him promise that he would return. The king and queen came out in mourning to receive the hearse. A posthumous title was conferred on the princess, and an enlarged guard of honor accompanied the hearse to the royal burial ground at Sleeping Dragon Mound east of the capital. In the same month, Zhou Bian's remains were also escorted back to the capital by his son.

Having been the prefect of one of the major prefectures for so many years, he had established close relations with members of the court and the army. There was hardly a nobleman that was not his friend. Since he was relieved of duty and now living in the capital, he enjoyed plenty of freedom and became more popular than ever. Even the king started to feel his prevalence. Just at that time, someone submitted a memorial saying, "The constellations show signs that a catastrophe is to befall our kingdom. Our ancestral temple will be destroyed; the capital will have to be relocated. All this is because of alien beings who are close by." According to popular understanding, it was his wanton excesses that caused the omens in heaven. The king removed his personal guards, forbade him from associating himself with high officials, and finally ordered him to stay at home.

He felt crestfallen. He had made Southern Bough stable and prosperous, and during his 20 years as governor he had taken no false steps, but now he was stung and humiliated by slanders. The king seemed to know his feelings, so one day he said to him, "It's too bad that my daughter should have passed away so early, leaving you alone in this world. You have been with us over 20 years. Why don't you take this opportunity to go home and see your own folks? I will send someone to pick you up in three years. You can leave your children in my palace. They will be taken good care of."

"Home? This *is* my home," he said. "Where are you sending me?"

"You belong to the human world," the king laughed. "This is not your home."

He seemed to be in a dream. After a long while, he felt awakened out of a stupor and remembered many things. Tears rolled down his cheeks as he pleaded to go home. The king told his attendants to take him back. He kowtowed and left.

It was the same two envoys in purple who brought him here, but the coach waiting outside was in the shabbiest condition. He was further dismayed to find that his own servants and drivers were nowhere in sight. Once out of town, the coach retraced the way from which he had come long ago. The hills and streams were the same as they had been, but the two envoys had lost their air of importance. The journey became unbearably depressing. He asked the two when they would arrive at Yangzhou. They didn't even care to interrupt the vulgar tune they were humming. "We'll be there in time," they grumbled through their teeth.

Gradually, the coach drove out of a tunnel into the familiar streets of his hometown. Nothing had changed. A sadness overcame him and tears trickled down his cheeks. The two envoys led him into his own courtyard and up the doorsteps. So surprised was he to see his own body lying on a couch on the east-wing verandah that his legs turned rigid. "Chunyu Fen! Chunyu Fen!" the two shouted several times and he suddenly woke up. Glancing around, he saw the houseboys were sweeping the yard, his two friends were sitting on a bench washing their feet, and the half empty glass of wine which he left on the window sill was still rippling in the slanting rays of the sun. How could time have passed so fast in a dream? He had spent a lifetime there!

Heaving a deep sigh, he motioned his two friends to his side and told them about his strange dream. They were fascinated, so that they followed him to the big locust-tree and detected a hole. "This is the very hole I drove down in my dream," he pointed and said. Thinking that it might have been a fox vampire or some tree spirits' mischief, his friends called for the servants to bring spades and axes to chop away at the gnarled roots and shrubs. Digging along a tunnel for about 10 feet they hit upon a large underground cavity, so large that it could probably hold a bed. In it were millions upon millions of ants. There was also piled earth in the shapes of walls, houses and palaces. In the center was a small platform of cinnabar red, occupied by two giant ants about three inches long, with red heads and white wings. Surrounding them were dozens of large ants, and ants of ordinary size kept themselves at a respectful distance. The giant couple must be the king and the queen, and this must be the capital of the Great Locust-Tree Kingdom.

A tunnel led southward. Tracing some 40 feet of winding path, they reached another cavity which was located right under the southern bough of the tree. There was also a square rise in the center with what looked like buildings and streets. Many ants lived there. No doubt, this was Southern Bough Prefecture where he had governed so long.

Another large cavity was found about 20 feet to the west. Wet with pockets of water, it looked somewhat like a deserted cellar. There lay a rotten tortoise, its shell big as a hat and covered with flourishing green mold. This could be none other than the so-called Tortoise Mountain where he and the king had hunted. Ten feet in the opposite direction they discovered a cavern around a stretch of twisted roots of the old tree, in which there was a mound of loose earth several inches high. Wasn't that the Sleeping Dragon Mound where he buried his dear wife?

Piece by piece, these findings brought back the details of his dream, making him sigh and lament over his momentary past. Unwilling to let his friends destroy the holes, he told the servants to cover them up again. That night a storm broke out. In the morning he went to inspect and found that all the ants had moved away—to where nobody knew. "Our ancestral temple will be destroyed; the capital will have to be relocated." Those omens in his dream had come true. He remembered the invasion from the Red Sandalwood. He sent for his two friends and asked them to join him again in a search.

Half a mile to the east of his house was a dried-up brook. By the brook stood a mighty red sandalwood tree with dense leaves and clinging ivy around its trunk. There was an ant hole beside it. Many ants crawled about the place. What could they be but the Red Sandalwoods?

Alas! If such small beings as ants could have a world to themselves, what about those bigger creatures living in the deep mountains or thick jungles? Could we even imagine what their lives were like?

He suddenly thought of Zhou Bian and Tian Zihua, both of them living in the vicinity of Yangzhou, and yet they hadn't shown up at his feasts for probably 10 days. He immediately dispatched servants to call on them, and learned that Zhou had died a few days before of a sudden illness and Tian Zihua was seriously bedridden.

The dream under the southern bough was nothing but hollow, and yet wasn't human life as transient as a dream? He decided to give up drinking and wanton desires, and to devote himself to Taoism. Three years later, in the year of Fire and Ox, he died peacefully at home at the age of 47.

A Kingdom in the Ear
(abridged*)

Zhang Zuo, a scholar of the Confusion school who passed the imperial examination in Kaiyuan reign, once traveled south of the capital. Riding along the road, he was joined by an old man astride a white-footed gray donkey entering from a back road. The man, carrying a deer-skin bag on his back, looked perfectly contented with life and dignified in spite of his plain attire.

Impressed, Zhang tried to strike up a conversation by asking where he came from. The old man only smiled. When Zhang made yet another approach, the man flared up. "What an insolent young man you are! How dare you question me as if I were a fugitive escaping with stolen money! Is it your business to know where one comes from and where one goes to?"

"I asked," Zhang replied apologetically, "because I admire your poised and knowledgeable air and was thinking of being your pupil. Does that deserve your anger?"

"But I don't think I have anything to teach you. I'm only an old man who has lived very long. You might be laughing up your sleeve at my shabbiness." So saying, he whipped the donkey to a canter.

Zhang spurred his horse and followed. That night they stayed at the same inn. The old man layed down promptly, pillowing his head on the deer-skin bag. But Zhang felt like having a drink to quench the exhaustion of the day and tentatively invited the old man to join him.

---

* The word-riddle and the text of the proclamation have been deleted.

The old man leaped to his feet. "That's the one thing I enjoy. I wonder how you figured out this weakness of mine."

As they drank, the old man's face seemed to soften. Seizing the opportunity, Zhang ventured meekly, "I'm young and ignorant. Does Your Honor mind enlightening me a little? I just wish to learn more about the world."

"What I've seen is but the rise and decline of the Liang, Chen, Sui and Tang dynasties. All that is now put down in your history books. Perhaps I may tell you something particular about myself.

"In the Northern Zhou Dynasty, I lived in Qi Prefecture. My name was Shen Zong. I was then 18, a lieutenant in an expeditionary force attacking Jingzhou City held by Emperor Yuandi of Liang. We captured the city and my general was to lead the triumphant troops back north.

"That night I had a dream. Two men in blue robes read me a word-riddle. Early in the morning I went directly to a dream-reader. According to his interpretation, it meant I must stay if I wanted to attain longevity. So I petitioned my superior and was permitted to remain and join the garrison force.

"I went again to see the dream-reader to tell him I had managed to stay, but I really doubted if longevity could be thus acquired.

"He told me I lived in Zitong County in my previous life, and my name then was Xue Junzhou. I indulged in taking exotic herb medicine and took delight in studying Taoist scriptures. Later, I moved to the foot of Honking Crane Peak, built myself a thatched cottage by a spring, and planted flowers and bamboo all around.

"Intoxicated on the full moon night of the eighth lunar month, I whistled and whooped into the crystal clear night. I loudly demanded why, as detached and transcendent as I was, there wasn't any supernatural being present to accompany me in my lone drinking.

"All of a sudden, I seemed to hear the rumbling of

carriages in both ears and for no reason at all I felt sleepy and dozed off. As soon as my head touched the straw mat, a tiny carriage a couple of inches high with red wheels and black canopy, pulled by a cinnamon-colored calf of comparable size, rolled out of my ear. Strange to say, it didn't seem to be a problem for them getting out of my ear. On the carriage were two lads, also about two inches tall, clad in blue cloaks with their hair done up in green headcloth. They leaned against the handrail and asked the driver to halt. Stepping down, they introduced themselves as envoys from the Kingdom of Divine. They came because they had heard my vibrant whistling under the moon, which they greatly admired, and they wished to converse with me.

"'You gentlemen just came out of my ear. Why did you say you came from the Kingdom of Divine?' I asked, not without some surprise.

"'The Kingdom of Divine is in our ears. How can your ear hold our kingdom!' they retorted.

"'With your height of two inches, how much room can there be in your ear for a kingdom? Well, granting what you say is true, your countrymen must be smaller than fleas.'

"'Be it so, there isn't much difference between our two countries. If you don't believe us, just come along and see with your own eyes. If you have the luck to stay in our kingdom forever, you'll escape the cycles of life and death.'

"A lad then inclined his ear for me to peep in. I saw flowers and trees, house after house, meandering streams and ragged mountain ranges extending into the boundless distance. I held his ear and threw myself into it. I found myself in a metropolis. The city walls were high, the streets wide and straight. I was wondering where to turn when the two lads appeared by my side. They told me that their country was as vast as mine, and since I was there, they suggested I pay my respects to Xuanzhen the Great.

"Xuanzhen lived in a palace of gold. The screens on the

doors and windows were strings of pearls. There he sat in the center of a grand hall, his robe embroidered with patterns of the sun and moon floating above rosy clouds, his hat tall and dangling with jade beads hanging from the front and back brims. Four virgin boys stood by his side. The two lads entered with bent heads and lowered eyes. An official in a tall hat and green robe proclaimed from a scroll that I was conferred the title of Grand Secretary of the Dossier. Four men in yellow cloaks led me to my office, where I soon discovered that the words in the documents were mostly unintelligible to me. Throughout the month, however, nobody came to make reports or receive orders. Whatever thought I might have in mind, my attendants would know before I could even utter it, and would see to all my needs.

"Idling about from day to day, I happened to ascend a tower. The scenery awakened a spasm of homesickness and inspired a poem:

> A gentle breeze across the land,
> Sends fragrance through the woods and dome.
> Staring out from this lofty stand,
> I realize this scene isn't home.

Later, when I showed it to the two lads, they were infuriated at what they called the impurgeable vulgarity ingrained in my nature. They said it was a mistake to have brought me to their kingdom. They had misjudged me as a man above temporal desires, and I still think of my worldly home!

"As they chased me, I felt the ground giving way under my feet. I only had time to look up to see that I had fallen out of the lad's ear and landed in my own courtyard. I looked again, and the lads were gone. When I talked to my neighbors, they told me that Xue Junzhou, that was me, had been dead for seven or eight years, though I felt it was only a matter of months. I did die soon afterwards, and was reborn as Shen Zong.

"The dream-reader then said that in his former life he was

296

none other than one of the lads from my ear. Because of my devotion to Taoism in my previous life, I was granted that visit to the Kingdom of Divine, but as my earthly roots were not entirely severed, I was not able to attain immortality, yet I could enjoy a peaceful life of 1,000 years. He retrieved from his mouth a foot-long strip of scarlet silk inscribed with magic figures and asked me to swallow it. Then, he revealed himself as the lad and disappeared.

"Two hundred years have passed since that day, and I've never suffered an illness during my constant tours through the sacred mountains. I've been through many strange events and had them all recorded. Here they are in my bag."

He opened the deer-skin bag and showed Zhang two thick scrolls. The words were tiny and illegible. Zhang begged him to read out a few passages, which he did.

When Zhang woke up in the morning, the old man was gone.

Several days later, someone who had met the old man in Ash Valley passed on his compliments. Zhang hurried to the valley, but could not find the old man.

Translator's note:

The motif of entering through a hole, be it a hole in the pillow as in "Into the Porcelain Pillow," an ant hole in "The Southern Bough," or an ear as is this story, symbolizes, according to some interpretations, a return to the womb—the reverse process of being born, where man seeks shelter from an alienating world. The ancient writers themselves, however, may have been less fascinated by symbolism than by the fickleness of life and the eternity of the soul.

Appendix I
The Dynasties and Period Titles*

The Qin Dynasty   221–206 B.C.
The Han Dynasty   206 B.C.–A.D. 220
The Three Kingdoms   220–280
The Jin Dynasty   265–420
The Southern and Northern Dynasties   420–589

The Southern	Dynasties	The Northern	Dynasties
Liu's Song	420–479	Northern Wei	386–534
Qi	479–502	Eastern Wei	534–550
Liang	502–557	Northern Qi	550–577
Chen	557–589	Northern Zhou	557–581

The Sui Dynasty   581–618
The Tang Dynasty   618–907

Zhenguan	627–649	Baoying	762–763
Yonghui	650–655	Yongtai	765–766
(*Empress Wu Ze Tian's reign*		Dali	766–779
	684–705)	Jianzhong	780–783
Tianshou	690–692	Zhenyuan	785–805
Dazu	701	Yongzhen	805
Shenlong	705–707	Yuanhe	806–820
(*Emperor Xuanzong's*		Huichang	841–846
reign	712–756)	Dazhong	847–860
Kaiyuan	713–741	Guangqi	885–888
Tianbao	742–756		
(*An Lushan-Shi Siming Rebellion* 755–763)			

---

* To keep the list simple, only the period titles of the Tang Dynasty appearing in the stories are listed.

298

Appendix II
Glossary of Place Names*

Anlu County: in Hubei Province, 100 miles to the southeast of Xiangyang

Bachuan County: Tongliang County in eastern Sichuan Province

Bianzhou City: Kaifeng City, Henan Province, a major town east of Luoyang

Bing Prefecture: an area around Taiyuan City, Shanxi Province

Canton Region: roughly corresponding to present Guangdong Province. It was a remote area at that time, where demoted officials were often exiled.

Chang'an (City): the capital of the Tang Dynasty, now called Xi'an, capital of Shaanxi Province

Changjiang County: in Sichuan Province

Changning County: in Shanxi Province

Chen Prefecture: Chenzhou City, in southern Hunan Province

Chengde Region: a garrison region centered around Zhengding County, Hebei Province

Chenliu: near Kaifeng City, Henan Province

Culai Mountain: to the southeast of Mount Tai

Deng Prefecture: an area at the eastern tip of the Shandong Peninsula

---

* The place name following the colon is the name used at present. If the name remains unchanged, it will not be repeated.

The distance mentioned is a rough approximation of the straight distance between two points on the map.

Dongping: an area in western Shandong Province near Dongping Lake

Duan Prefecture (Duanxi): Gaoyao County, Guangdong Province

Fan County: in western Shandong Province on the northern bank of the Yellow River

Fuchang County: near Luoyang City, Henan Province

Fuliang County: near Jingdezhen City, Jiangxi Province

Fuyang Prefecture: around Ci County in southern Hebei Province

Guangling County: in the northeastern suburbs of Yangzhou City

Guazhou and Shazhou: area around Dunhuang in western Gansu Province

Han River: a major tributary joining the Yangtze at Wuhan City

Handan (City): in southern Hebei Province

Hangzhou (City): now the capital of Zhejiang Province

Hannan: an area south of the Han River

Heng Prefecture: an area around Hengyang City, Hunan Province

Hu Prefecture: in northern Zhejiang Province

Hua Prefecture: centered around Hua County in northeastern Henan Province

Huai River: between and parallel to the Yellow River and the Yangtze River

Huaiyin County: a city on the Huai River, Jiangsu Province

Huan Prefecture: now in Vietnam

Jialing River: a major tributary of the Yangtze River in Sichuan Province

Jian'an County: in Fujian Province

Jiang Prefecture: in southern Shanxi Province

Jiangle County: in Fujian Province

Jiaxing County: in Zhejiang Province

Jingzhou (City): a large city on the Yangtze River, to the west of Wuhan City

Juyan: in western Gansu Province

Kai Prefecture: Fengjie County in eastern Sichuan Province

Lang Prefecture: Langzhong County in northeastern Sichuan Province on the upper reaches of the Jialing River

Liuhe County: 40 miles to the west of Yangzhou City

Lizhou Prefecture / City: Guangyuan County in eastern Sichuan Province

Lotus Peak: the second highest peak on Mount Hua, renowned for its precipitous slopes

Lulong: a garrison region in northeastern Hebei Province

Luoyang: a major city in Henan Province, the East Capital of the Tang Dynasty, where Empress Wu held court. It lies 200 miles to the east of Chang'an.

Mianchi: a town 40 miles west of Luoyang

Mount Heng: in Hunan Province, one of the five sacred mountains, also known as the Mountain of the South

Mount Hua: 70 miles to the east of Chang'an, and one of the five sacred mountains, also known as the Mountain of the West

Mount Ling: in southern Shanxi Province

Mount Lu: a beautiful mountain in northern Jiangxi Province, 300 miles up the Yangtze River from Yangzhou

Mount Tai: in Shandong Province, one of the five sacred mountains, also known as the Mountain of the East

Mount Yong: in Fujian Province

Nanking: now spelled Nanjing, a major city on the lower reaches of the Yangtze River

Nanpi County: in southeastern Hebei Province

Nanyang Prefecture: in southwestern Henan Province

Northern Hills: in the northern suburbs of Luoyang City

Penglai (Isle): a legendary islet off the coast of the Shandong Peninsula where the gods live

Pingyi: in Tong Prefecture

Qi Prefecture: in western Shaanxi Province

Qingcheng and Emei Mountains: both in Sichuan Province. Qingcheng is regarded as a sacred mountain in Taoism, while Emei is one of the four sacred mountains of Buddhism.

Qinghe County: in southern Hebei Province, 90 miles to the northwest of Dongping

Qinzhou City: in southern Shanxi Province

Qiongdu County: in western Sichuan Province

Ruen Prefecture: area around Zhenjiang City, Jiangsu Province

Runan County: in eastern Henan Province

Sanxiang: a small town near Luoyang

Shan Prefecture: in the northwestern corner of Henan Province, 60 miles east of Tongguan

Shanfu County: Shan County, Shandong Province

Shangyu County: in Zhejiang Province

Shen (Prefecture): in Hebei Province, 50 miles west of Zhengding County

Shifang County: north of Chengdu City in Sichuan Province

Shu: another name for present Sichuan Province, a geographical basin of rich soil surrounded by high mountains in the southwestern region of China

Silla: an ancient kingdom in the southeastern part of the Korean Peninsula. It was on good terms with China throughout its history.

Southern Hills: a mountain range south of Chang'an

Sword Gate: an important mountain pass on the northern route leading into Shu

Taihang Mountain Range: a north-south mountain range along the western border of Hebei Province

Taiyuan (City): the capital of present Shanxi Province, also designated one of the three capital cities of the Tang Dynasty because the House of Li originated there

Tang'an County: Guan County, Sichuan Province

Tong Prefecture: an area around present Dali County, Shanxi Province

Tongguan Pass: a strategically important mountain pass near Mount Hua on the eastern mouth of the Wei River valley, barricading the only way to reach the West Capital from the east

Wangwu Mountains: in southern Shanxi Province

Wei Prefecture: in the vicinity of Daming County in southern Hebei Province

Wei River: a major tributary of the Yellow River flowing through the loess plateau in Shaanxi Province, creating a stretch of rich farmlands along its valley, where Chang'an, the capital, was located

Weinan County: an area south of the Wei River

Xiagu Pass: an important mountain pass in the Southern Hills opening right onto the capital

Xiang Prefecture: in Hebei Province

Xiangyang City: a large city on the Han River in northern Hubei Province

Xianyang City: an ancient city about 15 miles west of Chang'an

Xinming County: Hechuan County in eastern Sichuan Province

Xu Prefecture: an area around Xuchang City, Henan Province

Xuan County: in southern Anhui Province

Xunyang: an area around Jiujiang City north of Mount Lu

Xuyi County: 70 miles northwest of Yangzhou City

Yangtze County: to the west of Yangzhou in the vicinity of Yizheng County

Yangtze River: see "Geography" in Appendix III

Yangxian County: Yixing County in southern Jiangsu Province

Yangzhou City: a big city and commercial center on the northern bank of the Yangtze in southern Jiangsu Province

Yanmen: an area in northern Shanxi Province

Ye County: near Linzhang County in southern Hebei Province

Yellow River: see "Geography" in Appendix III

Yi Prefecture: an area around Yi County, Hebei Province

Yilong County: bordering on Lang Prefecture in northeastern Sichuan Province

Yingchuan: another name for Xu Prefecture

Yixing County: in Jiangsu Province

Yiyang County: Huangchuan County, Henan Province

Yongkang County: in Zhejiang Province

Yue Prefecture: an area around Shaoxing City, Zhejiang Province

Zhenfu (County): Yang County in southern Shaanxi Province

Zheng Prefecture: an area around Zhengzhou City, Henan Province

Zhenwu Region: a garrison region in northern Hebei Province

Zhuji County: a county in Yue Prefecture

Zhushan County: Yun County in northwestern Hubei Province, 90 miles northwest of Xiangyang

Zitong County: in eastern Sichuan Province

Appendix III
Background Information

Administrative hierarchy

The Tang Dynasty cabinet was mainly composed of three councils (*sheng*). *Zhongshu Sheng* was in charge of policy making; *Menxia Sheng* reviewed and approved, while *Shangshu Sheng*, which was in fact the State Council supervising the six administrative ministries of personnel, finance, rites, military affairs, justice, and construction-production, implemented policies. The heads of these three councils were often concurrently appointed prime ministers.

Local governments were organized at two levels, the prefectures and counties. At the founding of the dynasty, the whole country was divided into 1,151 counties under 358 prefectures. All the officials holding key positions at these two levels were appointed directly by the central government.

In the middle period of the dynasty, however, a regional power had emerged over the prefectures, that is, the garrison commands which were established mainly along the northern border in defense against the nomadic tribes. At first they were purely garrison forces abstaining from local affairs, but after the An Lushan-Shi Siming Rebellion, a weakened central government resulted not only in the increase of their number, but also in their expanding power. The military commanders often became semi-autonomous warlords, usurping local administrative powers.

In the stories, the head of the county is called magistrate, the head of the prefecture is the prefect.

Buildings

Houses in ancient China, whether peasant huts or official mansions, were usually single-storied structures surrounded by a walled or fenced courtyard.

For richer families, the compound may have consisted of more than one building. With the main building facing south, it could have additional buildings flanking the east and west sides, thus forming an enclosed courtyard in the center.

The nobles and lords may have had a more complex structure by having two or more such courtyards within a bigger compound. The outer quarters were for official business and receiving guests, the inner quarters were the living area for the family.

Festivals

The most important festival of the year is the Spring Festival, or the Chinese New Year. It usually falls in late January or early February. Other important festivals include Qingming, Zhongyuan, and Mid-autumn.

Qingming is one of the twenty-four solar terms in the Chinese lunar calendar, coming in early April. It is one of the major festivals in memory of the dead, when rice, eggs, wine, and yellow money are offered.

The Zhongyuan, or *Ullambana* Festival, was originally a religious festival. It occurs on the 15th day of the seventh lunar month. On that day the temples held grand ritual services for lost souls.

The Mid-autumn Festival comes on the 15th day of the eighth lunar month when the moon is at her fullest. It is a time for family reunions.

Geography

China is slightly larger than the United States in area. From the Tibetan Plateau in the southwest, the land slopes down toward the east, thus the rivers mostly flow eastward into the sea. The Yangtze River, which stretches west to east, divides the land into the north and the south. North and parallel to it flows the Yellow River, the cradle of Chinese civilization. Farther north stands the Great Wall. Beyond the Wall are mainly deserts and grasslands occupied then by nomadic tribes. At the opposite end, the deep south remained underdeveloped and inhabited by numerous national minorities.

The Silk Road starts at the capital, Chang'an, leading northwest through what is known as the Northwest Corridor, a narrow strip of land sandwiched by the almost insurmountable Qilian Mountain Range on the south and the Gebi Desert on the north, into the Western Regions. The Western Regions consisted of many small kingdoms covering a vast area of what is now the Xinjiang Uygur Autonomous Region and extending as far west as the Aral Sea.

Marriage

In ancient times, the marriage of young people was arranged by their parents. Under normal circumstances, it was a breach of social etiquette for one to propose directly. The more common practice was to have tentative proposals conveyed through a matchmaker, a role which was often filled by a silver-tongued old woman.

Monogamy has long been established as a social norm in China, but a man was allowed to take concubines.

As life expectancy was much shorter in the past and family posterity was given supreme priority, people married at a much younger age than they do now. Girls of 16 were considered the right age for marriage. It would have been humiliating if she were not engaged or married by then. Men would usually marry before 20, unless he was too poor to afford a wife.

Measurements

The common linear measurements in China are *li*, *zhang*, *chi* and *cun*. As the measurements in the tales do not require scientific accuracy, the translation simply adopts their approximate English counterparts of mile (1 mile $\approx$ 3 *li*), rod, foot and inch.

Monetary units

In ancient China, the basic monetary units were copper coins and silver pieces. Gold being precious, it was not commonly used as a currency. The silver pieces are weighed in *liang* (roughly one ounce) and *qian* (one tenth of a *liang*). Copper coins, however, were the most widely used currency for daily exchange. They were about the size of a nickel with a square hole in the center so they could be strung together into denominations of 1,000, called *min* or *guan*.

If the denomination is not mentioned in the text, it refers to the coin. It might be convenient to think of it in terms of one U.S. dollar.

Names

The Chinese family name always comes first. In the Tang Dynasty and earlier, the given name was usually monosyllabic. Disyllabic given names gained popularity in the later dynasties. The translation keeps to the original order of given name following the family name, even when it is prefixed by such courtesy titles as Mr.

Period titles of the emperors

In feudal times, each emperor gave a name (or sometimes more than one name) to his reign. The years during that period were counted in numerical sequence until the next emperor ascended the throne, or until he changed the name with the idea of starting things anew.

Scholars and examinations

The word "scholar" in the stories refers to students of the Confucian school. We must remember that in the past learning was a luxury for the privileged few, and, except at the elementary level, for most scholars studying was more a matter of personal devotion than a schoolroom experience.

Those who could successfully pass the local examinations held by county and prefectural governments were nominated to enter the imperial examination conducted by the ministry of personnel (later by the ministry of rites) in the capital. Succeeding in that examination meant one could look forward to starting an official career. At first he would be appointed to a secondary position at the county level. After a three-year term, he could be promoted to a higher position or simply relieved, depending on his merits.

The imperial examination system was first established in the Sui Dynasty as a way to abolish the prevailing clan politics fostered through the Jin and the Northern and Southern dynasties. The Tang Dynasty adopted it as a way to select competent officials to govern its vast territory. The system lasted through all the dynasties that followed.

Taoism

Taoism as a religion was established in the later half of the Han Dynasty. Its theoretical base is Lao Zi's *The Fundamental Text of Taoism*. *The Way*, a literal translation of Tao, is the ultimate awareness of the ways of the world, as well as the universe. To attain it, one must not only observe the religious rituals and cultivate his personality, but also seek facilitation by such strenuous practices as regulating the "air" in one's body, fasting, and a patient quest for the elixir of longevity. Thus, many priests were devoted alchemists, and their power to change the elements inspired innumerable tales about their magic powers and how they transformed objects and even their own shapes.

Philosophically, Taoism holds a dualistic outlook on the world, which it believes is made up of the complementary forces of *yin* and *yang*. *Yang* is associated with the sun, the positive, the male, the south, etc., while *yin* is represented by the moon, the negative, the female, the north, and so on.

309

Appdndix IV
Source Titles in Chinese

Source Title	Source Book	Vol.
张老	《续玄怪录》	16
麒麟客	《续玄怪录》	53
阴隐客	《博异志》	20
三卫	《广异记》	300
陈袁生	《宣室志》	306
薛肇	《仙传拾遗》**	17
冯俊	《原化记》	23
陈季卿	《慕异记》	74
茅安道	《集异记》	78
掩耳道士	《野人闲话》**	86
杜子春	《玄怪录》	16
张山人	《原化记》	72
柳城	《酉阳杂俎》	83
京西店老人	《酉阳杂俎》	195
阳羡书生	《续齐谐记》*	284
张和	《酉阳杂俎》	286
板桥三娘子	《河东记》	286
襄阳老叟	《潇湘记》	287
新鬼	《幽明录》*	321
宋定伯	《列异传》*	321
黎阳客	《广异记》	333
赵泰	《幽冥录》	109
浮梁张令	《纂异记》	350
谈生	《列异传》*	316
华阳李尉	《逸史》	122
贾偶	《搜神记》*	386

---

* Books marked with one asterisk are believed to have existed before the Tang Dynasty; those with two asterisks were published after the Tang Dynasty.

李生	《宣室志》	125
士人甲	《幽明录》*	376
袁继谦	《玉堂闲话》**	500
卢虔	《宣室志》	415
光华寺客	《集异记》	417
陈仲躬	《博异志》	231
吕生	《宣室志》	401
僧晏通	《集异记》	451
田氏子	《纪闻》	450
户部令史妻	《广异记》	460
居延部落主	《玄怪录》	368
岑顺	《玄怪录》	369
黄花寺壁	林登《博物志》	210
鹦鹉救火	《异苑》*	460
永康人	《异苑》*	468
长须国	《酉阳杂俎》	469
升平入山人	《续搜神记》*	442
安南猎者	《广异记》	441
欧阳乾	《续江氏传》	444
乌君山	《建安记》	462
振武角抵人	《玉堂闲话》**	500
吃人	《启颜录》	248
苏无名	《纪闻》	171
嘉兴绳技	《原化记》	193
刘氏子妻	《原化记》	386
宁王	《酉阳杂俎》	238
尉迟敬德	《逸史》	146
李靖	《续玄怪录》	418
傅黄中	《朝野金载》	426
崔无隐	《博异记》	125
黑叟	《会昌解颐》	41
萧颖士	《集异记》	332

韦氏	《原化记》	421
瞻波异果	《酉阳杂俎》	410
新罗(二则)	《酉阳杂俎》	481
	《纪闻》	
宝珠	《广异记》	402
陈义郎	《干膜子》	122
圆观	《甘泽谣》	387
李诞女	《法苑珠林》	270
红线	《甘泽谣》	195
义侠	《原化记》	195
昆仑奴	《传奇》	194
胡媚儿	《河东记》	286
不识镜、啮鼻	《笑林》*	262
郭务静	《朝野金载》	493
简雍	《启颜录》	164
汉世老人	《笑林》*	165
纥干狐尾	《广古今五行记》	288
侯遹	《玄怪录》	400
太阴夫人	《逸史》	64
明思远	《辩疑志》	289
京都儒士	《原化记》	500
峡口道士	《解颐录》	426
娄师德	《御史台记》	493
薛氏子	《唐阙史》	238
定婚店	《续幽怪录》	159
崔护	《本事诗》	274
杨素	《本事诗》	166
王宙	《离魂记》	358
申屠澄	《河东记》	429
吴堪	《原化记》	83
张果女	《广异记》	330
画工	《闻奇录》	286
马士良	《逸史》	69

南海大鱼	《广异记》	464
檐生	《广异记》	458
邛都老姥	《穷神秘苑》	456
刁俊朝	《续玄怪录》	220
王布	《酉阳杂俎》	220
绛州僧	《广五行记》	220
杨务廉	《朝野佥载》	226
李邈	《酉阳杂俎》	390
范山人	《酉阳杂俎》	213
吕翁	《异闻集》	82
淳于芬	《异闻录》	475
张佐	《玄怪录》	83

图书在版编目(CIP)数据

太平广记选:英文/(宋)李昉等编;张光前译.

北京:外文出版社,1998

ISBN 7－119－02011－0

Ⅰ.太… Ⅱ.①李… ②张… Ⅲ.古典小说－中国－宋代－英文

Ⅳ.I242

中国版本图书馆 CIP 数据核字 (97) 第 24737 号

责任编辑:胡开敏

封面设计:王　志

插图绘制:李士伋

太 平 广 记 选

(宋)李　昉等编

张光前　译

*

ⓒ外文出版社

外文出版社出版

(中国北京百万庄大街 24 号)

邮政编码 100037

北京外文印刷厂印刷

中国国际图书贸易总公司发行

(中国北京车公庄西路 35 号)

北京邮政信箱第 399 号　邮政编码 100044

1998 年(36 开)第 1 版

1998 年第 1 版第 1 次印刷

(英)

ISBN 7－119－02011－0 /I·454(外)

03980

10－E－3174P